Been Searching for You

A Novel

NICOLE EVELINA

Been Searching for You

Nicole Evelina

Lawson Gartner Publishing
PO Box 2021
Maryland Heights MO, 63043
www.lawsongartnerpublishing.com

Printed in the United States of America
First Printing 2016

ISBNs
978-0-9967631-6-5 (print)
978-0-9967631-7-2 (e-book)
Library of Congress Control Number: 2015959292

Publisher's Cataloging-In-Publication Data
(Prepared by The Donohue Group, Inc.)

Names: Evelina, Nicole.
Title: Been searching for you : a novel / Nicole Evelina.
Description: Maryland Heights, MO : Lawson Gartner Publishing, [2016] |
    Series: [Chicago soulmates] ; [book 1]
Identifiers: ISBN 9780996763165 (print) | ISBN 9780996763172 (ebook) |
    ISBN 9780996763189 (audiobook)
Subjects: LCSH: Single women--Fiction. | Man-woman relationships--Fiction. | Love-
    letters--Fiction. | GSAFD: Love stories. | LCGFT: Romance fiction. | Humorous
    fiction.
Classification: LCC PS3605.V424 B44 2016 (print) | LCC PS3605.V424 (ebook) |
    DDC 813/.6--dc23

Editor: Cassie Cox, Joy Editing
Cover Design: Jenny Quinlan, Historical Editorial
Layout: Morgana Laurie, The Editorial Department

1. Fiction 2. Romance 3. Contemporary 4. Romantic Comedy

1. Fiction 2. Women's Fiction 3. Single Women

To "Paul"

CHAPTER ONE

February

To Whom It May Concern,

I think I wronged the love goddess in a previous life. How else do you explain that I've written you so many letters yet we've still not met? Everyone I know is either married or in a committed relationship, and here I am, pen in hand, writing to someone I can't even prove exists.

There's an old Chinese folktale that says soul mates are connected from birth by an invisible red thread and that they can feel one another's emotions, no matter the distance. It is this connection that eventually enables them to find one another. I believe it too.

As I write, I find myself trying to imagine your face, grasping at flashes of memory from dreams, wondering what name to voice in my prayers that you will soon be by my side. The irony is that by the time you read this, the color of your eyes will be second nature to me and your name will roll off my tongue as easily as my sister's.

So please, my unknown love, hold tight to your red cord and
follow it like a lifeline into the safe harbor of my arms.

"Are you ready yet, birthday girl?" Mia's impatient voice broke through my romantic reverie, scattering my lovelorn thoughts.

"Almost," I yelled back as I scanned what I had written. I wanted to say so much more, but Mia wouldn't wait. But there was one more thought I couldn't let go unsaid.

I just want you to know that I haven't given up on you. I don't
trust easily, but I trust in you. I'm still waiting, though not so
patiently anymore.

All my love,
Annabeth

The note was short compared to other years' letters, but it would be after midnight when we returned home, so this would have to be enough. My one rule in this long-standing tradition—I'd been writing these letters since I was sixteen—was that the letter to my soul mate had to be written on my actual birthday. I folded the paper, slipped it inside the matching envelope, and licked the flap, then I pressed down to seal it.

Mia stuck her head in the door just as I drew the big numeral on the front. It matched my age—thirty-four. She shook her head, making her flaming tresses bounce. "You and your letters. If you two don't meet soon, he's going to have to buy an extra plane ticket on your honeymoon just for that box." She nodded toward the big square hatbox that functioned as a hope chest for my letters to my future husband.

I slipped the newest letter in front, envelope awaiting further decoration. "Yes, but it's romantic, don't you think?"

"For a young girl, maybe, but you're well past that, hon." Her tone softened when I made a face. "You've got plenty of declarations of love. Maybe this should be the last one. You know, new year, new traditions?" She held up a shot glass filled with golden liquid. "Come on. We need to get this party started."

Still scowling, I took the glass and downed the tequila with a small shiver. "If you say so."

As I locked up, I cast one last glance at the box on my desk. She had a point about growing up, but I had no intention of giving up my beloved letters. It was only one each year, and it meant something to me. Those weren't just letters; together, they were my gift to my future husband. Old-fashioned? Maybe, but it was me. Anyone who wanted to marry me would appreciate that. I smiled with a sudden thought. It was good I didn't want to marry Mia.

⌢

Bass throbbed through the plate-glass doors of the Drake Hotel as we got out of the taxi. Next to the doors, a large placard illuminated by revolving spotlights and a dizzying dance of rotating heart-shaped lights invited passersby to "Meet Chicago's Top Singles at *Fifty Shades of Great*."

As we walked up the dark blue velvet stairs to the banquet room, the thrumming noise resolved itself into a song—"Marry Me" by Jason Derulo.

I rolled my eyes at Mia. "No one told me they were going to be playing themed music."

"The hearts on the sign weren't a clue?" She took a ticket from the attendant in exchange for her pashmina wrap. "You did name the event, remember?"

Heat flooded my face. My suggestion of a theme had come at the end of a long brainstorming session at the PR agency where I worked. We were all slaphappy and much in need of a drink. I'd meant it as a joke, but the organizers loved it.

I shrugged. "They wanted cheese. I gave them cheese."

"Speaking of food, I hope the hors d'oeuvres are edible. I'm starving," Mia said as we approached the registration table.

As one of the fifty top singles, she was greeted with a hug and a smile by our receptionist, who was doubling as hostess for the evening. I, on the other hand, was left to search for my own name tag. Mia found it before I did and handed it to me.

I squinted at my name. "Does it say 'spinster'? Because it totally should."

Mia peered over my shoulder. "No, but it does say 'foolish romantic who needs to get laid.'"

I threw her a dirty look and was about to retort, but I was distracted by a muscular ebony arm intertwining with mine.

My best friend and agency-mate, Miles, appeared at my side. "You're always complaining you don't know where the single men hide. Maybe tonight you'll finally meet a few."

Mia kissed Miles's cheek. "But you can't have this one. Even if I am playing single for the night."

So that meant the on-again-off-again couple was back on? Or were they off since Mia was going to be auctioned off later? I shook my head, resigned that I would never figure out their relationship.

"You are going to have fun tonight if it kills you." Mia poked me in the stomach with one hand while grabbing a glass of champagne from a passing waiter with the other. "Start with this."

"I'm heading to the bar," Miles said. "Anyone want anything?"

I pointed at the glass at my lips and mumbled into it that I wanted another.

While Mia gave Miles her drink order, I scanned the room, gauging what kind of night we were in for. When I first heard the plans concocted by our event team, I had feared walking into a bad facsimile of a reality dating show set, but instead I'd entered a Grace Kelly film. The event crew had used the room's ornate columns, glittering chandeliers, and checkerboard marble floors to transport guests back to the early twentieth century. Tall tables covered in shimmery white linens and sprays of long-stemmed roses fanned out across the room. A catwalk hidden in shadows split the ballroom in two. Artful lighting directed the guests' attention away from that area to the bars and posters displaying information on the Top Singles.

The honorees, designated by tasteful red roses pinned to the lapels of finely tailored suits or beaded gowns, weaved in and out of the crowd. Even the waitstaff was in black tie and serving from silver trays. Curious, I tapped the edge of my flute with a fingernail, waiting for the telltale chime of crystal, but I heard only the clink of glass. Still, I had to give the sponsors credit for maintaining the hotel's impeccable class while hosting an event with a silly name.

I was about to remark to Mia on the beauty of the room when we were approached by a middle-aged woman in a simple black dress and an upswept bun that pulled her face into a scowl. She put out a hand to Mia. "Miss LaRue? I'm Eva Stegman. I'm in charge of tonight's event. We need to talk about your dress. It's far too short. Did you not read the dress code that accompanied your invitation?"

Oh, she'd read it; she just didn't think it applied to her. Rules were for other people, not Mia. I took that as my cue to slink off before Mia could throw an *America's Next Top Model* diva fit.

I found Miles at the bar, deep in conversation with a handsome man with broad shoulders and just a hint of hard muscle beneath his tailored navy suit with white pinstripes. Long-legged and trim, he looked as if he'd be right at home on a runway. When the stranger ran his fingers through his wavy dark-blond hair, I glanced at his left hand. No wedding ring. Maybe tonight was looking up after all.

"So how's Regina?" Miles asked him.

The stranger looked down, contemplating his drink. "I wouldn't know. She left."

"Aw, man, that's rough."

"Yeah. Sometimes I still hope she changes her mind."

"Seriously, I hear you," Miles said. "I love Mia, but there's one woman from my past I'd welcome back in a heartbeat if I could."

"Violetta?"

Miles tipped his glass toward the other man. "The very same."

I froze, not liking the sound of that conversation. They were trading war stories. Apropos at a singles' event, but not exactly the time for a woman to interrupt. I changed course, aiming for an empty seat a few chairs down, but Miles saw me and waved me over.

"How is Mia doing?" he asked.

"I think they're making her change her dress. I left before she could get into full-on 'Don't you know who I am?' mode."

Miles shook his head. "I told her it wouldn't fly. But she didn't listen. Never does." His gaze flicked to his companion, who was watching us with obvious curiosity. "I'm sorry. Annabeth, this is Alex Grantham. Alex, Annabeth Coe. Alex and I were friends when I first moved here, but we had lost touch."

I reached out to shake his hand, but he surprised me by turning my palm downward and brushing the top of my hand with his lips, the slight stubble of his beard grazing my skin.

"Delighted to meet you, Annabeth."

My knees went weak. Here was a taste of the chivalry I'd always dreamed of but rarely encountered. And he was so handsome too. Did I dare hope he was available? Based on the conversation I'd overheard, he might have been, but then again, he seemed to be hung up on this Regina. Maybe I should have hovered a little longer.

Alex gazed at me with sparkling hazel-green eyes, awaiting a response, but my mind was so muddled that, "Uh-huh," was the best I could manage.

"Annabeth and I work together at Smith and Grenwick PR," Miles supplied, surrendering his seat to me. "We're a creative team. I design. She writes."

"You're a writer? How interesting."

My brain was beginning to recover, albeit slowly. "Yes. I'm much better with the words that come out of my fingertips than the ones that come from my lips, I'm afraid." I gratefully accepted the drink Miles held out to me, and I took a long swallow, praying I didn't appear too desperate.

Alex smiled. "I know that feeling all too well. What do you write?"

For some reason, the question caught me off guard, and I struggled to set my glass down steadily. "Oh, all kinds of things—articles, press releases, brochures, ads. You name it, I do it." I giggled wiping my sweating palms on my pale mint-green dress.

"She writes fiction too," Miles said.

I would have to thank him later for thinking for me. He was my guardian angel tonight. His job completed, Miles excused himself with a wink in my direction, leaving the two of us alone.

Alex raised an eyebrow, clearly intrigued. "What genre? What do you write?"

"Historical mystery mostly. Nineteen-twenties Chicago." I took a deep breath, grateful to be in comfortable territory. I was never very good at talking about my day job, but I could talk fiction for hours. "I've just finished my first book. It's about a flapper in love with a gangster. She's really smart, but instead of using her brains to help the police solve crimes, she uses them to help the mob cover theirs. Kind of a detective for the bad guys."

"That's a great premise. North side or south side gang?"

I beamed, excited that he knew something about the period. "Both, at least for now—a hired gun, if you will. She'll have to choose eventually, but I want the readers to form that alliance with her."

"I'd love to read a sample sometime if you're willing. I'm an English professor, so I may be able to offer some tips. You know, for what they're worth."

I looked at him through my eyelashes, pitching my voice to a sultry register. "Professor Grantham, is that your way of saying you'd like to see me again?"

He adopted a mysterious expression. "Perhaps." He shifted in his seat, changing the topic along with this posture. "So if you're a writer, you must also be a big reader. What's your favorite book?"

"Modern or classic?"

"You pick."

"Modern has to be Anne Fortier's *Juliet*. It's a retelling of *Romeo and Juliet* in dual time periods."

"So it's both modern and a classic. Nice. Does this one have a happy ending?"

"Yes and no. You'll have to read it to find out what I mean. What about yours?"

He narrowed his eyes at me. "If you were any other woman, I'd say *Ulysses* by James Joyce and try to convince you I actually understand it. But I have a feeling you're too smart for that." Alex rubbed his scruffy cheek with the back of a finger, considering me. "If I'm honest, I'm obsessed with Rex Stout's Nero Wolfe mysteries. That's why your stories intrigued me. Stout's books are light and fun, plus they touch on all the timeless themes: betrayal, revenge, fine food."

I laughed "That they do. They make me hungry."

"You've read them?"

I shook my head. "No, but I loved the A&E TV show that starred Timothy Hutton. I was a little in love with his Archie Goodwin."

His eyes twinkled. "Seems I have a lot to live up to."

I raised a mental eyebrow. So, he was comparing himself to my fantasy man. That was a good sign.

"Seriously though, A&E did a great job with adapting that series. But you should still read the books. As usual, they are better." He leaned closer to me. "Speaking of books, Miles said the two of you came up with tonight's theme? It's both culturally relevant and clever. You should be proud."

"Thank you. I thought it was rather silly, but I'm glad you appreciate it." I stared at my glass, suddenly unable to look at him even though that was all I wanted to do. I searched my brain for some way to turn the conversation back to him and forced myself to look up. "What brings you here tonight?"

He took a sip of his drink, some sort of scotch or whiskey judging by the color. "Supporting a friend—Paulo Rodriguez. He's a professor of Romance languages at the University of Chicago."

I knew that name. "Wait. Is he the one they called 'Hot for Teacher' in the *Chicago Magazine* article?"

"One and the same. I don't know if I'm embarrassed or proud to admit to nominating him for this event. You can see for yourself in a few minutes. He told me he was early in the lineup." His eyes swept over me from head to toe then back up again, leaving a tingling heat on my skin as they moved. "Will you be bidding tonight?"

"Me?" I croaked. Wait. Was that his way of finding out if I was single? "No, I'm here with a friend as well. She's up first actually."

Alex's brow wrinkled. "That's Mia, right? She's the one Paulo asked me to bid on." Seeing my confusion, he added, "The Top Singles can't bid on each other, but the rules say nothing about bids by proxy." He shot me a mischievous grin.

We lapsed into momentary silence, so I mentally leafed through my lackluster catalogue of topics to discuss with strangers.

"So you and Miles go way back? How did you meet?" I asked. It was such a banal question, but small talk had never been my forte. There I was, wanting to impress him with my sparkling wit, and the best I could do was basic niceties.

He started to respond, but his answer was drowned out by an ear-splitting squeal as Eva took the stage, manhandling the microphone.

"Welcome, ladies and gentlemen to the Windy City's most popular singles event of the year, sponsored by *Chicago Magazine* and Heart+Soul online dating. Each of our fifty Top Singles will be up for auction. All proceeds will benefit the University of Chicago Medicine Comer Children's Hospital, so please bid high. As each single walks out, I'll read a brief bio, and they'll explain which synonym of the word *great* they have chosen to describe themselves—no two will be the same. The bidding will begin when they have finished speaking." She gave a small nod, and the lights dimmed, plunging us into near darkness.

A moment later, they flashed to life as Lady Gaga's "Bad Romance" blared through the speakers, then it quieted as Eva read Mia's bio. I almost choked when Mia emerged from the wings, hands on her hips in supermodel style, long red hair swinging with each stomping step. I hardly heard Eva's account of Mia's time gracing the runways of Paris, Milan, and New York because I was too busy staring slack-jawed as Mia strutted down the catwalk in a one-shouldered metallic-silver cocktail dress ruched at the waist to accentuate her curves. It was longer than her other dress but left little to the imagination.

When she approached the end of the runway, she paused, turning once. Then the music quieted, and she addressed the crowd. "I'm Mia LaRue, and my synonym for great is wicked!" She made rock n' roll devil horns with the pinkie and forefinger of her right hand. "I chose this word because being great is about more than excelling at something. You have to have a special little spice to rise from good to great." She paused for half a beat. "And just so you know, I'm accepting bids from men and women." She winked at the crowd, which tittered in response.

Eva cleared her throat with a touch of disapproval. "Thank you, Mia. We will begin the bidding at one hundred dollars."

I tuned out as the room exploded in a volley of shouted figures, each higher and louder than the next. Miles emerged from the crowd and rejoined us at the bar. I leaned into him to be heard over the noise.

"How do you stand this?" I gestured toward the chaos. "When you're together, I mean."

He sipped his drink through a thin straw. "Comes with the territory. You don't like it, then you'd better run because you certainly won't be able to handle Mia. She's this multiplied by a hundred all by herself."

After only a few minutes of bidding, Mia's price was in the thousands and the auction was down to two contestants: Alex and a sultry brunette with huge doe eyes who looked as if she could have given Mia a run for her money. The bidding was up to five thousand dollars, and she wasn't backing down. Her bright, sparkling eyes and flushed cheeks betrayed the thrill she was getting out of the competition. Alex, however, did not look as excited. A muscle jumped in his jaw as he stared the woman down.

"Ten thousand dollars," he shouted.

The crowd gasped. All eyes turned toward the woman. She considered his offer for a moment then slowly shook her head.

Eva brought down her gavel. "We have a winner! Mia LaRue has just raised a record-breaking ten thousand dollars. Isn't that wonderful?"

As the crowd cheered, Mia winked at the brunette—whose number she would no doubt be in possession of by the end of the night—then blew a kiss at Alex before turning on her spiked heel and exiting the stage.

I had to rise up on my tiptoes to get near Alex's ear. "Does she know you were bidding for someone else?"

"I have no idea. I'm just glad I don't have to pay for her."

Was it my imagination or had his voice held a hint of disgust? So he wasn't interested in supermodel-perfect, trampy Mia. Good. Maybe his tastes ran more toward the girl next door.

Inspired by that thought—or perhaps it was the alcohol kicking in—I bit my lower lip and asked, "Would you have bid on me?"

He turned to me and looked me over again. "Now that's a different story." A breathtaking grin lit up his face. "I'd pay a lot more for you. Fine things are worth more than what's common for a reason."

My heart melted. I opened my mouth to respond but was interrupted by an auction official who'd come to collect Alex's—or rather Paulo's—payment information. By the time Alex had explained the situation to the official, Mia was strutting toward us as quickly as her sky-high heels would let her.

"There's the man with the best taste in the room," she yelled over the chaos of Paulo's auction. She grabbed Alex by the lapel and planted a noisy kiss on his cheek. "Hello, handsome."

So she didn't know he'd bought her for someone else. I couldn't wait to see Alex set her straight. But before Alex could even react, Miles took my hand and dragged me over to the nearest standing table.

"What the hell, Miles? We're going to miss all the fun."

He fixed me with his I-mean-business stare. "I heard what Alex said to you. Enjoy the compliment, but don't take it as anything more."

"Why not?"

"He referred to just getting out of a long-term relationship earlier. From the sound of it, the wound is still pretty fresh. I think he wants her back, and I don't want to see you get hurt."

"You just reconnected with him. What do you know about his heart?"

"I knew the woman. She was special to him."

"*Was* being the key word. So what if he wants her back? He doesn't have her right now, does he?" I narrowed my eyes at him as a thought occurred to me. "If the situation was reversed, would you be warning Mia off him?"

"Of course not. She can handle herself."

I threw up my hands. He was always big-brothering me. "Happy birthday, Annabeth! Here's a hot guy who might be interested in you, but Miles thinks you're too fragile to handle him. Thanks a lot." Before he could reply, I turned away and went back to Alex's side.

As I eyed a tall Latino man who had joined our group—had to be Paulo—Alex leaned down and whispered, "You okay?"

"Fine. Miles was just being an overprotective friend," I said, crossing my arms to show I didn't want to talk about it.

My face must have betrayed my emotions more than I thought because Mia leaned over to me. "Buck up, Pookie. This is no way to spend the last few hours of your birthday."

I gave her a withering look, not in the mood for her to patronize me.

"So where's the lucky lady who 'won' you?" Miles asked Paulo, mercifully changing the subject.

Paulo nodded toward the crowd, where a noisy volley of figures signaled the beginning of another auction. "Back into the fray. She's bidding on someone for her daughter. I'm supposed to call her tomorrow."

Behind us, two women erupted into a high-pitched yelling match over the current bachelor.

Paulo winced. "I don't know about you, but I'd much rather finish our evening somewhere quiet than listen to forty-seven more of these. Since we've all fulfilled our obligations, what do you say we head out?"

"I know the perfect place," Mia cooed. "There's a little jazz bistro on Eire that's just cozy enough for us to get to know each other." She squeezed Paulo's bicep while smoldering at Alex and Miles. "Oh, remind me to tell you what that *Vogue* photographer said to me last weekend. It's the funniest thing."

I rolled my eyes. So that was how the night was going to go. Queen Mia would hold court with her suitors and regale us with stories of her latest worldwide escapades. That was pretty much par for the course, but I didn't want to deal with it. With her in control, Alex and I wouldn't be able to get a word in edgewise, much less get to know one another, which was all I really wanted.

"Why don't we ask the birthday girl where she wants to go?" Miles said. "That's your agreement, right? You do what she wants tonight?"

Mia's face fell as she remembered our pact. "Yeah."

I could have forced the issue and insisted on getting my own way, but my inner introvert was exhausted. Finishing out the evening with a hot bath and a good book was sounding better by the minute, especially since I couldn't spend the evening talking with Alex.

I forced a smile. "Don't worry about it. Go wherever you'd like. I'm getting a headache—probably too much champagne. I think I'm going to head home."

"Are you sure?" Alex asked. "Maybe you just need some fresh air. At least let me walk you out."

I took his proffered arm. "That's very sweet, thank you." Looking over my shoulder, I called, "Have fun, you guys."

While we waited for the coat check girl to emerge from the sea of leather, down, and faux fur, Alex drummed his fingers on the countertop. "So what's with Mia calling you 'Pookie'? Is there something I should know about?"

It took me a second to realize he was asking if Mia and I were together. When I finally did, I burst out laughing. "No, no, it's not like that at all. I mean, she's into girls too, but I'm not." I found myself reaching out to touch him, but I changed direction to fiddle with my hair instead. "It's an inside joke. She says it to annoy me."

The girl returned with my coat, and Alex gallantly took it from her and helped me into it. "So what's the story?"

He walked me to the curb as I explained. "It goes back a few years. I told her once that 'The Tango Maureen' from the musical

Rent should have been called 'The Tango Mia' because she's as complicated and manipulative in her relationships as Maureen. She responded by calling me 'Pookie,' and it kind of stuck."

"Maureen's pet name for her lovers when she wants something. Nice."

I stopped in my tracks, turning toward him. "You know the musical? I'm impressed."

"It's one my favorites. I studied it when I worked as a dramaturge during my college internship."

Handsome English professor who knows Chicago history, studied theatre, and made an effort to say good-bye to me. . . could this guy get any more perfect? There had to be a catch. There always was—ask any woman. I knew he wasn't gay, so that left the ex.

She had to be it. But how could I ask about her without seeming all crazy stalker?

I looked around as though the perfect question would be written on the buildings towering over us. All I succeeded in doing was catching the eye of a cabbie who, guessing correctly that I needed a ride home, started his engine and pulled up to the curb in front of us.

"I guess this is my signal to go home," I said. The part of my brain that would forever be sixteen prayed he would ask for my number.

Alex hesitated, leaning toward me, then pulled back. He opened his mouth then closed it again. Instead, he took my hand and kissed it just as before. "It was a pleasure to meet you, Annabeth. Happy birthday." He squeezed my hand. "We'll miss you tonight."

My breath caught, and I cleared my throat. "Thank you. I enjoyed meeting you as well." He didn't say anything else or make another move, so if I wanted to see him again, it was up to me. I mentally took a deep breath. "Since I'm bailing on you tonight, what do you say I make it up to you over coffee sometime?"

Alex's gaze turned toward the pavement. He shuffled his foot. "Now really isn't the best time. Maybe in the future."

I held up a hand to forestall any further excuses. "Say no more. I had to at least ask." Inside, disappointment was hardening into a crust of ice around my heart, but there was no way I would let him know that. I reached into my handbag and withdrew a business card. "In case you change your mind."

He took it with a soft smile. "I meant what I said about wanting to read your book. I'll email you when my class load is light enough to give it due attention."

I turned toward the cab, and Alex opened the door for me. As I got in, I couldn't resist casting one last glance in his direction, drinking in the green and gold flecks in his eyes. A hint of sadness glinted in them as if he regretted our parting as much as I did.

I closed the door, gave the driver my address, and raised a hand in farewell. Alex mirrored my gesture, not breaking eye contact until distance forced us both to look away.

I sat back with a sigh and closed my eyes. The city passed by as brief spots of light behind my lids as the driver turned down Michigan Avenue. *Seriously, God, is this your idea of a joke? Give me a guy for my birthday, but he's not interested? Thanks a lot.*

The taxi crossed over the river, getting closer to my empty apartment with every second. I thought about the box waiting for me with its growing collection of letters. It didn't appear I was any closer to finding their intended recipient. But what did I expect after only one night?

I directed my thoughts to that soul at the other end of my invisible red cord. *Whoever you are, I hope you really can feel me. At least that way you'll know how much you're needed and how mad I am that you're so slow in getting here. I obviously can't leave our future up to you.* In that moment, I made a promise to myself and to him. *I will find you this year. . .one way or another.*

CHAPTER TWO

March

I was dreaming, but I couldn't wake myself. The past came to life in flashes, snippets of long-repressed memories jumbled together. I was back in Rome, during my senior year of college, with my best friend, a lanky boy with gorgeous baby blues and James Dean looks.

One minute I'm kissing him passionately, intent on crossing the line between friends and lovers by giving him my virginity. Nick's lips, the heat between us, is all I know.

Then there's the soft rumble of his voice as he whispers, "All this time you were writing those letters, and I was right in front of you. You could have just told me."

My stomach muscles seize up as I realize he's wrong; those letters aren't for him. The hard muscle of his chest as I push him away, babbling about him not being "the one." The bruising pressure of his fingers as he tries to convince me to relax, to give in. The jolt of pain in my arm as he tries to pull me back when I finally wriggle free of his weight to hide in the bathroom.

Now I'm trembling, naked on the bathroom floor as he hurls through the door an alternating string of curses about me being a tease and apologies for hurting me. A hole punched in the hotel wall. Dust motes floating through a golden sunrise as I peek out, relieved he's gone.

Nick's final words to me when we meet in passing weeks later. "I can't take this anymore. We're done."

I woke with a start, sitting upright, and looked around in wan light of my bedroom, dazed. What day was it? Sunday. Good, I could go back to sleep. I flopped back down on my pillow, images from my dream flashing in front of my eyes. Why, why had my mother mentioned Nick when we talked on the phone last night? If she hadn't, I wouldn't have thought of him, wouldn't have dreamed about him and had to relive our tumultuous past. It could have been much worse—he could have raped me—but his violent temper still traumatized me. No matter how much she wanted us to be together, I was not looking him up on Facebook. Best to leave the past buried.

A loud noise made me jump, and I realized someone was banging on my front door. I ran a hand across my face and considered pulling the covers over my head until whoever it was went away. *Bang, bang, bang*—fist on wood like the firing of a line of cannons. With a grunt, I forced myself into my robe and slippers. Glancing out the window, I noted not quite a foot of snow accumulated on the balcony. All I wanted was to veg on the couch with my laptop and a cup of tea. Whoever was at the door had better make it quick.

As soon as I saw Mia and Miles grinning at me from the other side of the threshold, all hope of that happening evaporated. "Can I help you?"

"Looks like we're snowed in. We thought we'd have a little quality time," Miles said.

"Plus, I'm craving pancakes," Mia added unhelpfully.

"So go to the diner down the street. My name is not Denny." I moved to close the door, wondering if they were drunk or just delirious on that annoying kind of happiness only rekindled romance can give a person. "Just because you live upstairs," I said to Mia, "does not mean you can drop by whenever you want."

Miles stopped the door with his palm, and Mia spoke up. "Pleeeaase, Pookie? It's not like you were going anywhere anyway. And besides, you make the best chocolate chip pancakes. Plus"—she reached into the bag Miles was holding and removed a bottle of champagne, probably from her seemingly endless supply—"I'm making mimosas."

"I hope there's OJ in there because I'm fresh out," I said, stepping back to let them in.

Mia squeezed Miles's shoulder. "He thinks of everything!"

I peered into the bag. A lonely jug of orange juice stared back.

"Except for the eggs, milk, mix, and chocolate it'll take to make your pancakes," I retorted, allowing bitterness to creep into my voice. To drive home my displeasure, I banged around a few pots and pans before bending down to find the only skillet large enough to feed three people. "I love you guys, but I just saw you yesterday. What gives?"

"Glad you asked." Miles plopped down on the sofa. He pulled my laptop onto his knee and opened it. "We are here to offer our expert guidance in filling out your Heart+Soul account."

I stood up so fast I nearly hit my head on the open cabinet door above me. "No. I take a lot from you guys, but I will not do the online dating thing. I meet enough crazies in real life. I don't need help from the Internet. Besides"—I gestured at Mia with a wooden spoon—"it's your account anyway, Miss Top Chicago Single."

She snorted, nearly in time with the popping of the champagne cork. "Like I need it. It's six months free, and I gave it to you, remember? You may as well try it. Consider it payment for the pancakes."

"Did you or did you not vow to find your soul mate?" Miles pinned me with a level stare.

"Yes, but—"

"And what exactly have you done in the last month to make that happen?"

Uh-oh, I had a sinking feeling I knew exactly where this was headed. "Um, nothing, but. . ." But what? I didn't have an excuse. I hadn't done anything because deep down, I was a chicken shit who was afraid of men. Was that what he wanted to hear?

"So what right do you have to say no?"

Crap. He had me trapped, and he knew it.

I let out a low whine even though part of me was curious. "If I do this, the two of you are never allowed to say another word about my dating or lack thereof. Got it? My vow, my problem."

"Scout's honor," Mia said, holding up her middle finger.

Setting down my load of breakfast items, I raised her index and ring fingers for her. "It's three fingers, genius."

She narrowed her eyes at me. "Oh, I know."

Miles sprang up and stepped between us in three long strides to hand out the drinks Mia was pouring. "All right, ladies, let's call a truce before someone breaks a nail."

I sipped mine gratefully before beginning to whisk the mix, eggs, and milk together. "Where do we start?"

Miles set down the laptop, angling it so I could partially see the screen. "Well, I know your name, birth date, and occupation, so we can skip that," he said, keying in the information. "It starts by asking you to describe yourself. What's your hair color?"

I pointed at my head. "You aren't blind. Can't you just fill that in for me?"

Miles held up a hand in self-defense. "Hey, hey, some people like to lie online. I was just giving you the chance. Brown it is."

"Mousy is more accurate," Mia said.

"I can still kick you out. Remember that." I beat the batter with extra vigor to work out some of my irritation.

"Eyes?"

"Hazel."

"Height?"

"Five foot six."

"On a good day," Mia chimed in. "And don't forget to mention her freckles."

"Not all of us are six-foot Amazons. Just for that, I'm burning your pancakes."

"Girls," Miles warned in his best dad-like tone, still clicking away. "Ah, now here, we're finally getting to the good stuff. What's the most important quality you look for in a mate?"

"I can only pick one thing?" I popped a chocolate chip in my mouth and thought as the first pancakes bubbled in the skillet, slowly releasing the scent of chocolate into the small apartment. "I have to be able to trust him, to know he won't abandon me."

I glanced at Mia. She gave me a pitying smile, knowing full well to what, and to whom, I was referring.

After a few seconds of tapping at the keys, Miles continued. "Got it. If you could build your ideal partner, what are three things his personality would have to include?" He pointed at Mia. "No comments from the peanut gallery."

"He has to be romantic in an old-fashioned sort of a way—you know, treating me like a lady. He has to be smart because I have to have someone I can discuss all my weird thoughts with, and he has to be honest. I hate duplicity."

"So basically, you want a guy who only exists in romance novels," Mia concluded.

I stuck my tongue out at her as I set down three plates, ready to dig in.

After a few moments of chewing in silence, Miles pulled the computer toward him again. "Three qualities for his looks."

"That's easy. Tall, dark, and handsome," Mia said before Miles could stop her.

"Actually, she's right." That came out more like "mapfully, she's white" through my mouthful of food.

Miles washed down his with a full glass of alcohol-laden orange juice. "Top me off? Biggest fear."

"Never falling in love."

"She means dying alone," Mia clarified.

"Same difference."

Instead of typing, Miles looked at me quizzically. "Really? That's worse than getting cancer or being buried alive?"

"Have you seen her box of letters? To her, it is."

"Mia! No one's supposed to know about that."

Miles ignored us. "I'm skipping over your favorite TV shows, movies, et cetera. You can fill that in later. Describe your worst dating experience."

"Which one?"

Mia laughed then coughed. "Um, I think mimosa just came out of my nose."

"I'm serious. Should we tell them about the guy who proposed after one date, the one who skipped bail to flee to Mexico, or perhaps the creep who stood me up twice then brought his male best friend on our date, who he proceeded to dump me for two weeks later?"

Mia waved her arm to stop me from continuing. "Oh, you should so mention the 'literary speed dating' event we went to. Miles, it was so sad. All old women, us, and three middle-aged, balding guys. What did you call them again?"

"The recently divorced trio," I answered.

"That's it! They kept staring at me the whole time. It was creepy."

"That's because no one believed you could read, much less have an opinion about a book."

She gave me a venomous look.

Miles tried unsuccessfully to cover a laugh, and Mia playfully hit him. "Moving on. What's your ideal date?"

I stood and cleared the dishes, pretending to think. I didn't want them to know I could answer that off the top of my head. I turned on the water and let one side of the sink fill with soap bubbles. "How do you pick just one?"

"Well, it gives some ideas here." He read from the screen. "'If money was no object, where would you want to go and what would you do for dinner that evening? Where do you want to be proposed to?' Things like that. They seem to want you to think big."

"Hmmm. . . well, if that's the case. . ."

Mia poked me in the ribs. "Come on, out with it. I know you already know. Where would you want Alex to take you?" Leaning in so only I could hear, she added, "I'd forget the date and take him straight to bed, but that's not your style."

Heat rose up my neck, a flush I couldn't really blame on the hot water lapping at my elbows. "He missed his chance. We're talking about guys who actually want to go out with me. I do love the Signature Room in the Hancock Building. It's got the best views of the city, the food is to die for, and the whole place has this art deco charm. I've only had dinner there once—my parents took me there on my first trip to Chicago when I graduated from college—but I kept waiting for Al Capone to step off the elevator. It's his kind of joint."

"You do love those gangsters, don't you?" Mia bumped my hip playfully. "But seriously, hon, you really need to join the rest of us in the present. It's the twenty-first century, not the nineteen-twenties. You're going to scare men off with an answer like that."

"You know, you could be helping dry the dishes instead of criticizing me," I snapped, cocking my head toward a dish towel hanging from the oven handle.

Mia opened her mouth to snark back, but Miles interrupted. "Just dinner or is there more?"

I shrugged. "I don't know. I haven't dated much lately. Aren't you supposed to say something about a horse-drawn carriage ride?"

"Only in the movies. Guys don't really go for that," Miles advised. "How about this? 'Then we'll see where the night takes us.' Leaves it to his imagination."

"Fine with me."

"The rest is pretty standard Q and A. Do you want children? How often do you drink? Do you have or want pets?"

"Yes, frequently since I've become friends with you two, and no. Are we done now?"

"I'll let you pick your own photos, but there's one more thing."

"What?" I asked over the rushing water.

"An essay."

I looked over my shoulder to see if I'd heard him correctly, and I caught Mia knocking him out of his seat to have a closer look.

"There's a test? Seriously?" She was aghast.

"Yeah."

I peered over Miles's shoulder while drying my hands and read the company explanation at the top of the page. *One of the things that sets Heart+Soul apart from other dating services is that we don't rely on a profile and a few photos to help you find love. We let you set the tone. Here you have the chance to say anything. Use it to tell people why you're here and who you're looking for. This free space is meant to give you a chance to convey what's important to you and give potential matches a sense of your personality. Use it as you will and have fun!*

I had never been at a loss for words at the keyboard, but the thought of writing about myself, something so intimate that would be read by anyone matched with me, was terrifying. As much as I loved Mia and Miles, I couldn't do this in front of them.

"Okay, you wanted pancakes, you got pancakes. Show's over." I removed Mia's glass from her hand. "Time to go home, M&M." I hadn't used my nickname for them in a while and was hoping it would get their attention.

"But you aren't done yet," Mia whined. "And I wasn't done with that." She swiped at the glass like a cat batting at a strand of yarn.

"Nope. My apartment, my rules. You got me to fill out the profile, and I fed you. Mission accomplished. Now I have to finish it on my own."

Miles stood and wrapped me in a bear hug. "We'd better not overstay our welcome. Thank you, Annabeth. It was a lovely visit." He took two steps back so as to better look me in the eyes. "Don't forget to hit submit when you're done with that thing. I'm expecting daily progress reports." He pointed a thick finger at me. "And don't think you can skip out either. I know where you work."

"Ha-ha," I said, ushering them to the door. "Your warning is duly noted."

I watched them wait for the elevator. On or off, they were cute together. Despite my irritation with them, I felt a tiny pang of jealousy as Mia hooked a finger into one of the loops on Miles's jeans, a small gesture not meant for the world—unlike ninety-five percent of what she did—but an intimate expression of possession. *You're mine, and I'm glad*, it said. I wanted that.

⁓

Eschewing the orange juice, I poured another glass of bubbly and stared at the glowing screen of my laptop. What I really wanted to write was way too brutally honest, but I had to start somewhere. What was it my English professor had said? *Get the words down; you can cut and polish later.* She was right. Taking a deep breath, I started typing.

> *They say everyone has a secret that will rip out your heart. Here's mine—I've never been in love. I thought I was once, but looking back on it, I see it for what it was—infatuation and the need for security. I've never had that head-over-heels, heart-melting kind of love. You know, the stuff people die for. And it's what I'm looking for.*
>
> *To all of you who look at my age and wonder how what I say is possibly true, I'll only say one thing—not everyone's life fits society's timeline. Some people are lucky enough to fall in love in high school or college and stay together for the rest of their lives. And that's great. I'm happy for them. But that's not the way things worked out for me. I've got a great life with a burgeoning career, a loving family, and loyal friends, but I don't have anyone*

to share it with. That's why I'm here. I know that person is out there, but I haven't found him.

So what are you getting with me? I've been called many things: old-fashioned, naïve, and quirky. But I prefer to think of myself as unusual. If you need proof, just take a look at the photos I've chosen. You'll see one with a kissing couple in a park on the left. That's my sister and her husband. The one on the right is me. Yes, you're seeing that correctly—I am kissing a tree. It started out as a joke since I didn't have anyone to pose with at their engagement shoot, but it ended up being emblematic of who I am. I'm that goofy girl willing to make fun of her situation if only to avoid crying over it. (I'm also the girl who danced with a mop at her senior prom, but that's a different story.)

I always wanted to be the kind of woman who could perch herself anywhere and look sexy, like the models in those ads who manage to be alluring on top of the kitchen stove. In reality, I'd probably fall off.

In the end, here's everything you need to know: I am who I am. I'm outspoken and honest, fun-loving and strong. I'm a romantic who, in some ways, will never grow up. I'm not one for a quick fling. I'm in it for the long haul or not at all.

Rereading what I'd written, I realized it didn't sound so bad. Honest? Yes, but that was me. If they didn't like it, they didn't have to contact me. Why should I pretend to be something I'm not just to get the attention of some guy I'd never actually met?

Mia would have a fit when she saw this. She believed in telling men what they wanted to hear—"alluring them rather than repelling them," as she'd explained once. She had tried time and time again to teach me her particular method of charm, but every time I tried, I felt wrong, as though I was misrepresenting myself—ironic since I worked in PR.

Oh well, it was my life, not hers, and I was going to live it on my own terms—online and off. I selected a few more photos—my most recent headshot, taken by a photographer who had let me play stand-in while he measured the light and waited for Mia to get into wardrobe; a few from last summer's vacation to Paris; and yes, the one with me kissing the tree—filled in the missing favorites section, and squeezed my eyes shut as I clicked "submit."

My love life was in the hands of the online gods. Maybe I'd have better luck with them than with Venus and Eros.

CHAPTER THREE

"Do you have any idea what this is about?" I asked Miles as I took my place around the conference table. Sunlight streamed in through the western-facing windows, so I had to squint to look at him.

"No idea. I just got the email meeting request like the rest of us."

My stomach tightened. The last time a group of creatives had been called into a room like this was during the worst layoffs our agency had ever seen. Within ten minutes, they were all jobless. I sent up a quick prayer that wasn't the case this time.

Nearly every seat was full by the time our boss, Laini Grenwick, took her place at the head of the table. Nearly fifty, she was one of the first female executives at the agency, and as such, she treated this business like her baby and was not known for putting up with nonsense. Today she looked every inch the career woman, from the dark twist of her hair and the subtle makeup highlighting her toffee-colored Indian skin to her mauve skirt suit and black pumps.

"I suppose you're all wondering why I've called you here." She looked each one of us in the eye before continuing. "Well, let me start by alleviating your fears. The fact that you are here is an honor. You've been hand-picked for a very important, high-profile assignment."

Miles and I looked at each other, intrigued and shocked. As my coworkers whispered to one another, I realized that collectively, we made up an account team. There was Jenna, the perky blond account executive; Miles and me, the writer and designer team; Rick, our creative director; and Kendra from media relations and the special events teams.

Laini adjusted her chunky black hipster glasses. "Some of you may remember the Fifty Shades of Great event we worked on earlier this year. Well, in addition to raising nearly half a million dollars for charity, it also brought some very attractive business our way. That night, I was fortunate to make contact with Dr. Gordon McAllister, Dean of the Department of English Language and Literature at the University of Chicago. They normally do their marketing in-house, but this is such a big undertaking that they need us. We've been tasked with helping with a yearlong campaign they want to launch in September aimed at increasing enrollment in the English program."

A collective groan went up. Four months to create a project of that scope was insane.

"I have chosen you for this project because you're the best we have. It goes without saying—but I'll say it anyway—that if this goes well, it could mean big things for our agency. So I'm asking you to clear your schedules this afternoon. We have a one o'clock meeting with the university president, the dean, and some of his professors. Listen to what they have to say, then get creative. I want your best ideas first thing tomorrow."

Miles raised his hand. "Are these billable hours?"

"Beginning with the meeting, yes. Track your time, and do what you have to do."

❧

The campus of the University of Chicago was sprawling, taking up two hundred eleven acres in Hyde Park on the south side of the city. Built in Gothic style, its turrets and ivy-covered walls immediately took me back in time to an era when learning was considered a sacred art. The Main Quadrangles—six courtyards each surrounded by buildings bordering one larger quadrangle—reminded me of the colleges of Oxford and Cambridge that I'd seen on a PBS special. Holding them all in a snug embrace was the Midway, a long green area constructed for the 1893 World's Fair that joined with two other parks to surround the campus in nature.

"Tell me again why I didn't go to school here," I called to Miles as we crossed the parking lot.

"I don't know, but I'm kinda having school envy myself. And I never thought I'd say that. I loved Drake."

A long hike later, we arrived, huffing and puffing, at our destination, a dark-paneled conference room down the hall from the dean's office. A long, rectangular wooden table dominated the room, flanked on all sides by luxe leather chairs that looked as if they were used to supporting the fattened backsides of rich board members rather than working stiffs like us. Along each wall, above waist-high mahogany wainscoting, was a row of oil paintings. The wall across from me bore likenesses of great men of English and American literature—Shakespeare, Byron, Whitman, Keats, even Fitzgerald and

Hemingway—on either side of arched triple windows. We each took a seat in one of the high-backed chairs.

"I could get used to this. Hey, Laini, what would it take to get one of these for my office?" Miles asked.

"About a thousand extra billable hours. Find them, and it's yours."

"Ouch!" Miles said, shaking his hand as if he'd just touched a hot stove.

Not long after an assistant returned, bearing cups of steaming coffee and glasses of water, two well-dressed men entered, and we all stood respectfully.

The one in the lead, a handsome man with a crop of thick black hair and the mercurial face of a politician, immediately put out his hand to Laini. "Dean McAllister. Wonderful to see you again, Ms. Grenwick." They shook hands, then he introduced his companion. "This is President Harrison."

The gentleman he indicated was about sixty with a ring of silver hair above bushy matching eyebrows. He was dressed in a fine, tailored three-piece suit that made even the dean's look lackluster, but he didn't have the bearing of an aristocrat. Rather, his warm smile betrayed a love of learning and genuine interest in his work. I immediately wished he was our main point of contact.

A third man slipped into the room, expression apologetic.

My heart stopped.

"Ah, good. He's here." The dean gestured toward the slightly tardy man. "Last but certainly not least, we have Professor Alexander Grantham. He is the head of literature for our department and will be your day-to-day contact on this project."

My mind went blank as I watched the man who had so captivated me at the singles event introduce himself to my colleagues. When he reached Miles, the two greeted each other with an affable smack on the shoulder. I wondered how long they had hung out that night after I left.

Then he was facing me, all tan skin and sparkling green eyes. His hand shake was strong, his grip firm. "How lovely to see you again, Annabeth."

"Likewise."

And then it was over. We took seats, and the meeting commenced like any other, everyone else unaware of what a momentous occasion this was for me. Well, everyone except for Miles. He elbowed me and flashed a playful grin. He knew full well what was going through my head.

"It would be very helpful to us if you could walk us through what brought you to propose this campaign, a situational analysis, if you will," Laini said to the three men.

"Of course." Dean McAllister interlaced his fingers and leaned forward as if confiding a great secret. "With the economy, fewer students are opting for the liberal arts, choosing instead to major in areas of traditional stability like business, health care, and IT, areas where they believe their employment and earning potential are stronger upon graduation. We want to convince them that that isn't the only path to a successful career."

"But first, you have to get their attention," Laini noted.

"Exactly. That's why Professor Grantham is here. He's one of our most popular instructors. Over the last several years, he has spearheaded an effort to teach literature using books teens and young adults are already reading. He teaches courses on popular literature like Harry Potter, and uses Percy Jackson to introduce his students to Greek myths and classics like the *Iliad*. Alex, why don't you tell them about it?"

Alex adjusted his position, mirroring the dean's forward posture.

"Those who love to read will naturally gravitate toward English as a major or minor. I'm looking to capture those undecided students who may read on the side as a hobby but have never thought to analyze its deeper meaning beyond which 'team' they're on." He chuckled at his joke, as did a few others. "For example, I use *The Hunger Games* and *Divergent* to introduce my students to dystopian literature like *1984* and *Brave New World*, which they may have previously shunned as outdated and boring."

"So you're meeting them where they are then taking them one step beyond," I said, admiring his dedication to connecting with his students.

He pointed his pen at me. "Exactly. If you throw a bunch of old dead guys at them, they think that's all English is—the study of things no longer relevant. But if you instead start with things they want to read or are already reading, you've got them on a completely different level. They can discuss how the book relates to their lives or what they would do in a given situation. Then later, when we move into the classics, they can take those skills with them and analyze the stories on a deeper level."

"So you'll want to take the same approach here. Start where they already are and draw them in," Miles said.

"Yes. But also show them literature is a living, breathing thing, something they and their peers can not only receive as readers but create. We're lucky to live in an age where, with tools like Wattpad and self-publishing, they can see their peers succeed."

"Your audience is primarily high school juniors and seniors, I assume?" Kendra asked.

The dean seemed to think for a moment. "Primarily, yes, but we also want to appeal to our students who haven't made a firm plan and those who might be thinking of changing majors. So if you're looking to generalize, I'd include our freshmen and sophomores in your list. By the time they're older than that, they're pretty much committed."

"What about the parents? Isn't their support important? I know if my parents wanted me to study medicine, I'd be less likely to waste my time with English classes, no matter how much I enjoyed them," Jenna said.

"Good point," Alex interjected. "Helping parents and students look beyond the obvious professions of beleaguered English teacher and starving writer is very important. English gives you a strong background for so much. If we can show them they're being prepared to be future online journalists, like Arianna Huffington, or big futuristic thinkers, like Seth Godin, we'll have a much better chance." He thought for a moment. "How many of you were English majors?"

Laini, Kendra, Jenna, and I raised our hands.

"Would you be willing to use your agency to show the range of career possibilities?"

Laini nodded. "We're always looking for interns, so certainly. Right here in this room we have writers, media professionals, and a creative director with a foot in both the design and writing worlds. That's another point. Perhaps we could collaborate with your school of design to show additional possibilities for dual majors or major/minor combinations."

President Harrison spoke up. "I'm sure they'd be happy to help. An increase in enrollment in any area is good for the school. I like the way this is shaping up. I have every confidence we've chosen the right team to help us." He glanced at his watch. "Unfortunately, I have to step out to attend another meeting. Is it reasonable for this group to gather again in a few days? I can't wait to hear your final plan." His excitement was palpable, the optimism in his voice infectious.

Laini thought for a moment. "Jenna will be in touch with your assistant by end of day, and we'll set something up."

The president excused himself, then Dean McAllister took control again. "Do you have any additional questions? What else can we tell you?"

"Obviously social media will be a huge part of this," Kendra observed. "Is there someone in your marketing department I can connect with on that? Actually, I'd like to liaise with your media relations team as well."

"Good point. In fact, I should probably introduce you to the team sooner rather than later. Perhaps we can tack that on after our final meeting with the president?"

"Got it," Jenna confirmed.

"Anyone else? Speak up or forever hold your peace." When no one else voiced questions, Dean McAllister brought the meeting to a close. "Thank you all so much for your time. I look forward to hearing your ideas. Jenna, Alex will send you the budget and contacts in the marketing department. He's my right hand."

Jenna flashed Alex her brightest smile and extended her hand. "I'll be in touch."

Alex gave her a small bow in response.

A pang of jealousy shot through me. Of course the perky blonde gets the contact with the attractive professor while the writer holes up in her cube like a mouse. Not this time. I would pour my heart and soul into this project not only to show I was capable of being more than just a penmonkey—I was a trained strategic advisor, damn it—but also to show Alex the difference between a charming saleswoman and someone who really knows her craft.

As we packed up, Laini gave her final instructions. "It's three o'clock now. Get out of here for the day. But remember, I want your best ideas first thing."

⌇

Less than an hour later, Miles and I were sitting in a bar on Rush Street in the midst of an evening of brainstorming. This was going to be a late night, and I wasn't happy about it, but times like this came with the territory. It wasn't my first or likely to be my last.

"Out with it," Miles said as I set down his second beer. "You are lit up like a Christmas tree, and I know it's not just because you're into this project."

"He's sooooooo handsome!" I squealed. "What are the chances we'd meet again like this? It has to be fate, right?"

Miles grinned at me. "Maybe. But remember, we're in professional mode. That means no flirting with the clients."

I hung my head in mock shame. "I know, I know."

"You know what they say, 'the fastest way to get someone's attention is to no longer want it.' Date someone else, and you'll be surprised how quickly he notices you. Take it from me. Women who are taken glow in a certain way that's irresistible to men."

"I'm trying to date other people, remember? And you think the glow is real?"

"I know so. Now, no more talk of men. We're here to work. What do we have so far?"

I read off our list, trying to get my brain to focus on the task at hand. "Tie-ins with local libraries and writing groups, the Chicago Review, online groups like the Chicago chapter of National Novel Writing Month and the River North chapter of Romance Writers of America. These are great starting points, but I think we need to get more specific. I jotted down a few ideas during the meeting. Did you see the shelf of books by well-known Chicagoans in the conference room? We need to check with the library to see if they have one too. If not, they need to get one. We need to show students and potential applicants what the program can prepare them for. That reminds me—we need to find out who the famous alumni from the program are and play them up." I wrote that down. "What if we work with Kendra's team to do a meet-and-greet with famous local authors and maybe even some outside of Chicago who wrote popular series? It would take a lot of work, a lot of coordination, but it would also bring in a lot of press."

"I think Laini will really like that idea. It would also give Alex a chance to highlight his classes and how current novels can and should be taught." Miles was typing away on his phone as he spoke. "Looks like there are a ton of famous alumni—John Scalzi, Philip Roth, and Susan Sontag to name a few. There's a whole Wikipedia page."

"If we got enough interest, we could even offer a series of weekend or evening lectures by famous alumni. I wonder if any would be willing to teach a workshop or something." I mused.

"It couldn't hurt to ask."

Five hours, nine beers—mostly consumed by Miles—and three baskets of wings later, we had a pretty solid plan.

"We still need to come up with a theme for this," I said.

"You're the reigning theme queen, remember?"

I scowled at him. "Lightning doesn't strike twice."

"I don't know about that. I'm sure Laini will make us all brainstorm themes tomorrow once we have the whole plan together, but it's probably a good idea for us to have some ideas ready, especially since we'll be the ones who have to write and design toward it."

"Good point." I twirled my pen between my fingers. "So far, the best I have is Year of the Book. Not so much."

Miles wrote it down. "No, but it's a starting point."

We spent the better part of an hour tossing ideas back and forth, a few good but mostly bad, with lots of silly wordplay and innuendo that had me laughing so hard my sides ached. Miles's latest, Peek Beneath the Covers, coupled with his double entendres about erotic literature, had me struggling for breath.

"Speaking of, how's the online dating thing going?"

I eyed him over the rim of my glass. "You're just dying to play bodyguard again, aren't you?"

Miles's stipulation the first time I'd expressed interest in one of my online matches was that he shadow us "just in case he's one of the crazies." Three times now he'd planted himself at the same restaurant or bar, a few tables or stools away but within sight, while the date happened.

The first guy was sweet, but there had just been no chemistry. By the end of the night, we both knew it wasn't going to work. The second, though in his thirties, spent the entire night talking about his older brother with an idol worship that should have ended in his teens. By the time he walked me home, I was convinced I should have been dating his brother instead.

"Hey, I did come to the rescue once."

"Yeah, yeah, rub it in."

That would be date number three. Something had been off from the moment I laid eyes on him, though I couldn't tell what. He was perfectly polite, chivalrous even, but something in his eyes had unnerved me. As the night wore on, I realized his questions and answers were a little too rehearsed, as though he had been on this exact date many times. Then when he asked me if I was interested in coming home to meet his wife, I knew he had.

I excused myself and frantically texted Miles. Ten minutes later, he "ran into" us and pulled up a seat, having a ball of making a pest of himself and doing his best to annoy my date into leaving. I'd give the guy credit for putting up with Miles. But when Miles got into the taxi with me at the end of the night, my date finally admitted defeat.

I shrugged, bringing my thoughts back to his original question. "Meh. For the most part, the guys either don't meet my personal qualifications or have something odd in their profile that screams, 'Run away.' I've chatted with a few a couple of times, and one I'd even consider meeting, but he hasn't responded to my last note, and that was like two weeks ago."

"His loss. At least you can say you've tried, right?"

"Yeah. Would you believe most of my matches don't even have pictures with their profiles? Why in the world would I even consider someone I can't see? No one likes a blind date."

"Men aren't really into details, in case you haven't noticed. They probably just haven't gotten around to it yet."

I crossed my arms. "Whatever. If they can't follow basic directions, I don't want to date them."

"And you wonder why you're single." I started to retort, but Miles held up a finger. He was scrolling through something on his phone. "Speak of the devil. . . I just got a Meetup invite to a traffic light party on Saturday." He looked up as though I was supposed to know what that meant.

I raised an eyebrow, willing him to explain.

"You don't know what that is? Jesus, you really did spend too many nights in the library at Drake. The Thetas had them several times a year."

I examined the table through the amber-colored liquid in my glass. The only time Thetas had paid me any attention was during freshman year when a group of assholes told my friends and me to go back to high school because there was no way they were letting us into their party. That was my first and last interaction with Greek life.

Miles was so absorbed in his own memories—he was a Delta—that he failed to notice my lack of enthusiasm and rambled on. "Traffic light parties are where a bunch of people get together and wear different colors based on their dating status. Green means you're single and looking, yellow that you're in a relationship but may be open to dating someone, and red means you're taken. It's an easy way to see who's fair game without having to look for a ring or engage in awkward conversation or guess."

I was confused. "Why would anyone wearing red go to one of those?"

Miles put an arm around me. "Well, for instance, I am taken by the lovely Mia, but I will be offering you my invaluable skills as a wingman. Therefore, I will be wearing red."

I stared at him. "I am not going to this. I didn't do keggers in college, and I am certainly not going to one now."

"You didn't do them in college, and look where it got you," Miles teased. "It's not a kegger. Actually, I'm willing to bet it will be a fairly nice affair. It's at Mockingbird, that new place over on State. I hear it's pretty swanky."

"With talk like that, should I expect to see you in a red leisure suit?" I drained my glass.

"With bell-bottoms. Only the best for you, babe. But seriously, you're the one who said you would try all measures to find Mr. Right, didn't you? Ergo, you can't say no."

I glanced at the clock on my phone. "Shit. Why didn't you tell me it was after ten already? If I don't get to bed soon, I'll be a wreck for our meeting tomorrow."

"Because most adults have bedtimes closer to midnight."

I gave him the evil eye. "All right, you win. I'll go to your stupid party. What time?" I riffled through my purse, looking for my keys.

"Mia and I will pick you up at nine. Wear something green."

"And Mia will be wearing yellow?"

"Most likely."

"Why do you put up with her?" I asked, genuinely puzzled at what he saw in her given her propensity to date and/or have sex with whomever she pleased whenever she pleased.

"I could ask you the same question. Besides, it's your fault for introducing us when I moved to town." He reached into my bag and produced my keys. "She's fun and unpredictable. Keeps life interesting. Come on, I'll walk you home."

CHAPTER FOUR

Mockingbird turned out to be a trendy lounge sandwiched between a retail store and a hotel on State, near Wacker, overlooking the river. I spotted the lounge's classic bulb-illuminated sign, similar to the iconic Chicago Theatre marquee, from across the street but took a moment to savor my favorite view in the city before going inside.

Walking down State toward the river, one was hemmed in by tall buildings on both sides until reaching the water. Then the city just opened up, laying itself bare as if to say, "Here I am in all my beauty. Admire me." At night, the view was especially grand, with the twinkling lights of the Wrigley Building and Trump Tower reflected in the lazy gash of the river, as though a courtier had just unlocked her jewel box and allowed a fleeting glimpse inside.

Normally I could stand quite contentedly for hours on the State Street Bridge and watch the people and boats go by, but not with Mia yelling at me from beneath the club's bright blue awning. With a sigh and a smile, I gave in and joined her.

"You look amazing," she said, admiring my emerald-green spaghetti strap tank and skinny jeans.

Mia didn't compliment others easily, so I basked in the praise. "I took a page from your book and splurged on something from Michigan Avenue that I really can't afford."

"That outfit will pay for itself many times over tonight. Just you wait and see."

I reached into my purse to pay the cover charge, but the bouncer waved us inside.

"Honey, put that away," Mia said, putting an arm around me. "You won't be spending any money tonight. In fact, by the end of the night, they'll be paying you just for the pleasure of your company."

"Isn't that the definition of prostitution?" Miles quipped, appearing from the brightly colored crowd.

Mia glared at him, but I tuned out the rest of their teasing argument, caught up in the glamour of the Jazz Age-inspired décor and the big band music piped in overhead. As Michael Bublé crooned away, I took in the crowd. Some were dressed for the room in beaded flapper dresses and feathered headbands, the men in fedoras and three-piece suits. Others had chosen a more modern approach, wearing chinos or frilly dresses and even jeans and T-shirts. But there was no shortage of variety, from lime green to the sparkling gold of Mia's sleeveless top to the blood-red of crisply starched business shirts.

The drink of the night appeared to be martinis. As we took a seat in one of the VIP alcoves—another perk of being with Mia—a waitress dressed like an old-time cigarette girl came by, balancing a tray full of clear gin and vodka martinis in addition to flavored varieties in stoplight shades. I took a pink Cosmopolitan while Mia chose a green appletini and Miles opted for the traditional gin.

Miles held up his glass. "To Annabeth, our lonely writer who will be single no more after tonight."

We clinked glasses and drank. We passed the time people-watching and enjoying our drinks, which magically refilled as we laughed and made snarky comments about our fellow revelers. By the time the dance floor was really filling up, I excused myself to visit the loo, and I was a little more unsteady than I'd expected. I tried to recall how many drinks I had consumed and failed. Who could count with the attentive cigarette girls exchanging one glass for another?

While I washed my hands, I looked in the mirror, inspecting my makeup, which was a little worse for the wear than when I'd applied it. But at least I didn't look like Tammy Faye. Yet. That usually came toward the end of the night.

As I was reapplying powder, Mia flounced out of one of the stalls. "Having fun?"

"Yeah, surprisingly, I am."

"Told you," she crowed. Her ears perked up at the first beat of a new song, and she practically shoved me out the door. "Get out there. You'll enjoy this."

I stumbled out to find the red, yellow, and green partiers divided up into six roughly parallel lines on the dance floor. Not knowing what to expect, I hurried over to the green section.

From some hidden sound booth came a booming voice. "Ladies and gentlemen, guys and dolls, welcome to Mockingbird's spring fling traffic light party."

The crowd cheered.

"Now, partiers of all ages, I'd like to remind you of the few rules of this evening. These folks dressed in red are not to be approached. Red means stop. They are either taken or otherwise not interested.

If you harass them, you will be ejected. But they're still here to have fun, so let's give them a big Mockingbird welcome!"

Those dressed in red took turns dancing down the center of their line, like members of a bridal party being introduced at a reception. Miles took full advantage of the song—"Highway to the Danger Zone" from the *Top Gun* soundtrack—to show off his best moves. His freestyle was a little jazz, a little tap, slides, and footwork as smooth as silk. In the middle, he spun around once before finishing his time in the spotlight with the moonwalk.

I yelled my appreciation while Mia let out an ear-piercing wolf-whistle.

When the reds were done, the lines shifted, the yellow group taking its place in the center.

"Now, let's hear it for our yellow team," the DJ boomed. "I'm not going to try to guess your situations because they could be anything. What all of you out there in dating land need to know is be careful with the yellows. Yellow means proceed with caution. They're some kind of trouble, but you'll never know what if you don't say hello. Just don't hold me responsible for any black eyes or slaps. Yellow, strut your stuff."

Men and women in shades from cheerful lemon to tacky gold lamé did the Hustle, the Electric Slide, and all manner of silly dances to Coldplay's aptly titled song, "Yellow." Mia waited until last, when she could have the spotlight all to herself, to show off her belly dancing skills, earning more than a few hoots and hollers.

Finally, it was my group's turn. The DJ must have been waiting for this because he took no small pleasure in harassing us.

"Now, this is the group you all came to see. We all know green means go, right?"

The crowd cheered again.

"Anything goes with this group, so take a look around. Scope each other out because these are the people who will be filling your dance card the remainder of the night."

He paused, giving us a chance to peek at our fellow green shirts. We were all grinning at each other self-consciously.

"All right, let's see if what they say about the green M&Ms holds true for those who wear the color."

John Legend's "Green Light" blared. I didn't like the lyrics to that song, but I was grateful we didn't have to dance to Kermit the Frog. The couple at the head of the line took a few beats to find their rhythm before starting the dance.

My heart rate increased with each step toward the front of the line. I had always had trouble walking and dancing at the same time. I was more of a twirl-my-hips kind of dancer, so I decided to go with what I was good at.

I took two bouncing steps to the middle of the group, set my hips spinning in a backward figure eight, and dropped down to the floor before popping up again. On the next beat of music, I paused, looked back over my shoulder, and shrugged it down in a burlesque-style trombone slide. I kicked up one heel and waved to the crowd before prancing back into line.

After the dance was over, Miles called as I neared the table, "Damn! Where did that come from?"

I smiled coyly as I sat beside Mia.

"Seriously, if you can do that, there is no reason for you not to be to fending men off with a stick," Mia said, still picking her jaw up off the floor.

"Don't look now, but I think you have an admirer." Miles gestured surreptitiously with one of the fingers he had wrapped around his glass.

Of course, my first instinct was to turn around. Luckily, Mia chose that moment to get up, and I was able to use the excuse of asking her to get me a glass of water to turn in the direction Miles indicated.

I was greeted by a pair of startlingly blue eyes looking at me from a face the color of luxurious hazelnut chocolate. *Hello there, handsome.* I smiled. His pillowy lips turned up at the corners, and he ran a self-conscious hand through his bushy black hair, which stuck out like dandelion fluff.

"Greens and yellows, can I have you back on the dance floor, please?" the DJ called. "All greens and yellows to the dance floor. We're going to play a little game."

We gathered in an uncertain mass on the dance floor, the waitresses corralling us into two groups, one on either side of the room.

"I need a volunteer," the announcer boomed.

Hands shot up all over the room. He picked a tall blonde to demonstrate. "How many of your remember the game Red Light, Green Light from when you were kids?" A smattering of applause and quite a few squeals answered the question. "Well, here's how we play it at Mockingbird. What's your name, sweetie?"

The blonde answered, but I couldn't hear her.

"Janice here is the stoplight. She'll give you directions by saying either 'red light' or 'green light.' When she says 'green light,' anyone interested in her should move forward. But don't go too fast, because if she says 'red light,' you have to stop. Anyone who doesn't immediately stop moving will be disqualified, even if you only stumble. All of you standing around will be the referees. Now, there's one more catch. If she wants to try to throw you off, she can also say 'yellow light.' That means you have to move in slow motion. If you tag the stoplight, you get to talk to her. Whenever she's got her share of admirers, she'll end her turn by declaring a blackout. Got it? Good. Take it away, Janice." He handed her the microphone, returned to his booth, and cranked up the dance music.

"Green light!" she yelled, and the game began.

Mia was third in line and took the game up a notch by holding up a silk scarf procured from her décolletage. Standing in the spotlight in her leather capris and gold sequined top, she could have stepped out of a 1950s film. She brought the scarf down dramatically, as if she was signaling a drag race, and called for her admirers to come forward.

Soon, we were fighting to form a coherent line, and as the alcohol kept flowing, chaos ensued as people forgot what red and green meant or the stoplight confused him or herself. On a few occasions, disqualified suitors jumped back into the game, and once, security had to be called when an overzealous guy picked up the stoplight and walked off with her against her will.

By the time it was my turn, the vodka had kicked in, and I was feeling saucy. Turning in a circle, I scoped out the men in the crowd, finding my admirer among them.

"Green light," I declared.

Having seen enough people disqualified, they moved forward at the pace of lions stalking prey.

"Red light." I paused, watching my suitors closely. "Red light."

Two guys weren't paying attention and took a step forward, disqualifying themselves.

I kept my eyes glued on my blue-eyed admirer, willing him to make it to me. He was dressed more simply than most people here, in jeans and a plain green T-shirt, but the laid-back look fit him.

"Green light."

They came forward again.

When I had men on both sides of me just out of arm's reach, I called, "Red light." I was teasing them, and they knew it. Then a rapid succession of, "Red light, green light, red light, green light," narrowed the field down to just three—my admirer among them— who all tagged me before I called "Blackout."

I spent the next two hours surrounded by them at the bar, having to insist they buy me water instead of alcohol so I didn't puke on their shoes. It became clear pretty quickly that one of them really just wanted to go home with me, so I pointed him in Mia's direction, grateful for the chance to get to know the other two without him as a distraction.

After a bit of conversation, I figured out the shorter one and I had nothing in common—he was very outdoorsy, into camping and hunting and other things I'd never do—so I politely told him I didn't think it was going to work. He made a half-hearted attempt to save his ego by saying he was thinking the same thing, but the slump of his shoulders as he disappeared into the crowd said he felt otherwise.

Now it was just my admirer and me, who, by this time, I had discovered was named Victor. He was a contractor by day and artist by night who lived not far from me, in Logan Square, where rents were a little lower but he still had easy access to the heart of the city.

"Finally. I thought I'd never get you alone," Victor said, shaking his head.

"I bet you say that to all the girls."

"That didn't come out right, did it?"

"Probably not the way you intended." After a pause, I added, "So you said you paint. Is that the only medium you work in?"

"No, I sculpt too."

"You're not going to try to seduce me by asking me to model for you, are you?" I batted my eyelashes at him and sipped my water through the tiny straw in what I hoped was a seductive way.

He feigned outrage. "Not on the first date. What do you take me for? Besides"—he stood, taking my hand—"I prefer other methods."

I pretended not to know what he was doing. "Such as?"

"Such as asking a lady to dance."

I gave him a slight nod and followed him to the dance floor. By now, the DJ had switched from the Great American Songbook to the usual club fare, heavy on the bass and perfect for hip shaking.

I cocked an eyebrow at Victor, daring him to keep up with me as I rolled my hips suggestively and shimmied my shoulders to the beat. He wrapped a muscular arm around my shoulders, his other hand resting lightly on my hips until he found the pace I'd set. Once he had matched it, his grip tightened, and we were off, grinding against each other under the flashing lights.

The DJ was announcing last call when Miles finally peeled us apart. "As much as I hate to break this up—and it really pains me to do it—I promised Annabeth that I'd walk her home."

My arms still around Victor's neck, I stuck out my lower lip in a pout. "But I'm having so much fun."

"I'm sure you are, but a deal's a deal. I'll be waiting outside."

"I can walk her home," Victor said.

Miles skewered him with a look. "No, you can't. For all we know, you're an ax murder."

"A really hot one with an amazing ass," Mia interjected as she leaned over to better admire it.

Miles ignored her. "But an unknown all the same. It takes more than a few games, five minutes of conversation, and an hour of sweaty dancing for me to let Annabeth out of my sight."

"Thanks, Dad." I glowered at him.

"Five minutes," was all he said before ducking out the front door.

I turned back to Victor. "He means well."

"Hey, no harm done. We should all be fortunate enough to have friends like that. So any chance I can get your number?"

I pretended to think. "Yeah, sure. Why not?" I put out my hand, and when he had unlocked his phone, I tapped in my digits.

We stood for a moment in awkward silence, not knowing how to bring the night to a close.

Victor put a tentative arm around me. "So I guess this is good-night then?"

I wanted to kiss him, but I wasn't good at being the aggressor. Actually, I couldn't recall the last time I had been the one to initiate a kiss. But I found myself leaning into him and whispering, "Not quite yet," before pressing my lips against his.

CHAPTER FIVE

"Miles!" I bounced up to his desk and perched on the edge. "You will never believe the email I got this morning."

"I doubt I will."

"Remember that essay I wrote as part of my online dating profile? Well, one of the guys who was matched with me liked it and asked if he could share it on his blog as an example of a modern woman's manifesto. It was pretty popular. I had people praising me as the next Gloria Steinem and others deriding me as a dried-up, bratty shrew—gotta love the Internet. Anyway, today I got an email from an editor at the *Huffington Post*. They want to run it as part of an article but have me expand on it a little. Isn't that exciting?"

Miles folded me into his arms. "That's incredible! Congratulations."

"It's due Monday, so I'm going to have to cancel on you for the game on Saturday. I promised Victor I'd be at his showing that night and if I don't get this thing written, I'll be a nervous wreck—"

"Say no more," Miles interrupted. "I get it. Work and the boy toy trump the best friend."

Laini poked her head into our shared cube. "I'm going to pretend I didn't just hear that last part, but I'm glad you're discussing work." She pointed at me with her notepad. "Jenna is out sick today, and she was supposed to meet with Professor Grantham to discuss plans for the event series. I need you to take this one." She handed me a manila folder. "This is what I could find on her desk. Good luck." Before I could respond, she raced off, sipping her coffee as she disappeared into a conference room.

When I looked up, Miles was doing his best Cheshire cat impression. "When it rains, it pours. First a handsome construction worker who wants to be an artist and now a one-on-one with your dream man. Try to keep at least one foot on the ground today, will ya? I've got some comps to discuss with you."

I whacked him with the folder before turning toward my own desk. The meeting was at noon. That meant I had three hours to discuss design with Miles, do my own work, and get caught up on Jenna's progress before hopping the Metra to the university. I opened the folder to find her notes were a mess, scribbled this way and that on both sides of the page as though she'd written down only what she pleased. *Jenna, why do you have to be as flighty as you look?*

⁓

The Rockefeller Memorial Chapel bell tower was just striking noon when I approached Alex's office. I would have been early, but I'd made several wrong turns before finally finding my way through the maze of Gothic buildings and bustling students. With the flowers and trees in full bloom, I had to fight the urge to stop and look around at every turn.

With its gabled roof and cross-like spires, Walker Hall looked more like a manor house or the dormitory of a seminary than a university building. But the similarities to one of Poe's haunted mansions stopped at the ornate façade. Across the threshold, the building was as utilitarian as any other school, with plain linoleum floors, a blue area rug, and boring beige walls set off by cork boards jammed with brightly colored flyers advertising jobs, roommates, and study abroad opportunities. Only the spiraling stone staircase gave a hint as to the age of the building, its treads worn in the middle from the shuffling of countless feet. Each step echoed like something out of a horror movie as I slowly ascended to the third floor. Beneath my palm, the wooden banister was worn smooth with age and discolored from the oil of thousands of sweaty palms.

I emerged at the end of a long hallway broken only by closed doors spaced at odd intervals. As I crept along the hall, trying to muffle the sound of my heels as I searched for room 332, snippets of lectures leaked out of the classrooms. In one, a woman suffering from sinus troubles was encouraging a debate between two students arguing over the symbolism and subtext of T.S. Elliot's *The Wasteland* while in another, a rich male voice was reading one of Shakespeare's sonnets aloud. I found myself slowing to listen, transported back to my own college days. A deep yearning to stay and learn stirred within my soul.

After what felt like an eternity—though the clock on the wall said it was only two minutes after noon—I found the room I was looking for. Alex didn't appear to have an assistant, so I was going to have to announce myself. As I raised my hand to knock, I caught sight of Alex sitting at his desk, casually sprawled in his chair and engrossed in a book. He brushed his left eye with his hand. At first I thought he was just scratching an itch, but when he did it again, I realized he was crying. I sneaked a peek at the cover—*The Fault in Our Stars* by John Green. No wonder. That book would have made even the most hardened criminal blubber like a baby.

Not wanting to embarrass him, I took a few steps back, made sure my footsteps made more noise as I reapproached, and knocked. "Professor Grantham? I hope I'm not disturbing you."

He looked up, momentarily dazed, then seemed to remember where he was and why I was in his doorway. "Yes, Annabeth, come in. And call me Alex. I think we know one another well enough to be on a first-name basis."

He flashed me a smile so full of warmth I thought I would melt into a puddle, leaving only a stain behind on his faux Persian rug. I took a seat in one of the chairs near the west window of the tiny office, hoping the glare from the sunlight would distract me from my two biggest temptations: staring at him and allowing my eyes to wander over the bookshelves crammed two deep. Some were sagging tomes peeling with age, others crisp and eagerly awaiting their inaugural read.

But as Alex adjusted the wooden blinds to shield me from the shafts of light, I caught sight of him and was momentarily undone. His look was classy and reminded me of a 1930s newspaper reporter—tan slacks held up by old-fashioned beige-and-mauve suspenders over a pink Oxford shirt with a white collar and cuffs. Gold and black cufflinks glistened at his wrists.

Instead of taking a seat behind his desk—and putting a barrier between us—as I'd hoped he would, Alex pulled up a chair just opposite mine. We were sitting so close I could have touched his knee. *You are here to work,* I reminded myself. *Get to it.*

I cleared my throat. "I'm sorry I was late, but I got lost trying to find the building. I appreciate your patience. You didn't seem surprised to see me though."

"No. Laini phoned this morning and said you would be coming in Jenna's place. Please tell Jenna I hope she gets well soon." He leaned forward, elbows on his knees. "I'm actually glad Laini sent you."

My heart fluttered into my throat. "You are?"

"Yes, I want to discuss our plans so far. From our initial meetings, I get the impression your heart is in this much more than some of the other members of our team."

Jenna. He meant Jenna. I smiled to myself, thrilled beyond measure he saw her for what she was.

"Passion is what will get us where we need to be. Like attracts like, right? If we aren't in this recruitment effort one hundred percent, the students will see that and react accordingly."

Alex's enthusiasm was infectious, and despite my best efforts to remain professional and rigid, I found myself leaning toward him. I placed a sheet of paper on the small, round table between us. "I couldn't agree more. That's why I've put together a list of possible scenarios for events, keeping in mind your principle of meeting students where they are."

He bent over the page, a thick wave of hair falling forward over his right eye and glowing gold in the muted sunlight. Silently, he read through the list. "I like what I see. Tell me more."

"Well, in addition to having a presence at recruitment events that take you into the high schools, you need to draw students here so they can experience the campus for themselves and get a feeling for what it would be like to be a student here. I know you do tours, but we need to think beyond those. Nearly every month has some sort of event we could capitalize on. For example, you said the desire was to launch in September. That's perfect timing to start with a bang because that's when Banned Books Week is held. Miles and I mocked up a sample brochure, web page, and a few social media examples for you to look at."

With the theme "We Don't Ban Books," the proposed event would be a daylong exploration of the juxtaposition of freedom of speech and rules of conduct in a private university setting. The event would include a few authors of recently banned or challenged works but would also go beyond the books themselves to cover censorship, the reasons used to justify banning, and the roles of parents, teachers, and students in the consumption and constriction of controversial works.

I set down another paper. "Here's a list of nearly one hundred banned books from the American Library Association, as well as those considered controversial over the last several years. As you can see, many of them are books you personally use in your curriculum. I'm sure your students would love to be involved. Perhaps some of your fellow professors could offer credit for appropriate participation. When prospective students hear from their peers, they're more likely to receive the message."

Alex nodded. "Yes, I see where you're going with this. In years past, our library has held staged readings of banned books with a local theater company, so I know the administration is open to the idea of participating in the week's activities. We'd of course have to get permission to expand it, but I see great potential here, especially for media coverage, which will extend our reach even more. What do you have planned for the rest of the year?"

Over the next two hours, I went over with him the ideas Laini had endorsed for National Novel Writing Month in November, the National Book Festival in January, Read Across America Day in March, and National Poetry Month in April. In the months between, we would hold workshops and events focused on well-known Chicagoans, university alumni, and competitions for current and potential students alongside ongoing calls for suggestions to curriculum and future events via social media.

"One thing I just thought of," I added. "You should consider inviting student journalists to cover the event. Give them special press passes and everything. That way, even those who don't attend have a chance to hear about it."

Alex was glowing with excitement. "I love that you're focusing on participation. From what my research has shown, that's something most schools don't do a good job of incorporating. We're all experts at talking to students, donors, and the like but don't often want to hear back. I think this has real potential to shake up the laissez-faire system and infuse some life into our stodgy old department."

"Oh, I'd say it's anything but stodgy with you around. What was it you were reading when I came in?"

Alex looked away, probably covering his embarrassment that I may have seen his unguarded moment, and reached for the book. He plopped it in my lap. "I'm just starting a six-week series on mortality and the choices we make. I'm also including *Sophie's Choice*, *Macbeth*, and in a twist, requiring my students to see the opera *La Bohème*."

"Again with the *Rent* reference. What is it with us and that musical?" I teased, expecting he would know that *Rent* was a modern retelling of the famous Puccini opera.

"I hope it isn't some sign from the universe that we're all doomed," he said, pitching his voice low to mimic a sinister force.

I laughed. "Seriously though, two novels, a play, and an opera in six weeks? That's more than we covered in a semester in some of my college classes."

"It's tough, but these kids worked hard to get in here. We accept on average less than eight percent of the students who apply, making our rate not much higher than Princeton's or Yale's and more competitive than Dartmouth's or Cornell's. I want my students to be on par with the Ivy League schools. That they chose not to attend those institutions should be irrelevant to the level of education they receive."

"Very well stated," I said, marveling once again at his determination to do right by his students.

A small clock with spinning crystal orbs chimed on his desk, followed shortly thereafter by a *bing* from his phone. Alex sighed and silenced the alarm. "That's my cue to depart for the dean's office. I'm meeting him between classes." His arm brushed a stack of papers, sending them floating to the floor like autumn leaves. "Oh, hell!"

I crouched to help him retrieve the fallen mess. One paper in particular caught my eye—a list of band names with a smattering of lyrics.

Alex caught me looking at it. "It's a rough sketch for a class I'm developing for the first spring term—Poetry and Storytelling in Modern Music."

"Interesting. But if you're looking for poetic lyrics, there's a band from right here in Chicago that you're missing."

"Who is it?"

Instead of answering, I reached into my purse and pulled out my phone. "May I?" I gestured toward his computer.

"Be my guest."

Less than two minutes later, he had two Kill Hannah albums on his laptop. "Give them a listen. If you don't like them, no harm done."

"Thanks." Alex tossed the untidy stack back on his desk then picked up the pages we had been discussing. "I'll go over these plans with the dean. I have a full teaching schedule tomorrow, but let's say I'll get back to you on Thursday?"

I rose as he put on his blazer. "Of course."

"Did you take the Metra in?"

I nodded.

"I'll walk you out. I'm headed in that direction anyway."

"A girl could get spoiled by this personal attention," I joked.

Alex merely smiled.

As we walked in silence, I mentally chided myself for making such a stupid remark. *Great, Annabeth. Open mouth and insert foot.* I had probably overstepped my bounds. What must he think of me now?

We reached the crossroads that led to the Metra in one direction and to his destination in the other.

I reached to shake his hand, determined to keep things cool and professional. "Thank you again for meeting with me. I'm pleased you liked our proposal."

He shook my hand as he would any other colleague's. "Miles says you're going to the baseball game on Saturday."

I shielded my eyes against the sun. "You've been in touch with Miles?"

"Yeah. He invited me."

Briefly, I wondered if that could be considered a conflict of interest, but I shrugged it off. "Oh." I couldn't hide the disappointment in my voice. "I can't make it. I've got deadlines to meet and then plans that evening." *Shut up, shut up, shut up. He doesn't need to hear about your date with Victor.*

Was it my imagination, or did his shoulders sag a little?

"Well, I hadn't made up my mind yet. It's not half as appealing now." With that, he walked down the opposite path, leaving me staring after him.

CHAPTER SIX

The whole time I was working on my essay for the *Huffington Post*, I was wishing I was at the baseball game with Alex. Why, why did I always have to be so dependable? Why did I always have to do what was right? *Because you're you, Annabeth.* Oh, great. Now I was answering myself too.

I rubbed my face with the heels of my hands and tried to concentrate. With a sigh, I went back and reread the introduction I had written.

Waiting for Love: A 21st Century Spinster Speaks

Tell me if this sounds at all familiar. You aren't even at a family event for five minutes when the questions start. "Where's your boyfriend?" "How's it possible that a pretty girl like you is still single?" "You aren't getting any younger. When are you going to start having kids? Tick-tock."

That last one is always my favorite.

I don't know about you, but I find myself immediately on the defensive, wanting to yell, "I don't have one, and you know what? That's my choice." "Damned if I know. Ask all the single guys in Chicago what's wrong with them." And, "First, thanks for the reminder. Second, whether or not I have kids—and how—is my business, not yours."

Believe me, it's not that I don't want to get married. I do. However, I don't want to marry just anybody. Many people have theorized that my standards are too high, but you know what? At least I have them. I have so many friends who married young and are now on their second or third failed marriage, sometimes with kids or bankruptcy trailing in their wakes. That's exactly what I'm trying to avoid. If I know you aren't likely to be husband material, why would I waste my time and yours and risk growing attached to the wrong person?

However, that hasn't stopped me from putting myself out there. Earlier this year, I joined the Heart+Soul online dating service. Part of the application was an essay in which I had the chance to tell potential matches anything I wanted.

A lot of girls probably would have used this space to make themselves appear as attractive as possible by telling men what they think they want to hear. And that's probably a very successful strategy. But it's not what I chose to do. My theory was that if you want to date me, I want you to know exactly what you're in for, warts and all. So I wrote four hundred brutally honest words and let the chips fall where they may. Heart+Soul was kind enough to allow me to reproduce my essay here, complete with the picture referenced within.

I skipped over my essay, which I'd read so many times by now I had it memorized. My thoughts were flowing as my fingers flew over the keys to type the conclusion.

Amazingly, my candor didn't make every guy run away screaming. I've even gone on dates with a few. But one was so impressed he asked me if he could share it on his blog. With great surprise, I found it resonated with so many people. That's how this column was born.

Nearly a century separates me and the women who first redefined standards for what was acceptable for women—the flappers of the 1920s. Yet we're still facing the same sort of attitudes. In the time between, we've seen working women become the norm, the Pill revolutionize sex, and feminism give us a greater voice in all aspects of life, yet the questions we're asked are still the same. Why is that?

Single girls, I feel like it starts with us. We need to be bold, be open with our opinions. That's never going to stop a concerned mother or grandmother from asking when you're going to start popping out kids, but maybe it won't be her first, or only, question. If we don't stand up for ourselves, no one else will. I'm not advocating saying exactly what you're thinking, but you can redirect the question to a different subject. If someone asks if you're still single, you could reply, "Yes, and I don't mind. It gives me more free time to focus on [insert your interest here]. And when the right guy comes along, I can't wait to share it with him." That shuts down their arguments in a respectful fashion.

As for everyone else, if they don't want you for who you are, there are plenty more fish in the sea.

Here's hoping all of you find your ideal mate.

I looked up from my laptop and blinked myself back into reality from the writer's trance. This was actually pretty good. Now all I needed was to proof it one last time. But first I needed to get some distance from it.

I glanced at the clock and pulled out my phone to check the MLB app. The Cards and Cubs were only in the fourth inning. I still had my ticket, and I had plenty of time to make it to Wrigley and catch some of the game.

When I opened the door to our company suite half an hour later, all eyes turned to me. Kendra, Angela, Miles, Christine the intern, Jenna, and Rick were all there along with Alex and a guy I vaguely recognized as Jenna's boyfriend.

"Hey, you made it," Miles called from the front row of seats. "What about the essay?"

"Finished it early."

"Well, I was hoping you'd change your mind. We saved you a seat."

I glanced at the empty chair next to Alex, where his date would have been sitting had he brought one. I took that as a good sign. Now he was in for some good-natured ribbing.

"I see you decided a game without me was worth your time." I made myself comfortable, and Miles passed me a beer.

"It was a calculated risk. Miles told me you hardly ever miss a game, so I took a gamble."

I eyed him warily, trying to decide whether or not to believe him. It was true I was a huge Cubbies fan, despite their abysmal track record, so I decided the best course of action was to pretend it didn't matter. "Well, you seemed to be having a swell enough time before I arrived."

"Swell? What is this, Prohibition?" He paused a beat. "In which case, you won't be needing this."

"Hey!" I squealed as he tried to take away my beer.

"No, no, no, doll. We can't let the coppers catch you with this contraband hooch. They'll send you up the river for sure." He was doing his best gangster impression.

I managed to free my wrist and get my drink back, but not without spilling some on his T-shirt, effectively ending our game. "Sorry."

"No worries. It'll wash out."

We spent the next few minutes in silence, watching the Cubs strike out one Cardinal after another.

"That's what I'm talkin' about!" Kendra yelled, doing a little dance of joy as the inning ended.

"Hey, Miles, where's Mia?" I called.

"Tokyo, I think."

"No, that was last weekend."

"Amsterdam?"

I shrugged. I couldn't keep up with Mia's jet-setting schedule. She was constantly off to one exotic locale or another. One day she was shooting a commercial in LA, then the next she was walking down a runway in London. We had to take her when we could get her.

"Hey, hey, guys, pay attention. They're about to put up the next question," Jenna yelled.

I leaned in toward Alex. "What's she talking about?"

"It's this new thing they're doing between innings to keep the crowd entertained. They ask a question, and you text your answer Then a few minutes later, they display the most popular answers and one lucky person who gave the top answer wins a prize."

"Huh," was all I could manage to say. Alex was leaning so close to me that I could smell the crisp, clean scent of his shampoo. It was affecting my brain, making my thoughts all fuzzy.

"Okay, everyone. The question is 'What's your favorite romantic movie?'"

A chorus of groans went up from the men.

"I'm not hanging around for this," Miles said, standing. "Rick, you wanna go for another round?"

I looked at Alex, wondering if he'd want to join them, but he said, "I'm good."

"*Casablanca*," Jenna shouted out her answer.

"Oh, that's a good one, but I prefer *Gone with the Wind*," Angela said.

Christine pretended to gag. "I say *Pretty Woman*."

"*Dirty Dancing*," I said. That was met by a series of low whistles and at least one poorly delivered line about a corner.

"*Avatar*."

Everyone became silent, staring at Kendra.

"What? To me, it's romantic." She crossed her arms and scowled.

"Alex, what's yours?" I asked.

He scrunched up his nose and closed one eye as if trying to decide. "I'm going to have to go with *Roman Holiday*."

"Oh, Audrey Hepburn. A classic. Good choice," Jenna cooed as she texted in our answers from atop her boyfriend's lap.

I wanted to smack her—and not just because she was flirting with Alex in front of her boyfriend.

A few seconds later, when the answers appeared on the board, it was Jenna's turn to dance. "Woo-hoo! *Casablanca* at number one."

"I hate that movie," I muttered, not realizing I'd said it aloud until Alex turned to me.

"Seriously? Me too."

"I've never met anyone who dislikes it before. They're all"—I pitched my voice to a falsetto—"'But he walked away because he loved her.' Bullshit. If he loved her, they should have found a way to stay together."

"Amen!" Alex clinked his plastic cup with mine. "I don't like tragic endings—even with a well-written purpose. I've always felt that the hero should get the girl in the end. That's the way film, if not life, should be."

"And literature," I added.

"I bet you hated *Wuthering Heights*."

"Not as much as *Tess of the d'Urbervilles*."

We both groaned. We carried on this way, happily discussing our favorite and most abhorred books—he loved *The Road* and hated *Waiting for Godot*, and we both agreed that *The Great Gatsby* was way overrated—oblivious to the ball game until Miles and Rick returned and doled out drinks.

"What did we miss?" Miles asked.

"Besides Jenna missing out on a trip to Cancun?"

Jenna scowled. "Some bitch named Carrie from Skokie won."

"Top of the eighth, three to two, Cubs. Runners on first and second. Lamros is up," Kendra answered, her attention focused totally on the game.

Craig Lamros was our newest recruit from the minors. He'd proven himself in the outfield but had yet to show any consistent hitting power. With two men already out, this could be his chance to shine.

We watched with great anticipation as he fouled the first pitch off into the stands. Strike one. The next was a wide curveball the umpire called as a ball. Lamros swung at and missed the next pitch. Strike two. The third pitch was a fastball, low and away, but Lamros managed to connect with it solidly and send the ball screaming into the stands for a three-run homer. The crowd went wild.

In our little suite, the roar was no less deafening as we all shot to our feet and cheered. Soon we were all hugging and tapping glasses. That was when I noticed Jenna was drinking water, which was unusual. Before I could process that observation, a familiar song spilled from the speakers, celebrating the home run by welcoming the fans to the city, followed by an expletive covered by a guitar riff.

"That's a Kill Hannah song," I yelled to Alex.

He bent down to be near my ear. "I know. I recognize it."

"You listened to them? What do you think?"

"They aren't traditional poets, but I can see where my students could identify with their lyrics. I'll keep them in mind as I construct the course."

My heart fell. I had really hoped Alex would understand the subtle beauty of their lyrics.

Even after our group had quieted down, Miles was in full-on victory mode. "Fly away little birdies. Go on home to roost on the Arch where you belong," he sang a little drunkenly.

I raised an eyebrow at Rick, who nodded and said, "Don't worry. I'll get him home safely."

I was about to thank him when the clock on the scoreboard caught my eye. "Oh geez! Is that the time? I have to meet Victor." I shot to my feet, thanking everyone for a good time.

Alex touched my arm. "Are you sure you can't stay till the end of the game?"

"I would love to, really, but I can't. I promised Victor I'd be there."

"No, I get it, the boyfriend takes precedence," Alex said.

Oh, a hint of petulance. I couldn't help relishing the idea that he might be just the slightest bit jealous. I removed his hand gently. "You got my afternoon. He gets my night. Sounds like a fair deal to me."

⌇

I flew up the stairs to my apartment. In less than five minutes, I was out of my jeans and into a black cap-sleeved dress and had traded my tennis shoes for jeweled pumps. If I touched up my hair and makeup quickly and the taxi gods were with me, I'd have just enough time to be considered fashionably late.

Just my luck, traffic was horrible. As I walked the last five blocks to the gallery, I heard my fellow pedestrians complaining about a malfunction with one of the bridges. At least I'd have an excuse for not getting there on time.

Navigating on autopilot, I replayed my encounters with Victor since that night at Mockingbird, looking for some sign that he also thought our relationship was headed somewhere. We hadn't had much time to see each other thanks to our crazy, and often conflicting, work schedules. We'd met for lunch a few times, and he'd accompanied me to a few of my work functions, but we still hadn't been on a proper date. Now I was on my way to one of his art shows. Sometimes I wondered if we'd ever get a few minutes of alone time. I craved emotional and physical intimacy, and that was something we wouldn't get until we could block out the rest of the world. He might be the one I could move on with. He might just erase the scars Nick had caused. A host of faeries danced in my abdomen at the thought.

When I was only a few buildings away from the gallery, music spilled out into the street as guests came and went. As I entered, I took in the white walls lit here and there by small spotlights that shone on canvases brightly splotched with paint or illuminated pedestals for his clay-and-glass sculptures. I still had a lot to learn about modern art, but I was willing to try for Victor.

Victor spotted me as I stepped past the reception table. He kissed me on the forehead, nearly singing, "Hello, beautiful."

I hugged him briefly before he whisked me off to meet some of his friends, the owners of the gallery.

"Annabeth, I'd like you to meet Katrina and Peter. They're the curators here and also work as buyers for a well-known auction house I'm not allowed to name."

"Hello, Annabeth, so nice to meet you." Katrina's smile and grasp were warm, but the genuineness she sought to project never reached her eyes.

Peter, on the other hand, looked more like a basset hound than a man, with his droopy, bag-ringed eyes and loose jowls. He never let go of his drink but instead nodded in my direction. "A pleasure."

"It really was kind of you to open up your gallery to Victor tonight," I said.

Peter scoffed. "Oh, it was nothing. This boy has immense talent, and it's time the whole city knows it."

"The city? Darling, you think too small. We're telling the world." Over my head, Katrina saw someone she knew and gave a small finger wave. "If you'll excuse me." She brushed past us, then more quietly in my ear, she added, "This is a private collector from Japan I've been wooing for months. One sale to him could set your boy up for stardom."

I swallowed hard, suddenly nervous for Victor.

"What was that all about?" Victor asked.

Not wanting to rattle his nerves, I told a white lie. "She was just telling me there are several pieces here I can't miss."

Victor's face lit up. "There are. I want to show you a few of my favorites. Peter, please excuse us."

"No worries, my boy, no worries." Peter quickly returned his attention to his scotch.

Victor led me to the wall of bright paintings I had seen through the front window. In the sea of color, a somber black-and-white triptych commanded attention. On each canvas, Victor had painted a recently extinguished candle, its wick still a burning ember, the smoke lazily forming something akin to an ink blot test. The first time I glanced at it, all I saw was swirling white paint; the second time, the smoke resolved itself into the profile of a ballet dancer *en pointe*. Next to it was a similar piece, only this one was a couple dancing the tango. The final piece in the triptych was a couple—depending on how you looked at it, it could have been a man and a woman, a man with another man, or two women—in a passionate embrace.

"This is the one I wanted you to see." He pointed below the black to a colorful portrait of a woman in profile.

She was gazing slightly downward as if deep in thought, her flowing hair a mass of swirling color around her face. It tumbled like a rainbow waterfall over her shoulders to the top of her white gown, where the canvas ended.

I looked at the plaque beneath it. "'Annabeth's Essence.'" I gazed at Victor in wonder. "You painted me?"

He nodded, barely able to contain his excitement. "The night we met. Right after the party, I went to my studio, flooded the place with light, and started working. There was something about you. I just had to capture your spirit. You're unlike anyone I've ever met—shy yet fun, brilliant and sweet but with this unexpected wild streak. Your little dance made quite the impression on me."

I leaned toward him, up on my tiptoes so my lips nearly brushed his. "Oh, it did, did it? Well, there's more where that came from." I leaned in to kiss him.

"I look forward to it," he purred, then our lips met. When he finally pulled away, he reluctantly scanned the crowd. "I should probably get back to circulating the room. Drinks after the showing?"

"Sure. I'll mingle. I think I saw a few people I know from a PR association."

"I'll find you by nine. We should be done by then." He kissed me quickly, this time on cheek. "You're a doll for understanding. I promise you a real date Monday night. That sound good?" he called over his shoulder as he approached a group of artfully chic thirty-somethings admiring one of his sculptures.

"I'd like that."

I was still watching him when Peter shuffled up to me. "I couldn't help but overhear. If you ask me, that's not how a lady should be treated. If he valued you, you'd be his top priority even on his night. He should keep you by his side and introduce you to everyone, make you part of his career."

Before I could reply, Peter rattled the ice in his glass, took a sip, and disappeared into the crowd without further commentary, leaving me to wonder if he was right and I was a fool.

CHAPTER SEVEN

Monday came far too soon, as it always did. I barely had time to set down my purse and turn on my desk lamp before Laini called me into her office.

Pen and paper in hand, I knocked on her doorframe before stepping inside. My normally calm and collected boss did not look well. It was only nine in the morning, and her curly hair was already coming loose of its hastily pinned updo. Her normally smooth skin was etched with deep lines, and her knuckles were white as she lifted her coffee cup to her lips.

"Are you okay, Laini?"

She motioned for me to sit. "Not in the least. Meetings started at seven this morning, then I got the most charming phone call." She allowed me to absorb her sarcasm, then she sighed. "Jenna quit. Just up and quit. No two weeks' notice, nothing."

I didn't know what to say. Jenna was a flake, but I'd never expected her to do something so unprofessional. "What? Why?"

"She's pregnant. Apparently that gives her leave to put us all in a bind." Laini leaned on her elbows, resting her forehead on the warm base of her mug. She didn't look up as she spoke. "I suppose you realize this is the worst possible time for her to abandon us. We're in the thick of so many projects. I've handed off some to our other account execs, but they can only do so much." She looked up then, straight into my eyes.

I shifted in my seat, wondering what was coming next.

"You've been here a few years; you know how we operate. You've also been intimately involved in the University of Chicago account. That's why I'm handing that one over to you. As of today, you are both account exec and writer for this project. If you have other things on your plate that would compete with these duties, let me know, and I'll reassign them to the other writers."

I sat back, stunned. This was a huge opportunity for me. If I could show the leadership she desired, I might qualify for a permanent promotion. Plus, it meant a lot more time with Alex. "I—thank you. I won't disappoint you."

"I know you won't. That's why I asked you. You're in charge through September, when the project launches. Most of our work will be done by then, at least on the creative side. We'll fill Jenna's position before then. Once the university's first-term needs become purely coordination and media relations, it'll be a good project to hand off to our new person. But I don't want to leave them without a contact in the meantime."

"Thank you again. I'll get in touch with them right away and let them know of the change." I started to rise, but Laini stopped me.

She held out a spiral notebook with a leather cover. "You might want this. It's Jenna's master plan for the project. I'm sure you'll find more in her computer files, but this should get you started."

Jenna had a plan? All in one place? Maybe I'd underestimated her. I took the book from Laini, swallowing hard as the full weight of what I'd agreed to pressed on my shoulders. I flipped through the pages, which were just as messy as the file folder had been. Nope. Pegged her right. Once I sorted this all out, I'd be up to my ears in meetings for the next several months, not to mention writing all the creative we still had to produce.

"Oh, and Annabeth?" Laini called after me. "I'm counting on you. If we do well on this, who knows what other business the university might send our way."

No pressure.

❧

"Damn it!" I yelled, slamming the eyeliner on the faux marble bathroom counter. I was lucky the brown pencil didn't break. All I was trying to do was line my eyes, but that was impossible with my shaking hands.

Mia appeared in my doorway with a glass of some amber-colored alcohol. "Drink this."

I glared at her, offended by the idea that I would need to start drinking before my date.

"What? It's not like you're driving, and you really do need to chill out."

"You really are not helping." I took the glass anyway and took a big sip, regretting it a moment later when the Grand Mariner burned my throat. I gagged and coughed.

"Could have fooled me," she said, returning to the depths of my closet to choose appropriate accessories to go with the lacy, violet empire-waist sheath dress she had picked out for me earlier.

She was back from whatever exotic locale had recently spit her out and was in full "give Annabeth a makeover" mode. I reluctantly tolerated it because I didn't want to be alone while I was getting ready for fear my nerves would eat me alive—or at least make me back out of our plans.

"You and Victor have been on plenty of dates, so why are you acting like a virgin on prom night?"

Because I am *a virgin, you ding-dong.* I widened my eyes while passing the mascara wand over my lashes. "Yeah, but this is our first real date, something that doesn't involve his art or my work. I'm really starting to care about him," I added more quietly.

Mia's eyebrows shot up. "Are you in love?"

"No, but I really like him, and I think this could last a while."

"So you want to impress him. Understandable. Not necessary, but understandable." Mia handed me a chunky necklace I didn't recognize. "It's mine. He's an artist. You have to show him that you have an artistic side too. Your stuff is too. . . petite. Just wear it."

Scowling, I fastened the necklace then took the earrings she offered.

"So where is he taking you?" She played with my hair, experimentally twisting it up then letting it flow free.

"He wouldn't tell me. He just said to dress up and that tonight was special."

"Oh, a mysterious man. Sexy," she said around a mouthful of hairpins. She'd just put the last one in place when the doorbell rang. Mia hugged me. "Aw, my little girl's going to get her flower plucked," she drawled with mock pride. "It's about time." I gave her a wry smile. It was true my encounter with Nick in Rome had made me reluctant to trust again, especially when it came to sex, but that didn't mean I was as pure as she thought. I may have had morals, but I also had needs. I'd had some experience with the few guys I'd dated, just not as much as she thought I should. I hit her playfully. "Shut up. And don't embarrass me."

I opened the door. Victor stood before me in a gray sweater over a blue shirt and gray slacks. The blue really brought out his eyes.

"You look lovely," he said before I could say hello.

"Thanks." Remembering Mia, I shoved her out the door past him. "You remember Mia. She was just leaving."

"Bye." She wiggled her fingers at us. "Don't do anything I wouldn't do."

"That rules out absolutely nothing," I muttered.

"Best way to start an evening," Victor said, grinning and taking my hand. "No rules, just all the possibility in the world."

✌

The restaurant Victor chose was upscale and trendy, perfectly in keeping with his world and predilections. Looking at the other patrons, I felt a little overdressed, but I subscribed to the Mae West school of thought that said a woman can never be overdressed or overeducated.

"So you never wanted to do anything other than paint?" I asked as the waiter set a colorful salad in front of me.

"No. I swear, from the first time I touched finger paints, I was in love. I can even still picture that first painting." His eyes went dreamy with the memory, then he barked a laugh. "Actually, it wasn't all that different from some of the abstract stuff I do now."

I laughed, trying to keep the water I had just swallowed from spraying out of my nose.

"But all through school, art was really the only thing that held my attention. I kind of liked math but only geometry and other things

I could apply to my art." He looked at me shyly over his glass. "I have to admit I wasn't the best student. I went to the Art Institute for college, so I don't really have what you would consider a traditional education."

"That's okay—not everyone follows the same path. How's your contractor work going?"

"Well, with the success of the gallery showing, I'm getting to use more and more of my time on my art. Right now I'm focusing on a new sculpture collection." He wiggled his eyebrows. "I'm pretty good with my hands."

"I bet you are." Mia probably would have followed that up with a request for a demonstration, but I couldn't force the words past my lips.

He met my gaze with smoldering eyes. "You have no idea."

Our entrees arrived then, and conversation turned to more mundane topics as we both balanced speaking with eating. He asked about my writing, and I told him about my ongoing struggle to balance a full-time job with writing my second book and a social life.

He looked concerned. "I don't want to hinder your art. Believe me, I know what it's like to struggle to find enough hours in the day."

I placed my hand over his with a gentle squeeze. "You could never hinder me. In fact, I've noticed I'm more inspired when I'm with you. The day after the gallery opening, I wrote two thousand words after work. Most nights, I don't write anything at all, so that more than doubles what I get out on a normal night."

He placed his other hand over mine and leaned toward me. "Maybe I'm your muse."

"Maybe you are." I leaned in so that our lips met ever so softly.

Our waiter chose that moment to offer us dessert, and we pulled apart sheepishly.

Once a piece of something chocolate that likely would someday give me a heart attack sat in front of me, I asked Victor, "So how did your meeting with the guy from Japan go? Was he interested in your work?"

Victor visibly brightened. "Yeah. He said he really liked what he saw. He bought three pieces right then and there and said he wants to talk to some of his artist friends and other collectors back home. He thinks there may be some opportunity for me in his country."

"That's so exciting! I bet Katrina was thrilled."

"Oh, she is. She's determined to make me an international superstar."

"As you should be."

I held out my fork to him. He leaned across the table and ate from it, closing his eyes as he savored the rich chocolate and made sounds of delight. Before he could sit back in his seat, I stopped him.

"You have a little bit right here." I dragged my thumb down next to his lip, then I licked the chocolate off it.

His expression turned sultry. "Just so you know, dessert doesn't have to be the end of the night."

I played coy. "Whatever could you mean?"

"Whatever you wish me to." But his eyes told a different story. They betrayed how he hoped the night would end, and his plans went far beyond a good-night kiss.

I smiled at him as the waiter took away my plate and left the check for Victor. "All right, Don Juan. What do you say we pay the man and see what kind of trouble we can get into? I hear paint can be all kinds of fun."

He grinned. "I love the way you think."

Back in his cozy apartment in Logan Square, it didn't take long for things to get hot and heavy, clothing discarded in favor of the kiss of moonlight on bare skin. I was panting by the time we broke apart, skin slick with sweat.

Victor was already fumbling in the bedside drawer for a condom, which brought me sharply back to reality. Here was the dreaded moment of truth. Victor knew about my past, or lack thereof, but it made sense he thought it was time. And it was—or least it should have been.

Was I ready? I was way too old to be having this internal debate, but the knot in my stomach told me the answer was no. Damn Nick and his violent temper. Damn my romantic fantasies. If it wasn't for them, I wouldn't have this sexual hang-up. I could just ignore it, do what everyone else did, and get this over with. I willed myself to say yes, but instead I shook my head.

"I'm sorry, Victor." I sat up, my back toward him, and hugged my arms around myself. "I can't—not yet at least. I should go. You deserve someone better, someone who can meet all of your needs. I can't. I'm. . . broken."

Victor kissed my shoulder softly. "You aren't broken. You just need time. We haven't really been together that long. I can wait."

I looked over my shoulder at him. "Are you sure?"

"Yeah." He turned me back toward him, his expression suddenly devilish. "Besides, there are plenty of other things we can do to keep each other entertained."

CHAPTER EIGHT

July

I had a mental image of cartoon calendar pages flying off the wall—that was how fast the next few weeks passed. I was constantly with Victor or Alex. For a girl who was used to being alone, having two attractive men in my life daily was a pleasant shock.

My days were spent either writing at my agency office or with Alex at his, working out the particulars of the rest of our plan for the next nine months. Most of my nights were with Victor—he and I were actually able to see one another on a regular basis—and he was being incredibly patient as I struggled to get over the complex mental hurdles that kept me from making him my lover. I couldn't help but feel stupid going through this at my age, but his willingness to wait for me, to try to understand my inner conflict, made me like him all the more, though I wasn't quite yet in love with him. Yet, some part of me knew his patience had its limits and I'd better figure out what was wrong with me soon.

But there was so much to do on the University campaign I hardly had time to think. When I wasn't writing, I was contacting publicists and literary organizations, libraries and publishers, making arrangements for our events. When he wasn't teaching, advising students, or grading papers, Alex was on the phone with or emailing donors, parents, and prospective high schools. He reached out as far away as St. Louis, Bloomington, and Kansas City for financial backing, support, and pledges of participation. Because of his teaching schedule and my other responsibilities, we often ended up meeting late in the day and into the evening.

One hot evening toward the end of July, the air conditioning in Walker Hall faltered, doing little to relieve the sweltering summer heat trapped in the old stone building. We flung open all the windows in his office, capturing a soft cross breeze that I liked to imagine came off the lake even though we were too far away for that.

"I'm really surprised by how much easier this is flowing with you. I think it's because you're so organized." Alex gestured at the color-coded folders strewn around us on the floor of his office as we went over each aspect of the campaign.

Self-consciously, I tucked my hair behind my ear. "It's in my nature. I have to have a plan for everything, or I freak out."

Alex sat back, watching me. "What else is in your nature, Annabeth?"

I looked up from the box of Chinese takeout I was picking at, trying to figure out if he was joking or if that was a real question. "Seriously?"

"Yes. I'd like to get to know you. God knows we spend enough time together."

I hugged my knees, suddenly uncomfortable. "Okay. Um, I'm a worrier, but you probably guessed that." I racked my suddenly empty brain for things to say. "I'm absolutely no good at small talk." I laughed nervously.

Alex smiled. "Say no more." He stacked our folders into a neat pile next to him. "I think we're done with these for tonight, right?"

"Yeah, I don't think I can think about books anymore this week. Says the girl who should go home and write." I started to get up, but Alex grabbed my arm. The pulse that passed between us was so strong I sat back down without meaning to.

"I didn't mean I wanted you to leave," Alex said, sitting down with his own carton and chopsticks. "It's Friday night. We deserve a little downtime. I was serious about wanting to get to know you. You say you're not good at small talk, so let's try it this way—remember those 'getting to know you' quizzes that used to go around by email in the nineties? Let's pretend we're filling out one of those. It'll give us a place to start." He gazed out the window as if a list were written the stars. "I already know Mia calls you 'Pookie,' so we can dispense with the nickname question—"

"No, no, no. It doesn't work that way. We both have to answer the question. I don't know yours yet."

He shrugged. "I don't have one."

"Oh, I'm sure you do. Everyone has at least one. I bet your students have names for you."

"They probably do. But there are many, many legal reasons why I don't want to know what they are." He popped a strip of beef and broccoli stem into his mouth.

"Come on, your parents had to call you something. I'll give you another one of mine. My dad calls me 'kitten.' Come on, think. If you don't give me one, I'll make one up for you," I threatened.

He chortled, chewing. "My mom used to call me 'Alexander the Great,' but I doubt that counts now."

"It counts. And I like it. I may start calling you that."

He wagged a finger at me. "If you do that in public, I will fire you."

I held up my hands in a gesture of surrender. "All right. I give up."

"Now, as I was saying before I was so rudely interrupted by the writing pixie—that's your new name, by the way—what's your favorite color?"

"Oh, so now I get another nickname when you won't divulge a current one. That's fair. But I like this one, so you're forgiven. And the answer is blue. Yours?"

"Same."

"Flower?" he asked.

"Blue hydrangeas. My dad and I grew them back home."

"Where is back home?"

"Des Moines. My parents still live there. What about you? Are you a lifelong Chicagoan?"

"I am. Except for four years at Princeton, I've always lived here. This city has been in my blood for generations."

"Princeton, eh? Did you row crew?" I figured he probably had. It was one of their most competitive sports, even turning out Olympians.

"Of course. I actually coach for one of the boys' schools here in town. It's the only sport that I ever felt was worth my time."

"Why is that?"

"I don't know. There's something about being on the water and moving in time with seven other people that's almost. . ." He searched for the right word.

"Meditative?"

"Yes! I don't suppose you row?"

"I have. I took lessons for a while, but I never really got the hang of the oar. I kept knocking it into the person in front of me. Plus, I lived in fear of falling into the water while trying to get into or out of the boat. I'm not exactly graceful."

"I have a hard time believing that."

"Oh, give me time. I'll fall over or off of something. Or nothing. It doesn't really matter." I nervously picked at my fortune cookie, getting crumbs all over my lap as I broke it open.

"You have to read it out loud," Alex said.

I rolled my eyes. "And add 'in bed' to the end. I know the drill." I opened the narrow slip of paper. "'You will prosper if you speak your truth with sincerity.' Wow. That's generic."

"But it fits you. That reminds me, I saw your piece in the *Huffington Post*."

"You did?" I asked, wishing the floor would swallow me.

"Yes. I thought it was very well done. Being single is hard, especially as we get older. It's like society brands you as abnormal if you haven't committed to someone, anyone, by a certain age. I'm willing to bet what you said resonated with a lot of people. I know it did with me, and I'm a thirty-seven-year-old guy. Women probably related even more."

"The comments were interesting. As on the blog, some people loved it and said I was spot on while others said it was no wonder I'm still single." I crossed my legs and leaned toward Alex. "But I'm surprised you related to it. You seem to have it all together."

Alex emitted a self-effacing snort. "Hardly. It's tough when you want to be with someone who is really ready to commit and everyone around you just wants to have a good time."

"Or when you have standards you can't express but aren't willing to compromise."

"Exactly."

We lapsed into a pensive silence then, both lost in our own

thoughts. Outside, crickets sang from the bushes while other insects clicked and chirped their own contributions to the music of the night.

"You know, I've always loved the sound of summer evenings. To me, there's nothing more relaxing than the chirping of crickets." I turned to look at him. "Have you noticed that they get more active as the weather cools? I like to think they're singing the earth to sleep for winter."

"'And, down the mist-enfolded lanes/Grown pensive now with evening/See, lingering as the twilight wanes/Lover with lover wandering,'" he recited.

"That's beautiful."

"'Autumn Twilight' by Arthur Symons. He wrote in the early nineteen hundreds." Alex rose and crossed over to one of the many bookshelves. He pulled down an old, fraying hardback with a red cover long since faded to pink and held it out to me. "His collected works. I think you'll really like him."

Fingering the gilt lettering, I looked at him. "Thank you. How do you know about him? I don't think he's someone we studied in school."

"I did. Poetry was my minor. It's kind of a passion of mine."

"Hence your poetry in music class. I think I'm starting to understand you, Alexander the Great." I stood, brushing cookie crumbs off my skirt. "Do you write it as well?"

"Occasionally. I never fooled myself into thinking I could make a career out of it. It's more of a hobby than anything else."

"Hey, we all need those. But don't undervalue yourself. I bet you have more talent than you think."

He smiled. It may have been my imagination, but there seemed to be so many unspoken words in that small gesture. I silently wished the words out of him, begging him to say the things voiced only in my dreams, deep within my heart.

That was when I realized I was falling for him. I liked Victor, but I was developing quite an affection for Alex. I'd found him attractive from the moment we met, but my lust had been slowly transforming inside the chrysalis of our professional obligations into something much deeper. But there was no way I could tell him—not while we were working together.

And what of Victor? We were getting more serious, and I was happy about that, but if given the chance, I'd still have picked Alex over him. What did that say about my feelings for Victor? Was I just biding my time until Alex was available, or did I truly care for Victor? Was it possible to carry a torch for two men at once?

Silently, I cursed the ill timing of my duplicitous heart. I'd seen enough romantic movies to know no good could come of this. Someone was going to get hurt; I just hoped it wasn't me.

CHAPTER NINE

The following Monday, I came in to work to see Jenna's old office lit up and clean. Gone were her messy piles of unfiled meeting notes and stacks of project folders. For the first time in my three years at the agency, I could see the top of her desk. It had even been dusted. In place of the mess was a welcome basket filled with a coffee cup—bearing the agency logo, of course—assorted teas and coffees, snack foods, and a few gift cards to local eateries within walking distance. In the center of the desk was a fresh notepad, waiting to greet its new owner.

They must have hired Jenna's replacement. That was fast. Whoever they'd found must have been perfect for the position. Although anyone would have been better than Jenna. I glanced at the name plate on the door, but it hadn't been filled in yet.

Before I could retreat to my cube, Laini and Rick flagged me down.

"Annabeth, good. I'm glad you're here. I'd like to introduce you to our new account executive," Laini said.

The two pressed their backs against the walls of the narrow hall, allowing a man to pass between them. When he looked up, my heart iced over. Those eyes, so blue, like hidden pools of the purest water. I had spent most of my life looking into them, but the last time they had been cast my way, they were filled with hatred and pain. I'd certainly never expected to see them in this city, my new home, much less in my workplace.

"Annabeth, this is Nick Zarrino," Laini said. "Nick, this is Annabeth Coe. But I believe you know each other. Is that right?"

Nick put out his hand to shake mine. "Yes. We're old friends, but it's been a long time. How are you, Annabeth?"

"Fine." The word came out high and cracked as I took his hand. Part of me wanted to melt into its familiarity, to forget the past and just remember the good times, but I couldn't erase the memory of our parting. Finding my voice, I added with my most professional smile, "Welcome to Smith and Grenwick."

"Since you two already know one another," Laini said, "Annabeth, I'd like you to spend the next two days orientating Nick. He'll be taking over the corporate social responsibility account of Northwestern Memorial Hospital and the foundation work from Roger Harris. Eventually we'll transition him into the U of Chicago account but not yet."

Laini's assistant, Angela, piped up from behind her superiors. "There's a meeting at ten with the Northwestern team. We're taking him to lunch at noon—you're welcome to join us—then he's meeting with Rick for the rest of the afternoon. Tomorrow is open until three, when Mr. Harris has agreed to a conference call."

"I really appreciate you doing this, Annabeth. I'm in meetings solid for the next few days," Rick said as though that justified the situation he'd unwittingly put me in.

I smiled, readjusting the tote bag and purse on my shoulder. Rick was my boss as well as Nick's, so it wasn't as if I could say no.

Laini gestured us into Nick's office. "Have fun, you two." She and Rick ambled off down the hall.

Nick and I looked at each other, the tension of more than a decade of grudges crackling between us like the lit fuse on a stick of dynamite. Neither of us spoke, each trying to figure out how to bridge that gulf. Part of me wanted to rail at him, another part was brimming with questions, and the greater part warned me to remain professional. There would be time for the rest later. I decided to listen to that part and treat him like a stranger.

"Would you like something to drink? I'll show you where the break room is, then we'll swing by my cube so I can set this down." I gestured toward the bags digging into my right shoulder. "Then I'll give you a tour, and we can get started."

Nick's eyes were pleading. "Baby, I'm so sorry for what happened—"

I held up a hand to cut him off and said with a forced smile, "This is neither the time nor the place. Let's just forget about it for now. We have work to do."

♌

"You will never believe who appeared at the office today," I said to Mia.

Along with Miles, we had just ordered our dinner at a popular new Mexican restaurant and were nursing drinks on the rooftop terrace.

Mia arched an eyebrow at me. "Judging by the rate you're sucking down that margarita, I'm guessing it wasn't someone good."

I glared at her, but the object of my wrath wasn't here. In fact, I didn't have a clue where he was. Probably charming something blond in a short skirt. "Remember the guy who broke my heart senior year of college? Well, we're colleagues now. He was hired in to replace Jenna."

"Seriously, what are the chances that Nick the Dick would end up at our firm?" Miles asked. "I mean, I didn't keep in touch with him but last I heard, he wasn't even living in this part of the country."

"I know, right?"

Mia was looking at me as though appraising my ability to handle this odd situation. "So what are you going to do now?"

"What do you mean?"

"I mean, are you going to clear the air or just let the obviously bad blood between you fester?"

"I'm going to be professional when I need to be around him, which is apparently eight hours a day for a while, and the rest of the time, I'm going to pretend he doesn't exist."

"Fester it is then." Mia sat back in her chair as if she couldn't care less about my choice.

"Well, what would you have me do?"

"Wait, why don't you sound surprised by this whole situation?" Miles asked, narrowing his eyes at his girlfriend.

Mia grimaced, turning her lips downward and wrinkling her brow. "Well. . ." She drew out the word. "I may be indirectly responsible."

I nearly knocked over my drink by lunging at her. "What?"

Miles grabbed my waist and pulled me back into my chair. "Down, girl. Let's hear her out."

Mia's eyes widened, and she backed her chair up a little before speaking. "A few weeks ago, I was out with the Ford girls at some club. I met this cute guy who said he was new to town. Eventually, he mentioned where he went to school, and I said my boyfriend and friend went there. When it turned out you were in the same class, I mentioned your name, and he said he knew you. Later on, when he said he was still looking for a job, I told him about the opening at your company. I figured since you knew each other. . ."

I gripped the lip of the table, fighting to keep my temper in check. "And when he told you his name, you never once thought it could be the same Nick I've wailed about over and over again?"

"No."

Mia's expression radiated lamblike innocence, but I didn't believe her for a second. She had a nasty habit of forgetting about relationships when it suited her. "You didn't make the connection, not even for second? Just like you didn't realize your roommate's girlfriend was the same woman you slept with on St. Patrick's Day? You knew them for months. And you've known about Nick for three years. Who else could he have been?"

"Be fair, Annabeth," Miles chided. "If the situation were reversed, you may not have made the connection either, especially if you'd been drinking. Plus, Nick still had to make it through the interview process. This isn't all Mia's fault. He could just as easily have found the job on the Internet."

Leave it to Miles to be the voice of reason. But I still couldn't believe that was the whole story. If I had learned one thing about Mia, it was that she rarely did anything without it somehow benefiting her.

I started to ask her more, but the waiter arrived with our food, and by the time he left, she and Miles were chatting about the cattle call for Chicago's fall Fashion Week coming up in October.

"Hang on," I interrupted. "Back the truck up. We're not done talking about Nick."

A shadow of annoyance passed over Mia's face, but she tried to cover it with a sigh. "What more is there to say?"

"A lot more." I stabbed at my enchilada with my fork. "Like, what's in it for you?"

"What are you talking about?"

"Helping Nick. Why did you do it?"

"Ah, hello? I was being nice."

"Uh-huh. Since when are you nice?"

Mia looked to Miles to defend her, but he only chuckled.

"He was cute, all right? I wanted his, um—" She glanced at Miles apologetically. Miles frowned but said nothing. Something in the set of his shoulders said he was used to situations like this. "Attention, if you catch my drift."

"Two peas in a pod," I muttered, shaking my head. Then, more loudly, I added, "If that's all it was, why didn't you tell me about it?"

Mia rolled her eyes. "Because I was afraid you'd react like this."

"Like what?" My voice rose with each word. "Like someone blindsided by a demon from her past? Because I have no right to act like that, do I?" I shoved a forkful of enchilada into my mouth.

"Annabeth. . ." Miles' tone was a warning.

"What?" I asked, mouth too full to say more.

"Calm down."

I swallowed and narrowed my eyes at Mia. "You thought I'd be jealous, didn't you?"

"And you're not?" she asked, voice lazy as though she was bored with the topic.

"No. I'm mad that you didn't warn me this bastard was creeping back into my world." That I needed to prepare, to protect my heart. To my chagrin, tears of frustration spilled into my refried beans. "A real friend would have at least given me a head's up."

Mia looked hurt. "Look, I'm sorry I didn't think to tell you, but as I said, I didn't realize who he was. It's not like I make a habit of reporting to you on every guy I meet." She crossed her arms defensively, expression crumbling into an unattractive sulk.

"And now it's time to change the subject before your friendship is ruined over a silly misunderstanding," Miles said, putting a hand on each of our shoulders. "How about them Cubbies? I think they may have a shot at the post-season this year."

❧

Only one hour to go before Nick becomes Rick's problem not yours, I told myself as Nick questioned our way of doing things for what felt like the millionth time in two days.

Willing myself to have the patience of a saint, I forced my expression to remain neutral while I took a deep breath and explained—again. "A log of all of our meetings with clients is important in tracking our billable hours in case a conversation ever comes into dispute or if, as in your situation, someone has to take over an account in progress."

"Yeah, but summarizing every single conversation just seems like busywork. Can't I just hand over my notes to Angela and have her type them up?"

"Angela is Laini's assistant, not ours. We don't have one, so we do this work ourselves."

Nick frowned. "When I took this job, I thought I would be doing more liaising and less paperwork." He tapped the paper clip he was fiddling with on the desk.

"You'll get used to it. Think about this way—these reports are helpful to you as well. Sometimes you'll have half a dozen accounts in flight at once, some of which are likely to be similar clients. This will help you keep Northwestern Memorial's events straight from those associated with the University Medical Center. Besides, Laini presents these to the board and uses them to make sure she knows what's what with our clients."

Nick tossed down his paper clip, and it skittered across the desk like a skipping stone before finally coming to rest next to his stapler. "Great, so my activity is being monitored too."

"Yes, Nick," I snapped. "We all are. It's part of agency life. If you don't perform, you're out. We're not two kids playing in the sandbox together anymore. This is work. It's fun, but it's no easy ride."

He looked at me then, those blue eyes of his piercing straight through my workaday demeanor. "You could just let me fail, you know. Why are you being so nice to me?"

I looked at my lap, eyes tracing the pattern of my houndstooth skirt, not wanting him to see the emotions warring within me. *Because what happened was my fault not yours. Because part of me will always love you even if you are a bastard.* "Because it's the right thing to do."

He grimaced, clearly not happy with my answer.

"Why are you here, Nick?"

"What do you mean?"

I flailed my arms, gesturing around me. "Here. In this office. In this city." In my life.

Nick watched me for a moment before answering, his eyes searching in the way I'd come to know meant he was sizing me up, trying to decide how much to tell me. "Things haven't been going so great for me. My parents are gone. My sister doesn't speak to me. I needed a friendly face."

"And so you decided that the woman who hasn't spoken to you in over a decade was a good place to start?"

Nick let out a long breath through his nose. "Yeah. I mean, I looked at my life, at my past, and wondered where I went wrong. I realized it was in Rome, and that led me back to you."

I snorted. "You always were a smooth liar. You'll do well bullshitting our clients."

"I'm serious, Annabeth. I had no right to hurt you, to pressure you—and I am sorry for that; it was an accident—but I shouldn't have left you alone in a foreign country like I did."

"Stop being so melodramatic. It's not like I was actually alone. I had twenty other classmates to hang out with once you left."

He nodded, accepting my point. "If you had it to do all over again, would you still make the same choice, still say no?"

I stilled, thrown off by the intimacy of his question. For a few heartbeats, I didn't even breathe. I imagined what it would have been like if Nick and I had been lovers, if we had stayed together through the final months of college. I probably would have followed him around as he'd pursued his dream of being a music manager. It was a hard scenario to swallow given that it would have changed everything. We may have even gotten married.

"Yes," I said quietly. "Something in my gut told me you weren't the one, and I always listen to my instincts."

Nick's face darkened, and he glanced at my hands folded in my lap. "Your gut seems to be doing a great job of keeping you single."

I pulled back as though he had burned me, pressing deep into the back of my chair. "I don't see a gold band on your finger either."

"But that's by choice. I don't want to be tied down, not yet. You always wanted to be. Let me guess. You're still chasing a fantasy, still waiting for your Prince Charming. Am I right?"

My cheeks burned, and I glared at him, refusing to answer. But there was no need. Nick had known me since we were four. He could read me better than my own mother.

He leaned forward, resting his elbows on his knees. "Still writing those letters on your birthday? God, I'd kill to see what those say." He chuckled darkly.

I smacked him across the cheek.

Nick's head jerked. A second later, he was rubbing his jaw. To my great astonishment, he smiled slyly and catlike. "There's the Annabeth I've been waiting to see. I was wondering when the she-devil would come out. Jesus, girl, you're not a fucking saint. It's been ten years. Let me have it. Let's get it all out in the open."

I stood, smoothing my skirt, and fought to keep my voice level. "I've done all I am required to with you. Now leave me alone. We may have to work in the same building, but that doesn't mean we have to talk to one another."

Nick got to his feet, placing a hand on my shoulder. "Come on, love, I'm sorry. I didn't mean it. I was just trying to rile you."

I shrugged him off and whirled to face him. My index finger was less than an inch from his nose. "Never ever call me that again. If you must say anything, call me by my name. We are adults. Professionals. Nothing more. Got it?"

He nodded.

I gathered my things and headed toward the door, fighting the tears pricking at my eyes. "Angela will call you when the clients are here."

Instead of going back to my desk as I had planned, I took a detour into the bathroom and locked myself in a stall. Immediately, my whole body shook. Working with Nick was going to be its own special kind of hell.

CHAPTER TEN

August

"Come on, Annabeth," Mia said, dragging me by the arm toward the black-clad doorman at the CopaKaraoke. "It won't be so bad. You'll see."

"No. I swore I would never do karaoke, and I don't plan on changing my mind now."

She stood between the street and me, blocking my escape, hands on her hips. "It's my birthday. Therefore, you have to do what I want. That's our rule, remember?"

Ugh. She was right. "Fine."

The doorman waved us through. "Happy birthday," he said to Mia with a wink.

She responded with a smile that could only have been described as delicious.

As an off-tune couple crooned a popular duet, we found the rest of our group at a cluster of tables in front of the stage. Scanning the faces, I realized most of them were Mia's friends and every one of them a model. Suddenly, I felt very pedestrian.

So Miles and I were onlookers into Mia's glamorous world tonight—again. Goodie. I sat and ordered a vodka martini, knowing I'd need something strong to get me through the night.

"All right," Miles said, rubbing his hands together. "Who is going to rescue us from this terrible tragedy happening on stage? Someone has to go first."

I pointed at Mia. "The birthday girl should go first."

"Yeah," one of the models chimed in. "Birthday girl!"

Soon they were all chanting the phrase. Mia stood, smiling coyly, but she was enjoying every second of it. She went over to the guy in charge and consulted his list before whispering something in his ear. Then she took the stage. A few seconds later, she was seducing the audience with a sultry rendition of Katy Perry's "Dark Horse."

Sometimes I thought she'd missed her calling. Not only did she have perfect pitch, she was a true showman, making up dance moves off the top of her head perfectly coordinated to the music. By the time she pulled Miles up on stage to rap Juicy J's part, she had the audience eating out of the palm of her hand. Plenty of people were cheering, catcalling, and whistling.

As they exited the stage, one particularly sharp whistle came from directly behind me, making me jump and spill my drink all over my sequined shirt. Thank God vodka was clear. I turned around, ready to spear the whistler with a dirty look, but I froze when I saw it was Alex. What the hell was he doing here?

I grabbed Mia's arm when she walked by, purposefully digging my nails into her arm. "You invited Alex?"

"Miles did. But I'm glad he's here." She looked him up and down appreciatively. Turning back to the group, Mia called, "I want to do shots! Who's with me?"

As the models raced to the bar, Alex pulled up a chair next to me, signaling to the waitress to bring me another drink. "Sorry about that. I didn't mean to frighten you."

"No, I—I just didn't expect to see you here."

"Neither did I. Karaoke has never really been my thing. When Miles invited me, I tried to beg off, but Mia made it sound too good to pass up."

"She could sell a prostitute to a priest."

Alex laughed, choking on the beer the waitress had just set before him. "That I would like to see."

I smiled at him over my glass. "What are you doing next Sunday?"

He grinned at me.

Soon, there was a shot glass in my hand. Tequila. Oh, this was going to be an interesting night. The next thing I knew, we had created a dance floor in the middle of the room, shaking our booties to the good, the bad, and even the ugly. After a few more shots, the group decided it was time for me to take the stage.

"No, no, no, I don't sing. You really don't want me to," I protested.

"I've heard her sing. She's telling the truth," Mia said.

"When have you heard me sing?"

"Please, how many nights have we spent at Howl at the Moon, singing with the dueling piano guys?" Mia's eyes sparkled. "Actually, there is one song you manage to stay on key for." She snatched my wrist and dragged me toward the coordinator.

"What song?" I called, suddenly terrified.

"You'll see." She fixed her large green eyes on me. "Pookie, it'll be fine. When have I ever steered you wrong?"

I could think of a thousand times.

Standing on the stage, a microphone clutched my hands, my heart pounding, I thought I would faint.

"Just keep your eyes on me," Mia said. "Pretend we're in the crowd at the piano bar. You sing along every time. Just follow my lead."

The familiar six-beat guitar lead-in to Rick Springfield's "Jessie's Girl" poured from the speakers, and I relaxed a little. Mia wasn't kidding. This was a song we, and every other club-going woman, knew far too well. She was right. I could do this.

Even before Mia sang the first line, the crowd cheered. I waited for her to get through the first few lines, and I joined in at the part about the girl's eyes, doing the classic disco move of framing my own eyes in sideways peace signs before running my hands down my body in time with the reference in the song.

I couldn't see the crowd very well through the lights, but I heard Miles and Alex cheering. Emboldened by their support and the alcohol flowing through my veins, I took the lead on the second verse. When we got to the bridge, Mia and I harmonized. I couldn't resist playing air drums during the extended solo, and Mia mimicked rocking out on the guitar.

When the song ended, the crowd was on its feet, led by Mia's friends. The coordinator said something about the birthday girl over the mic, but I couldn't hear him over the roar. Plus, my head was starting to ring from the alcohol. Perhaps it was time to switch to water.

Mia bounded down the stairs into the arms of her friends, and I struggled to keep up. Just as I was taking the last step, my heel caught and I stumbled forward, right into Alex, who dropped his drink to catch me.

"Are you okay?"

My cheeks were on fire. "Other than my wounded ego, I'm fine. I told you, hang around long enough, and I'll fall over something." I glanced at his empty glass on the floor. "I suppose that makes us even?"

"I suppose so."

"I'll get you another one," I said, starting off toward the bar.

Alex pulled me back. "No, you won't. A gentleman doesn't allow a lady to buy him a drink. It should be the other way around even in this day and age."

I started to argue, but the announcer called for the next singer.

"That's me." Alex turned toward the stage.

"I thought you said you don't do karaoke."

He winked. "There's a first time for everything."

Sliding into my seat, I watched Alex say something to the announcer. He nodded, flipped a switch, and handed Alex an acoustic guitar.

"Oh, he plays guitar," Mia slurred, putting an arm around me. "You've always had a thing for musicians."

She was right. It was as if I had musician radar. You could put me in a room filled with a hundred men, only one of whom was a musician, and I'd head straight for him, like a moth to a flame. Come to think of it, it was surprising Victor wasn't a musician. But he was an artist, so maybe that was close enough to fit the pattern. My stupid weakness for men with guitars had been part of the reason I'd succumbed to Nick's charms all those years ago. *Ugh, bad Annabeth, no. Don't think about Nick.* I shook my head to clear it.

When I opened my eyes, Alex had finished tuning the guitar. He looked up and played the opening chords, which quickly resolved into Chris Issak's "Wicked Game." Looking straight at me, he sang, his voice deep and sonorous.

The world around me faded away until only the two of us remained. His song melted into my skin, into my veins, and flowed straight to my heart. And all the while, his eyes never left mine. A soft smile formed on my lips, and he smiled in response. With his voice swirling around and within me, I felt as though he was holding me. I could almost feel his hands caressing me, his lips burning my skin. As he sang, the intimacy grew until it was as if our souls were dancing. This was it, the feeling I'd been waiting for since I was sixteen.

Tears were in my eyes by the time he strummed the final chords. I stood to meet him at the bottom of the stairs, but Mia beat me to it.

She threw her arms around him and purred, "That was so hot." Before I could move a muscle, she kissed him, long and deep. Then she whispered something in his ear.

Alex shook his head, untangled himself from Mia and steered her over toward Miles. "I think it's time you took her home."

Miles stood to steady Mia, who didn't appear to quite know what was going on. "I think you might be right. Besides"—he clapped Alex on the shoulder—"no one could top the performance you just gave. That was solid, man. It really was."

"Thanks."

"Will you make sure Annabeth gets home all right?"

I cut between them to grab my purse. "Annabeth can take care of herself, thanks."

I started to berate Mia, but she was nearly passed out on her feet. No sense in wasting my breath on someone who wouldn't remember any of it in the morning anyway. With her in this condition, there was no sense in sticking around, especially since I didn't know how to face Alex after that kiss. I strode toward the exit.

Halfway to the door, Alex caught up with me. "Annabeth, wait, please."

I turned and found his eyes were pleading. I sighed. "What?"

He gestured over his shoulder. "Please know that I—I didn't want—it had nothing to do with her. It was all for you."

"I know. Thank you." My voice cracked despite my attempts to keep my emotions in check. "I know this wasn't your fault. I'm mad at Mia and taking it out on you, which isn't fair. But you do have lousy timing."

"Why?" He put a hand on the small of my back and ushered me out the door, raising the other to signal for a taxi.

"Victor. . .Nick. . .work. . .now Mia pulls this stunt." I buried my face in my hands and shook my head. "It's just all too much. I need some time to straighten out my head."

Alex's lips curved in a wry half smile. "Believe me, I understand that. I'm here if you need someone to talk to." He opened the door of the cab that had pulled to the curb.

I smiled up at him. "Thank you. You know, this reminds me oddly of the night we met."

Alex gave me a quick squeeze, not quite a hug. "Yes, but this time we won't have to wait months to see each other again."

And this time, I know how you feel about me.

CHAPTER ELEVEN

September

The Cubbies were finally in the playoffs, and tickets were at a premium. None of us could afford them, and with Mia in the Bahamas on a photo shoot, even her connections couldn't get us in. So we settled for watching the game at Bugsy Malone's, our neighborhood bar, along with a few hundred of our closest friends.

"Oh, come on!" Victor yelled at the TV, his voice blending into the general mayhem around us. "He was safe. Even a blind man could have seen that."

From somewhere behind us, someone threw popcorn at the screen, and I grabbed my drink, spinning out of the way. I walked away from Victor and over to the other table our group occupied. Alex was debating the team's pitching strategy with Kendra when I arrived.

"Uh-uh," she said. "No way is he going to risk bringing in a lefty at this point in the game."

Alex looked up. "Care to venture an opinion, or were you just bringing over free snacks?" He extracted a piece of popcorn from my hair and held it up.

I touched my hair, removing two more pieces. "Thanks. I would have walked around like that all night."

"And you would have looked charming," he said.

An arm snaked around me, and for one wild moment, I thought Alex might be making a move, but it was Victor.

"Hey, babe, I have to jet for a sec. My manager is here, and I need to go talk to her. I'll be right back, okay?" He kissed my cheek.

"Okay."

"Since when does he have a manager?" Kendra asked.

"Since that guy from Tokyo bought those pieces at the gallery exhibit. He's been talking about moving there if he can convince Mr. Kobayashi to sponsor him, become his patron."

Kendra frowned. "What would that mean for the two of you?"

I drew patterns on the tabletop with my finger and the condensation from my glass. "I don't know. We haven't really talked about it since nothing is for sure yet."

"I'm sure everything will work out fine," Alex said.

Wishing to change the subject, I turned my attention back to the game, shouting my encouragement at the player at bat. When he struck out, ending the inning, I excused myself to use the ladies' room.

Weaving through the press of sweating, swearing fans, I caught sight of Victor and Katrina in what appeared to be a heated debate. He was leaning casually against the wall, but she was towering over him, clearly trying to get some important point across. Curious, I hung back, just close enough to listen in on their conversation.

Katrina was speaking. "I mean seriously, where did you get that girl from, a consignment store? She's cute, yes, but you're a star on the rise. You need to think about your reputation."

"What, exactly, is wrong with her?" Victor's voice was edged in steel.

"Well, for one, she's so average. Girl-next-door is fine for a starving artist, but you need someone more sophisticated, someone who understands the world you're moving into. When you get to Tokyo, no one will pay you any mind with Raggedy Ann on your arm. She's friends with Mia LaRue, right? So trade up. Dump her for her friend or one of Mia's model friends. She's bound to have a million of them."

"And what if I love her? We have been together for a while now."

Katrina scoffed. "Please. You're about to move halfway around the world. How much of a hold could she possibly have on you?" She crossed her arms. "Does Little Miss Midwest even know about Tokyo?"

Guilt clouded Victor's expression. "I haven't told her yet—"

"Then don't. Just go. Send her a text once you're there. She'll never know the difference."

Victor looked uncertain.

"Look, I'm your manager, and I'm just trying to do what's best for your image. If you arrive with a model on your arm, you're fresh and mysterious. Everyone will be dying to get to know you, find out who that beauty is and what your secret is. With your name on everyone's lips, the value of your art will skyrocket."

"And if I arrive with Annabeth, I'm just another artist." He sounded resigned.

"You got it. What's one girl's broken heart in comparison?"

Victor seemed to think for a minute, digging his hands in his pockets. "I really don't want to hurt her, but I guess I can see your point. We really don't have a future together anyway." He shifted from foot to foot, his gaze on the floor.

Katrina's lips formed a serpentine smile. "You can do it. Hell, I'll even text her for you."

Victor looked up then, his eyes bright with excitement. "So what are you thinking? California blonde, or should I go for someone a little more exotic?"

My heart constricted, and for a moment, I couldn't breathe. No future together? Apparently he was done waiting for me, especially since Katrina had presented him with a better option. Who did he think he was? I'd given him four months of my life, and now he was going to discard me like a piece of garbage just because I didn't measure up to Katrina's idea of a sophisticated woman? No, he wasn't getting away with this.

I pushed through the people separating us, shoved Katrina aside and grabbed Victor by the shirt. He was taller than me, but my rage and his surprise gave me enough leverage to pull him down to my level.

"You forgot one thing about us Midwestern girls—we know an asshole when we see one." I slapped him so hard he stumbled backward. "Don't bother trying to defend yourself. There's no excuse. We're done."

I stormed into the ladies' room and took my rage out on a jammed stall door. There was no way I was sticking around and pretending everything was fine. After I washed my hands, I was out of here.

As soon as I emerged into the bar, a commotion drew my attention.

"If you're stupid enough to think her plain, then perhaps you need some sense knocked into you."

I heard the threat, but it took me a moment to realize Alex was the one who had issued it. Apparently I wasn't the only one who had overheard Victor's conversation.

"Really, man, I wasn't going to leave without saying good-bye. I was just saying what Katrina wanted to hear."

"You sounded pretty sincere to me. How would you like to arrive in Tokyo with a broken hand? Not much use if you can't paint, are you?"

I rushed over then, yelling for Alex to stop and shoving gawkers out of my way, but I wasn't fast enough to prevent the first blow. Alex's fist connected with Victor's cheek before I could get between them. Victor stumbled backward but quickly recovered and launched himself at Alex. Tables tottered and tall chairs tipped while Kendra and I tried in vain to pry the two men apart. Security arrived within seconds. The two burly bouncers hoisted Victor off Alex as though he weighed no more than a barstool.

A few moments later, we were all standing in the street, our entire party ejected for causing a fight. Alex's face was scratched, his shirt ripped, the tails untucked, but he seemed no worse for wear. Victor was dabbing his swollen and bleeding lower lip with a paper napkin. While Miles talked Alex down, Victor pulled me aside.

"I never meant for things to turn out like this." He brushed a lock of hair that had come loose back behind my ear, and I shrank away from his touch. "I was going to tell you about Tokyo, I swear. I just found out myself."

I stared at him, willing all my anger into a piercing gaze. "And when were you going to tell me you we were trading me in for a fancier model?"

He shook his head. "I never planned to leave you for someone else."

"Not until Katrina put the thought into your mind. I saw your face, Victor. You were as excited about the idea of dating a model as she was. If you really cared about me, that wouldn't be more than a fantasy."

I had him there, and he knew it. "I guess this had to happen sooner or later."

"What do you mean?"

"I mean, I'm going to Tokyo. Your life is here, and I'm starting a new one halfway across the world—"

"One without me, you mean. One with models and women who can build up your image. Women who will sleep with you right away. Ones who aren't broken."

"It's not that. I didn't think—"

"No, you didn't, and that's exactly my point." I stormed off, passing Miles and Alex on my way. "Hit him one more time for me, will you? I don't want to break a nail," I hissed at Alex.

Rounding the corner onto Michigan, I looked back just in time to see Victor picking himself up off the ground.

CHAPTER TWELVE

I couldn't remember the last time I'd had a day off. Sitting on the outdoor patio of my favorite café, I savored the autumn sunshine, letting it warm my face as a temperate breeze lifted my hair. I leaned back, perfectly content to let the world pass me by. I was free. For the first time in months, I had no one to worry about. The Banned Books event had gone off without a hitch, garnering national press for the University of Chicago, with Dean McAllister and Alex at the center of the attention. To say they were happy with our management of the first phase of the campaign was an understatement. The rest was now Nick's problem; I could return my focus solely back to copywriting, which was my first love. Victor was long gone; he had been smart enough to not try to contact me after the scene at the bar. Mia was caught up in preparations for Fashion Week, so even she couldn't bring me down.

"Excuse me, miss."

I opened my eyes to see the waiter delivering my glass of sauvignon blanc along with a basket of baked cheese and herb artisan crackers. He took my order, then I relaxed again in the wicker chair, pulling my sunglasses down over my eyes as I sipped the crisp, fruity wine.

I pulled a book, an epic fantasy about a slave woman who discovers she has the power to control the elements, out of my bag. But after only a few pages, I found I couldn't concentrate on the story. My mind kept drifting back to two nights ago, when Alex and I had had one last late-night working session in his office to debrief after the Banned Books event. He had convinced me to read him some of my historical novel. Of course, in reading it aloud, I'd found a million typos, but he seemed to really like it.

"You've got a great authorial voice," he said. "And your main character is very fresh. There are a lot of flapper stories out there—*Dollface*, *Ingenue*, and *The Diviners*—but Millie stands out as spunky and strong. I think she's someone today's women, especially the eighteen-to-thirty demographic, would really relate to. You should think about getting it edited and seeing if there's any agent interest."

"Wait. You think this is good enough to get published?"

He turned on a hundred-watt grin as he perched on the corner of his desk. "Not yet, but it's got great potential. It needs some polishing, but you're certainly talented enough to make a career out of this if that's what you decide you want to do."

I glanced at him, still afraid he was going to tell me he was just joking. "Thank you. I—that's a lot to take in."

He opened his desk drawer and pulled out a business card. "Here. This is the name of a professor here who does editorial work on the side. If you decide you want to take the next step, give her a call. I think you'll like her."

We talked for the next hour about what he particularly liked, what he thought could be improved, and I told him the rest of the plot. He had some great insights on things that didn't fit and ideas for things that could tie some of the main points together. In the end, I promised him he could read the whole thing once I'd taken another pass through it. I wasn't sure if I wanted him to see it before or after I talked to his editor friend.

I'd stayed up past midnight that night, scratching down ideas and marking up a printout of my manuscript. Now that I was thinking about it, a flood of new ideas came to me. Back into my bag went the book, and out came my manuscript. I rearranged the table so I could make the story bleed with my red pen while I ate. When I wasn't chewing on my salad, I was chewing on the cap of my pen, working through a particularly rough plot point in my head and on the back of the previous page.

Eventually, I had to stop. I was full, and my fingers were greasy from the crackers, which I'd kept eating alongside my salad. I grabbed my purse and went inside to wash my hands. When I returned to my seat, a decadent chocolate ganache-filled cake topped with raspberries waited for me along with a glass of sparkling wine.

I stopped the waiter when he approached. "There must be some mistake. I didn't order this."

"A gentleman asked that it be delivered to your table."

I looked around but saw no one. "Who?"

He searched the surrounding sidewalks in vain. "I don't know, ma'am. He was just here."

Slightly unnerved, I moved the dessert aside and flipped the page on my manuscript, intending to continue my work. It took me a moment to realize there was a note tucked between the pages.

I was having lunch across the street and couldn't help but notice you. You are more beautiful today than I've ever seen you. You must be meant to be a writer. You put the sun to shame when you are working, and there is nothing sexier than a woman doing what she's passionate about. I couldn't let another day go by without asking you what I've been wanting to say since the night we first met.

(Read this part to the tune of "Out Tonight" from Rent.)

Will you go out with me tonight?
I want to be by your side in the moonlight
Can't you see the stars in my eyes?
Well, say yes and we'll dispense with the excuses and lies.
Come with me for a surprise.

Alex

I let out a little whimper, covering my mouth with my hand. He had adapted Mimi's plea to Roger to ask me out. I thought things like this only happened in movies. I looked around, searching for some sign of him, hoping he could see the tears of joy he had brought to my eyes.

My phone chimed with a text message.

Look up, first balcony.

Alex was there, across the street, standing at the wrought-iron railing on the second floor, with a huge grin on his face. He waved.

I waved back tentatively. Then, emboldened by his gesture, I tossed some money on the table to cover my bill and scurried across the street to stand below the balcony, gazing up at him.

"Is that a yes?" he called down.

"Yes!"

∽

If I'd thought I was nervous before my first date with Victor, it was nothing compared to how I felt that night—at least until Alex showed up on my doorstep with an armful of blue hydrangeas.

I was so surprised to see him holding my favorite flower that, for a moment, I couldn't move or speak. As I searched my vacant mind for some words, he simply watched me, drinking me in as though he was appreciative of the extra moments to admire me.

"I—how did you know?" I asked when I finally recovered use of my voice and the synapses in my brain started firing again.

"You told me, remember?" He stepped past me into my living room, his head turned to keep eye contact with me. "That first night in my office, back in July, when we were still planning the year. When you teased me for not having a nickname? You told me you and your dad used to grow them. I thought it might be a nice way to show you that despite our rocky start, I really am a good guy."

I stroked his cheek, running my hand across the stubble that so resembled a freshly harvested field. "I already knew you were a good guy." I took the flowers and spun away toward the kitchen before he could catch me up in his arms. "But I appreciate the gesture all the same." I grabbed a vase from the cabinet under the sink and turned on the tap. "So where are we going tonight?"

Alex perched on the arm of the loveseat while I arranged the flowers. He raised his voice over the water. "Well, anyone can take a girl to dinner or a movie, so I thought we'd do something a little different, something quintessentially Chicago."

I peeked out from behind the spray of azure blooms. "You've certainly piqued my interest. Is my outfit okay?"

We both looked down at my flouncy white tank, capris, and jeweled sandals.

"Actually," he said, "it couldn't be more perfect if you tried. You'll see."

Our cab smelled like curry and stale tobacco, but I didn't care. I sank down next to Alex in the grimy leather seat, leaning my head on his chest with a casual air that shocked me yet felt perfectly natural. Maybe all the time we'd spent working together had broken the ice that usually stretches between strangers on a first date. Whatever it was, I was grateful to be at ease already.

He must have felt the same way because as we sat in the warm car amid bumper-to-bumper Friday-night traffic fighting our way down East Illinois, the radio chattering away in a language I couldn't understand, he twined his hand in mine and sighed contentedly. When I tilted my head back to look at him, his temple was resting on the doorframe. He looked as relaxed as a cat in the sun.

I must have drifted off because I started when the taxi came to a halt outside the tall red gates of Navy Pier.

"Have a nice nap?' Alex teased after he'd paid the cabbie and we'd gotten out of the car. He pulled me to him with one arm around my neck in a sexy "she's mine, I've claimed her" kind of way.

"Mmmm. . . hey, at least you know I'll be alert the rest of the evening."

"No worries, I dozed off too. I blame the heat and the curry."

I laughed. "What now?"

"Now we wander."

We ambled down the boardwalk, chatting idly and making snarky comments about the tourists.

"I'm guessing they're from Michigan," I said, discreetly pointing at a family stirring up a ruckus as their unruly toddler screamed for cotton candy. The father, who resembled a lumberjack, was fishing in his wallet for cash while his wife tried in vain to silence the child and mask her desire to beat him into submission.

"No fair," Alex protested. "One hint of their accent and the game was over. What about them?" He indicated an older couple in nearly matching track suits and straw hats.

"Florida. Gotta be."

"Nope, not tan enough. I say New Jersey."

"I dunno. Wouldn't they be tanned too?"

"Nah, that's only the young ones with reality TV shows." Alex stopped at an old-fashioned photo booth complete with ratty black cloth to block out the light. "We have to have a souvenir of our first date, right?"

We piled inside, me on Alex's lap and my arms around him, to make faces and bunny ears in the first two pictures then grin like teenaged idiots in the third. Just before the camera was due to flash for the last time, Alex kissed me, a gentle, reassuring gesture of his affection. He was warm, his lips soft, but his arms around me were strong, just as I'd always dreamed. Though our kiss lacked the overt passion of a romance novel, there was something to it, a connection and innate understanding that I'd never felt with anyone else—not Victor, not even Nick. Far too soon, the flash lit the space behind my eyelids, and we pulled apart, foreheads touching for just a moment longer.

Out on the noisy pier again, Alex handed me the ribbon of images, and I held them to my heart. "I will treasure these always."

"You'd better. I don't go around kissing girls in front of cameras every day."

"You don't? That's not what I hear. . ."

He pressed me against his chest so that I had to stop talking. I breathed in the spicy, sharp scent of his cologne, perfectly content to stay right there for the rest of the evening.

"Come on, Miss Smarty-pants." He released me except for looping one finger in my back pocket.

We passed the Ferris wheel with its long queue of tourists and decided it wasn't worth standing in line since we'd both been up in it multiple times.

When we reached the mini golf course, Alex threw me a daring look, one eyebrow cocked. "You game?"

"Bring it on."

But my bravado didn't translate into mad skills as I'd hoped. After three holes at least two strokes over par, I finally admitted my weakness. "I have no hand-eye coordination."

"Nah, you just don't know your own strength. This isn't the PGA. You have to tap the ball gently." He came around behind me. "Here, I'll teach you." He bent over, his body folding around me so his arms and hands covered mine. "So, stance is the first key. Bend your knees just a little."

I did, fighting the urge to melt against him while my heart skipped beats in reaction to his nearness.

"Not that much. There you go. Now swing back just a little and tap the ball." He held on as I did so, controlling my speed with a gentle squeeze to slow me down. He was still holding me when the blue ball stopped just short of the hole. "See?"

"Sure," I said over my shoulder as I moved out of the way so he could take his turn. "It's easy with you guiding me, but what about—"

Something solid connected with my foot, then I was sprawling forward in slow motion. *I'm falling. Don't let me fall in front of him,* was all I had time to think before I met the ground with a thud, my palms burning as they caught my weight on the Astroturf.

"Annabeth?" Alex was standing over me before I could even turn over. "Are you okay? Are you hurt?" His strong hands lifted me by the shoulders.

"I'm fine, really. Just extremely embarrassed. Why do I fall over things every time we're together socially?"

He shrugged, fighting back a grin. "Law of averages?"

I laughed. "Probably."

By the time we finished the game—he won, and I managed to not fall over the course separators again—Alex's stomach was growling.

"Dinner?" I asked.

"Yeah. Where do you want to go?"

I scanned the row of restaurants, their entryways packed with waiting patrons, then looked at my phone. "Do you trust me?"

The look he gave me was dubious, but he said yes.

"Good." I took his hand and headed toward the gates in a trot.

"Where are you taking me?" Alex asked.

"You'll see. It's not far."

We strolled through the tiny square of Jane Addams Memorial Park that faced the pier. Just west of the hidden patch of beach behind the park sat a white van with a giant neon taco painted on the side in street graffiti style.

I stood next to it, showing off the logo like a spokesmodel on a game show. "Best tacos in the city. Trust me, you don't ever have to eat at those overpriced tourist traps again."

Alex's shoulders shook as he laughed. "All right, Vanna, I'll take your word for it." He wagged a finger at me. "But these better be good."

Ten minutes later, we were headed back toward the park, hands full of white bags. The scents of beans, beef, and cheese wafted all around us. I wanted to have a picnic on the beach, but Alex said he had something even better in mind. We walked the length of the pier, snatching tortilla chips out of one another's bags as we went. When we reached the far end, Alex nodded to a middle-aged man standing guard over a small two-seater speedboat.

"All set?" he asked the man.

He handed Alex a small silver set of keys. "She's yours for the evening. Just watch out for the cruise boats and have her back by ten thirty."

Alex stepped aboard, set the bags of food in one seat, and held a hand out to me. I took it gratefully, hesitating at the edge of the dock. This had always been my least favorite part of rowing, and tonight, I wasn't any more certain.

I looked at Alex. "I don't think I can do this."

He squeezed my hand. "Yes, you can. I've got you. I won't let you fall. Just put one foot in. I'll pull you the rest of the way in."

Shaking, I lifted one sandal and carefully placed it into the boat. The boat's owner took my other hand and held it until I safely had both feet in the boat.

"Thank you so much," I called to the boatman.

He doffed his red newsboy cap in acknowledgement.

Alex settled me in, and I arranged the bags of food at our feet while the engine roared to life. Alex drove us out onto the lake.

"You teach, you row, you appreciate theatre, you write poetry, and now I find you sail too. Do your talents never cease?"

"I wouldn't exactly call this sailing, but yes, I do that as well. My dad is big into boats. He doesn't care what size. If it floats on the water, he loves it. I think it's in the blood and he passed it on to me. My brothers all sail too. But we don't share his love for tall ships. They're beautiful but way too much work. This is more my speed."

"Your brothers? How many do you have?"

"Three. One older and two younger. I have a younger sister too. What about you?"

I nodded. "One sister, older by two years. She lives in North Carolina now."

By the time Alex stilled the boat in an open stretch of water, the sun was beginning to set, making the skyline a dramatic backdrop of pink and peach.

I rummaged in the bags and held up two paper-wrapped packages, pretending to balance them on scales. "Taco or burrito?"

Alex scrunched up his face for a second, weighing the options. "Whatever you don't want."

I held the burrito to my heart. "Oh, aren't you chivalrous." I handed him the taco then a drink.

Alex touched a few buttons on his phone, and suddenly Otis Redding was crooning "Stand by Me." I sank into Alex's arms, content to enjoy the food, the view, and the company. "This might just be the best date I've ever been on."

Alex stroked my hair with his free hand. "And it's nowhere near over yet."

"Promise?" I asked around a mouthful of burrito.

His chest shook as he laughed. "Of course. And I don't make promises lightly."

I swallowed. "So what made you ask me out now? And how did you think to leave me that note? Why not just ask me in person?"

"The last part of your question is the easiest. I wanted to do something you would remember. As with dinner and a movie, any bloke can ask a girl out. Not everyone can do it using a musical reference." The shell of his taco crunched as he bit down.

"Another echo of your dramaturge days?"

"Oh yes." He took a minute to chew and swallow before continuing. "I was bitten by the theatre bug a long time ago. If I could sing or dance or act, I swear to you I'd be on the stage." His eyes shone with an inner fire that was beautiful to behold. They were like smoldering sapphires, lit by the passion he felt for the arts. "But as that way was barred to me, I work it into my teaching when I can." He looked down at me. "And very occasionally, into my love life. But it's rare to find a woman who can match me quote for quote."

"And we haven't even really thrown down yet. Just you wait. Hey, we should go see a show together. That would be so much fun."

"As you wish. Consider it done."

"Okay, Westley."

"Hey, I have yet to meet a woman who doesn't appreciate a good *Princess Bride* reference."

I tossed the empty burrito wrapper into the bag and settled back against him. "You do get bonus points for that one."

When I looked up again, he'd finished eating, and his expression was pensive, eyes distant as he looked through rather than at the skyline. "Your original question is a little harder to answer." He cleared his throat. "I wanted to ask you out the moment we met at that silly singles party, and I very nearly did, but I decided that wouldn't be fair to either of us."

"Why not?"

"I was just out of a long-term relationship and still very, very hurt. At best, you would have been a rebound relationship, and I couldn't do that to you. You deserve so much more. So I decided to let you go. More than once I wondered if I had done the right thing."

He was bouncing his knee as he spoke. I placed a hand on it, willing him to calm down. "You wanna know a secret?"

He stilled as his curiosity took over. "What?"

"I've wanted to be with you from that same night. It's been so hard being professional these last few months."

"Tell me about it." Alex rubbed the back of his neck, turning the conversation back to his original story. "You came back into my life so unexpectedly. It wasn't so much that I was your client that stopped me then. It was more that. . ." He seemed to search for the right words. "That I wasn't sure I was ready. But yet, you were always there, waiting for me to heal but not pining away. You were living your life, and I have the utmost respect for that."

He went quiet for a moment. I was unsure if he would go on, but after a few deep breaths, he did.

"Honestly, I was overwhelmed by my feelings for you, by how attracted I was not only to your body but also your intelligence. I had finally found my equal, and I didn't want to mess that up. Besides, you were with Victor. So I waited."

"Now it makes sense that you said you understood when I told you I needed time to figure out my mind."

"That's exactly why. But by that night, I was losing my battle." Alex smiled and stroked my hair, growing visibly calmer. "I decided that even if I couldn't be with you, I could tell you how I felt. That's why I picked that particular song. Then when Victor insulted you, all the pent-up energy I had been suppressing came out in that punch." He grinned at me. "Or should I say 'those punches'? That was when I knew we were both ready."

"I'm honored. I don't think a man has ever put that much thought into my feelings before."

"I highly doubt that. If you're right, they've all been fools."

I snorted. "I won't argue with you there. Not that there have been that many. I don't date much."

"What? You haven't found your soul mate on Heart+Soul yet?" His eyes crinkled in the corners with amusement.

"Not exactly. My friends put me up to that, by the way."

"Let me guess—it involved the word 'Pookie.'"

I laughed. "It most certainly did."

Alex's fingertips traced lazy lines up and down my bicep. "Do I get to call you Pookie?"

"No. Not even if you give me a kidney. You can call me baby, sweetheart, lover, whatever you want—but not that. Hell, even sugar tits would be better than Pookie."

"Wow, I never thought I'd be on a date with Mel Gibson." He pretended to shiver. "I don't really know what to do with that."

I propped myself up on one arm, sliding up his body until our faces were level. "What about this?" I kissed him softly, tasting his lips and just barely catching his lower lip in my teeth. "Do you know what to do with that?"

In answer, he pulled me to him, tangling one hand in my hair and caressing my back and butt with the other. My mouth was just as hungry as his, our tongues dancing as we sought to quench a thirst so long denied. I pressed myself against him, savoring his warmth, seeking to get closer and aching for skin-to-skin contact. His lips pressed against mine with an urgency that betrayed his own desire, especially when he pulled back and slid his lips down my chin to the hollow of my throat. I lost myself in him, arching my back as he pulled down one of the straps of my tank top.

Just then, a loud boom, followed by several successive pops, startled us both, breaking the spell. We both turned toward the sound. Sparks of red and gold lit up the evening sky over the pier. Then a line of blue shot into the sky before exploding into a dozen points of light.

"Fireworks," I breathed. When I glanced at Alex, he wore a smug smile, and I shoved him. "You knew about this, didn't you? But how? It's after Labor Day."

"It pays to have friends who work for the nonprofit that runs the pier."

"Is that how you got the boat too?"

He waited for a gaggle of screaming, undulating gold firecrackers to explode before answering. "No, that was old-fashioned commerce."

He pulled me back into his arms, and we watched the remainder of the show in silence punctuated only by the occasional "oh" and "ah" as we reverted to childhood beneath the glittering, dancing lights. Once, a particularly loud boom made me jump, and his arms closed protectively around me.

When it was all over, we lay in a silence, not unlike after a night of passion, listening to one another's heartbeats.

"Can we stay like this forever?" I asked.

"Mmmm," he murmured into my hair. "Fine by me."

A few minutes later, his phone beeped, stirring us both from our reveries.

Alex grunted as he sat up to silence it, still holding me. "How does time go by so fast?"

I rubbed my face sleepily. "Oh, that's right. We have a curfew."

"Well, we don't, but the boat does. Are you up for a little more adventure?"

I smiled at him. "Somehow I doubt you could top what's happened so far even if you tried."

"Milady, is that a challenge? If so, I accept."

CHAPTER THIRTEEN

November

Alex was already seated on my gray microfiber couch when I breezed in the door, announcing, "Honey, I'm home!" peeling off my coat, and kicking off my heels.

Alex looked up from the papers he was grading and kissed me. "Hello to you too. How was your day?"

"Meh. It was fine. Yours?"

Alex's hands came around my shoulders, and he kneaded them without me even having to ask. "I've had better. I could use a glass of wine with you, though."

I hopped up, heading toward the kitchen. "Say no more. What made your day rough?"

"Two interminable hours in conference with Dean McAllister. Need I say more? He was complaining about Nick, bemoaning that you were abandoning us. Honestly, you were much more on top of things, and you have unique ideas. Nick is just—" He struggled to find the correct word.

"An ass? Lazy? I could go on if you'd like." I pulled on the cork of an already-open bottle of Shiraz, and it opened with a satisfying pop.

"No, I think you've about covered it. He's more interested in schmoozing than being a coordinator."

Red liquid flowed into two glasses as I tipped the bottle over them. "I'm sure he loves rubbing elbows at the special events. I've always thought he missed his calling as a fundraiser—or maybe even a politician. The man could convince a miser to part with his last penny."

Alex laughed. "See, that's the problem. He's so busy chatting people up at these things that he can't be bothered to be our gofer. That's what we need him for. We have our own bamboozler."

I carried two glasses back to the couch, offered one to him, set mine on the glass coffee table, and snuggled in next to Alex. "There shouldn't be much for him to do this month. Your professors are coordinating your National Novel Writing Month activities, right? Maybe this is the perfect time to tame him."

"And how do you suggest I do that? A whip and a chair? He doesn't listen to anyone," Alex said, taking a long swallow of wine.

"Tell me about it. He should respect your wishes and methods as a client though. If he doesn't, you need to talk to Laini."

"I think the dean is going to. What does that mean for us if they replace him?"

I shook my head. "I don't think they will, at least not right away. He's just now officially your rep, so she'll be lenient for a while. He'll get a verbal warning first. If I know Nick, he'll shape up for a while then backslide when he thinks no one is paying attention. You may have to keep on top of him."

Alex sighed. "If I wanted to babysit, I would have hired an intern. Can't we just have you back for the next six months?"

"Well, I can't date clients if I'm managing their accounts." I sat up, snaking an arm around him. "Can you wait six more months for this?"

I kissed his lips, leaving a matching trail of kisses down to his collarbone then to his bellybutton, slowly unbuttoning his shirt as I went. My eyes flicked up to his, and I let them fill with longing and desire. His pupils dilated, and he readjusted me in his lap so that I was straddling his hips. I slid my skirt up over my hips, giving him a glimpse of the lacy thong beneath.

"I know I can't," I purred as I nipped his earlobe.

Alex pulled off his shirt. "No, you're right. I'll put up with him if I know this is what I'll be coming home to."

"Every single night."

The next morning, Laini steered me into her office after our weekly staff meeting. Once she had taken her place behind her desk, she fixed me with a stern look that made it clear we were not going to be discussing upcoming writing assignments as I had expected.

"I had a most unsettling conversation with Dean McAllister last evening."

I wrinkled my brow. "Oh?"

"Yes, 'oh.'" She laced her fingers together on the desk. "He told me at length, and with more than a little color, of his displeasure with Nick Zarrino." She was silent as though she expected me to speak.

"I'm sorry, but I don't understand what this has to do with me."

"You trained him, didn't you?"

"Yes." I still didn't know what she was driving at.

"Then the dean's displeasure is just as much of a reflection on you as it is on Nick. I will speak with him, but you need to correct his behavior. I must say I am highly disappointed in you, Annabeth." She was looking at me like a disapproving schoolteacher chiding a student.

I would not let Nick do this to me. I would not be a victim of his games. I summoned all my courage, balling my hands into fists at my sides, and took a deep breath. "With all due respect, I don't think it's fair for you to blame me for Nick's missteps. I trained him as carefully as I could, but he is a grown man. I can't be held responsible for his choices. If he blatantly ignores what I've shown him, that's on him. I am not his mother, nor am I his boss. If you expect me to act in that role, then promote me. Give me the power I need to put him in line."

Laini considered me, sliding her glasses down to the tip of her nose. For a while I thought she might fire me then and there, then her expression softened. "Be careful what you wish for, my dear. For now, go and talk to him, and I'll do the same." Her phone buzzed, and she picked it up. "Yes, Angela?" She motioned with a wave for me to leave.

I was shaking as I closed her door behind me. I paused to catch my breath, then I straightened my plaid skirt. At one time, I would have hidden in my cube for the rest of the day, mortified that Laini had called me to the carpet unjustly, but not now. I was determined to use this frustration-born adrenaline to put Nick in his place.

I didn't even bother to knock before bursting into his office and slamming the door shut.

At first he was startled into silence, pushing back from his computer to face me in his chair. "Annabeth, I always dreamed one day you'd burst in and take me in this office, but I didn't expect it to be today." He adjusted his tie as though that was exactly what he expected me to do.

"Shut it, Zarrino." I towered over him, taking advantage of our relationship to get right in his face. "Your childish insistence on following your own whims has cost me respect it took me three years to build. Do you have any idea how it feels to be dressed down for something you did simply just because I trained you? Well, that will not"—I emphasized the word with a shake of my finger—"happen again. Do you understand me?"

Nick stared at me, open-mouthed and unblinking like a fish.

"Here's the deal—Dean McAllister wants you fired." So I was exaggerating a little. Maybe the fear of unemployment would straighten him up. "The only thing that saved your ass is that you're new and we can't terminate you right away simply because you aren't living up to the client's expectations."

"I—what did I do?" Nick spluttered.

I leaned back from him, crossing my arms. "Apparently you spend too much time chewing the fat with guests at the events and too little time being available to our clients. Laini will be talking with you later, but I'll give you a little piece of advice. From now on, consider yourself an intern, a lackey, because that's the crux of your job. You do whatever the clients need you to do. Volunteer doesn't show up? You fill in. Speaker spilled coffee on his notes? Hand him the fresh set you just happen to have. If the mic isn't working, find someone to fix it. Get the picture? You aren't the head of philanthropy or one of the boys. And when you're in this office, you are the go-between who relays information from us to them and vice versa, nothing more. The sooner you get that through your head, the longer you'll have a job."

I headed toward the door, keeping an eye on him. Nick opened and closed his mouth a few times, but before he could formulate a response, I was leaning over his desk.

"And one more thing," I said. "If you ever, ever get me in trouble again, I swear you will regret it. If I go down, you're going with me. So shape up, or find another doorstep to darken because no one here has time for your bullshit. This isn't college anymore."

∽

"How goes it?" Alex kissed my temple after he closed the door to his Hyde Park apartment one cold November evening about two weeks later.

We were practically living together already. I had half his closet space and rarely went home, especially now that National Novel Writing Month was consuming all of my waking hours.

Tearing my eyes away from my laptop, I smiled at him, watching him unwind a bright blue scarf from around his neck. It had been my "just because" gift a few weeks before. "Slowly. But I only have another five hundred words to make my daily word count."

"Does that mean you're caught up?"

I rubbed my eyes. "Hardly. At this rate, I need to write two thousand words a day in order to win."

Alex hung his coat in the closet and leaned back on the closed door. "I still don't understand the fascination with writing fifty thousand words in one month."

"It's fun."

He made a derisive noise. "You haven't looked like you were having fun since the sparkle of the first few days wore off."

I rolled my eyes, not wanting to admit he was right. "Fine. It's a challenge."

"It sounds like torture to me."

"You've been around enough writers to know we're all a little crazy."

"True enough." Alex ambled over to me, wrapped his arms around me, and read over my shoulder. "So this is another Millie mystery, right?"

"Yeah. In the first one, we got to know her world and saw her work with Dean O'Banion's gang. Now she's caught Capone's attention. The only problem is she kinda likes the guys on the north side, so she's conflicted. By the end of this book, she'll have made her choice as to where her loyalties lie."

"You know the North Side Gang really only held power until the St. Valentine's Day Massacre. If she's going to get with anyone on the north side, you're going to have to play that very carefully so you don't end up with Capone having to whack her in the end."

I opened my mouth to object, but then I realized he was right. "Crap." The screen blurred as I thought through the whole plot. "What if the whole thing is set up wrong?" I looked at him for some sign of reassurance. "I'm already thirty-seven thousand words in. I can't abandon it now." I ran my fingers through my hair, pulling on it as I went. "What am I going to do?"

Alex squatted so that his face was level with mine. "You're going to finish writing your story. You know better than anyone how much stories evolve as you write them. There may be snags now, but they'll be gone by the time you're ready for anyone to read this. Let your characters tell you how it's going to work. They haven't let you down so far, have they?"

I hugged him, burying my head in his shirt collar as tears of fear and frustration ran down my cheeks. "What would I do without you?"

He didn't answer, only chuckled.

I pulled back, shooing him toward the living room. "Now get out and let me write."

"Have you eaten? Silly question—of course you haven't. I'll make us some dinner. How does stir-fry sound?"

I inhaled, imagining the pungent scent of sesame oil and ginger. "Lovely."

Alex disappeared into the kitchen and rattled pans around as he began to cook. A minute later, he stuck his head around the corner. "Just don't have any of your coppers say, 'Welcome to Chicago' with a Scottish accent or run any baby carriages down the stairs, okay?"

"Noted."

The world around me faded away as I sank deeper into the writer's trance. Alex was right—I just needed to get out of my own way and let the characters take over. And they did. My fingers flew over the keys, and their story slowly diverged from anything I'd ever seen or read. *Untouchables* be damned. This was its own creation.

But when I read back through it, just before obeying Alex's summons to the table, I realized it was also horribly written.

"You can fix it in January. Don't worry about it," he said, pulling out my chair for me. "Just keep going. But not today. For the rest of the evening, you are mine."

"Yes, I am." I forced myself to smile through the frustration churning in my stomach and threatening to eat me alive. "How was your day?"

Alex huffed. "You don't want to know."

"Of course I do." I hoped I sounded more sincere than I felt. My mind was still half on my story, teasing at a rough plot point I'd either have to skip or unravel before I could make progress. I blinked, pushing it to the back of my mind. "Try me."

He took a fortifying sip of wine. "Okay. Well, in my first period, I caught two students cheating and had to discipline them. Then Dean McAllister wanted a word. I like the guy, but sometimes he can be such a buffoon. He kept going on and on about this inane idea to match current English majors with potential recruits as pen pals. Pen pals? Do kids even have those anymore? Anyway, he talked for so long he made me late for my next class. Then I had a student drop by during the office time I was hoping to use for some research for my next journal article." Alex ran his hands through his hair, tousling it attractively, and let out a forceful breath. "It was just one thing after another."

"It sounds like it," I said, but my heart wasn't in the comment. My brain had drifted back to my story, and I was trying to mentally record the dialogue running through my head.

Alex was quiet for a moment. "Are you even listening to me?"

I shook myself to attention. "Yes. You had one thing after another go wrong today."

"What was the last thing I said?"

I searched my brain. The last thing I remembered was a mental image of Dean McAllister in a harlequin costume when Alex had called him a buffoon. But that hadn't been the last thing he'd said.

My hesitation was enough to set Alex off. He threw up his hands. "Jesus, Annabeth! You're as bad as my students. I swear NaNo Brain is a debilitating condition. I'm starting to recognize the dreamy look in their eyes when it comes on, and you just had the same expression. Is it really too much to ask you to listen to me rant about my day?" He threw down his napkin, pushed back his chair, and stormed into the bedroom before I could attempt to respond.

I should have called after him, tried to stop him, but I wasn't in the mood. All I'd done was tune out of a conversation. Men did that and got away with it all the time. Grumpily, I poked at the last of my meal, skewering a mushroom and a cube of chicken, before deciding Alex's tantrum had robbed me of my appetite.

When Alex hadn't returned by the time I'd washed our dishes, I decided to let him sulk. I heard the TV chattering in the bedroom, so he couldn't be too upset. Two could play at that game. I sat back down at the keyboard, smiling wickedly. His display of immaturity had given me an idea. The old saying really was true; irritate a novelist, and you'll end up in their story—as a corpse.

The next morning, I woke up groggy just moments before my alarm was due to go off. I turned off the ringer before it could buzz Alex awake.

Thinking about it while brushing my teeth in the half light provided by my cell phone so as not to wake him, our whole argument seemed trivial. Both of us had behaved irrationally. If I had simply gone to him and apologized, offered to listen and that time really, truly tried, we could have made up by now, and I wouldn't have the sinking feeling that I'd slept next to a stranger last night.

As I got dressed in the closet, shielding Alex from as much light as possible, a plan formed in my mind. While I did my makeup with the bathroom door firmly closed, I scribbled, "I'm sorry for being a flighty writer," in eyeliner on a sticky note and affixed it to the mirror in a place he'd be sure to see.

When I emerged into the living room, hair pinned and pumps on,

Alex was sitting on the loveseat, staring out the window, his navy bathrobe hanging half open to reveal his bare chest. He didn't stir when I passed him, so I poured two cups of coffee and doctored mine before approaching him from the opposite side.

"Hey," I said tentatively.

He looked up, blinking at me as though I'd woken him from a daydream. "Hey." His voice was groggy.

"You sound like you could use this." I held out the cup, which he took with a small smile and a quiet thanks. "Look, Alex, I'm sorry about last night—"

He held up a hand. "Annabeth, stop. There's something I need to talk to you about. It's what was really bothering me last night. I took it out on you without you even knowing it. . ."

I tossed my shoes on the floor and pulled my hosed legs beneath me. "Alex, what is it? You're worrying me." From how serious he looked, I thought he was going to break up with me or tell me he had cancer.

He twisted his head from side to side, cracking his neck like a boxer about to enter the ring. "Did you notice what time it was when I got home last night?"

"No. I was so absorbed in writing I guess I lost track of time." Oh God, he was going to tell me there was someone else.

"It was around nine. The reason I was late was that I was having drinks with Nick."

My eyebrows raced for my hairline. "Okay. . . I thought you hated him."

"I do, but the dean thought it would be a good way for us to bond, then he got called away on some crisis, so it was just the two of us."

I watched his expression change as though he couldn't decide whether to be mad, anxious, or hopeful. Stomach tightening, I silently willed him to go on, to get to whatever bomb he was going to drop.

"How long have you known Nick?"

"I told you, since we were kids." I exhaled nervous laughter, muscles unclenching now that I knew this was the big mystery topic.

"And the two of you were friends in college?"

"Yes."

"Just friends?"

"We dated for about a year. But it ended badly."

"What happened? He told me to ask you about Rome."

I squirmed, the leather upholstery squeaking in protest. Rome. That was the one thing I'd hoped to never have to discuss with anyone ever again, much less with the love of my life.

"I know his version of events, but I want to hear it from you," he said, standing and pacing.

"No doubt they're two totally different stories," I muttered, watching the little dots of creamer dance in my coffee as my breath ruffled the surface. Best to get this over with. "You really want to know? Here it is, the whole ugly truth—our senior year of college. Nick and I were part of a group of students who went to Rome as part of a music competition." I looked at him. "I played cello and he the bass, in case you were wondering. I never touched my instrument again after that school year. In fact, I sold it to pay for my move here. Anyway, he decided that Rome would be the perfect place to seal our relationship by finally sleeping together." I put the cup down, pulled my knees up, and hugged them as though I could close in on myself like a bud at twilight. "Things were progressing, but I stopped him at the last moment. I can't even really explain why. I just knew I couldn't go through with it. He wasn't 'the one,' and that's who I was saving myself for."

Alex stopped pacing, turning to face me. "So you didn't sleep with him?"

"No. Needless to say, Nick got really mad. At first he tried to get me to relax and submit, but when I shoved him off of me, he grabbed my arm, wrenching it pretty hard. Then he hit me. I think it was an accident, but I was scared—of him, of his temper, of us. I hid in the bathroom, crying until I knew for sure he was gone. He had never been violent with me before, so I chalked it up to a mistake in a tense moment. But he didn't come back, not for the last day of the competition—luckily we had a substitute—not for the trip home. I saw him around campus not long after, and he told me it was over. We never spoke again until he turned up at Smith and Grenwick." In my memory, his voice repeated his final words—*I can't take this anymore. We're done.*

Alex sank down next to me. "So basically he walked out on you—after physically hurting you, accidentally or not—because you wouldn't have sex with him. Wow. That is not the story he tells." He shook his head, idly running a finger over the stubble on his jaw. "Wait. Is that—is that why you were so nervous the first time we made love?"

I nodded. "Yeah, you're the only one I've ever been able to trust enough." I gave him a small, shy smile. "It's not like I didn't tell you beforehand I wasn't experienced."

"I know, but in context it's an even bigger honor. What made me different?"

I thought for a long moment. "You get me in a way no one else does. It's hard to put into words. You seem to understand my soul. It's like you know what I need before I do." Alex watched me for a long moment as though appreciating me in a different light. When

I couldn't take the silence any longer, I prompted him to continue. "So what's Nick's version of the story?"

"That you two were lovers, that you were the love of his life, and that it isn't over yet, so I'd better watch my back."

I burst out laughing. "And you believed him?"

Alex sprang up, apparently incensed. "Well, what would you think?" His face reddened. "You work with him all day. You're in close proximity for long hours. Things can happen. Passions can take over."

Wow, jealous much? I grabbed his wrist, pulling him back down to me. "Maybe for some people, but that's not going to happen to me." I forced him to look at me. "I didn't date anyone seriously for eight years after Nick hurt me. We hadn't spoken in thirteen years when he showed up in Jenna's old office. There's no way I'm going back to him. You have nothing to worry about." I kissed him softly.

"Next time I see Nick, I'm going to pummel him for lying about you," Alex muttered, fists balling at his sides. "I'm sorry I believed him. It's just—I'm a little gun-shy."

I snuggled into his arm. "Why?"

Beside me, Alex tensed. His eyes were distant, looking past me as though remembering and deciding how much to reveal. "Regina. She was a real piece of work. We'd been together three years when she got a job opportunity in Washington, DC. She asked me to go with her. Even though I'd just recently become tenured, I was considering it." A note of bitterness crept into his voice. "Then I found out she was cheating on me with one of the other lawyers in her new firm. Rumor had it they'd met at a convention and had been hooking up every time she had business in town."

"Oh, Alex, I'm so sorry."

He grunted, not really hearing me. "When I confronted her, she denied everything and accused me of choosing my career over her—again." He gnashed the last word through clenched teeth as though mimicking the way she'd said it. Silence stretched between us, echoes of past memories filling the void. "The next thing I knew, she was gone. It was all so sudden. Even though she'd betrayed me, I wanted to try to work things out. What a fool." He shook his head. "I need to know you won't ever screw me over like that."

"Of course not." I moved to kiss him to seal my reassurance but stopped when I saw the darkness in his eyes. *Note to self: mentioning Alex's ex, not a good idea.*

"I know you won't. You are an entirely different kind of person." He forced a smile that didn't quite reach his eyes.

I shouldn't have brought her up. Now he was in a bad mood, and I was late for work. But at least I knew a few more things that pushed his buttons. As long as I didn't get together with Nick or cheat on Alex with one of my coworkers, we should be fine. But that little word "again" bothered me. When had he chosen his job over her before and how? Silently, I added one more rule to our relationship list: I'd better not stand between him and his career or else I would be history too.

～

"Well, Aunt Deloris broke her hip," I told Alex, staring at my now-silent cell phone. "Mom says Thanksgiving is canceled."

"Isn't she going to step in and host? I would think that's the logical thing to do." Alex glanced sidelong at me from the couch, where he was reading the paper.

I snorted. "You don't know my mom. Everything has to be a grand affair with her. It's two days before Thanksgiving. There's no way she'd have time. Besides, she has to go play Florence Nightingale to her sister." I laughed at the mental image of my mom hovering at my poor aunt's bedside, driving her crazy. Then I shrugged. "At least the plane ticket will transfer to Christmas, so I'm not out any money." That was a stroke of luck considering Laini had announced our firm was going to be going through a restructuring before the end of the year. If there was any possibility I wouldn't have a job come New Year's, I needed to save every penny.

"Well, you are not spending Thanksgiving alone. You're coming with me." He pulled me down to the couch next to him.

I swallowed hard. "Don't you think it's a little soon? I mean, we've only been dating like a month." I pulled my knees up to my chin and poked at him with the toe of my fuzzy pink slippers.

Alex nipped at my ear. "Says the woman who practically lives with me. Think of it as a casual get-together. My whole family brings their significant others, and one of my brothers has a new girlfriend so you won't be the only new person there. Besides, everyone should experience a party at the Grantham compound at least once."

I cocked an eyebrow at him. "Compound? Are you closet Kennedys or something?"

Alex laughed. "Or something. Our lake house is the only place big enough to fit three generations of my family at once. It's gorgeous. Trust me."

∽

Thursday morning, I found myself on a downhill road, approaching that very structure, in the passenger seat of Alex's black Mercedes, windshield wipers sluicing away a light rain. He was right. It was its own compound, sprawling over several acres on the shores of Lake Michigan. A large main house dominated the landscape with smaller wings trailing off on three sides.

I let out a small puff of air. "I am totally out of my league here." I turned to him. "I suspected your family had money, but I never expected anything like this." I shoved him to mask how truly over-whelmed I was. "Here you are giving me the underpaid teacher act, and you're loaded."

Alex held up a hand in surrender. "Hey, I never claimed to be underpaid. That part is on you." He gave me the side-eye. "But yes, my family is wealthy. Millie would be proud. The Grantham for-tune has its roots in the bootlegging of Prohibition." He shrugged, eyes back on the road. "All of this has never mattered much to me. It's just a part of my life, like my siblings are. Speaking of. . ."

Alex pulled up next to a large black SUV in the circle drive and rolled down his window, letting in a blast of cold, damp air.

"Hey, Will, where do they want us?" Alex called to a guy leaning into the trunk of the massive car.

The man straightened and leaned in to clap Alex on the shoulder. I gasped. He could have been Alex's twin if his hair wasn't so short in the back. "Just leave it here. Someone will move it."

Alex pulled up in front of the SUV and killed the engine. "You ready?"

I nodded. "As I'm ever gonna be."

We walked into a spacious living room dominated by a large glow-ing fireplace surrounded by dark wood paneling. Men and women in festive oranges and browns, a few in early red and green, stood in clusters chatting while children wove between them or jumped on beige upholstered furniture. Jazz music set a relaxed tone amid the popping of champagne corks, laughter, and the buzz of happy conversation.

"It appears we're the last to arrive," Alex noted. "Before the others notice us, I'll give you the lay of the land." He gestured toward a loose knot of people about thirty paces in front of us. "The guy in the gray sweater is my brother Arthur. He's the eldest of us, a lawyer. The blonde in the red tunic shirt is his wife, Gemma. Next to them are my brother David and his wife, Marcie, both also lawyers. The brunette is my little sister, Casey."

"Let me guess—she's also studying law," I said dryly.

"Family tradition."

"Then how did you become a teacher?"

Alex frowned. "That's a sore spot. I'll explain later."

Alex's younger could-be-twin emerged from a side door, carrying a drink in each hand, one of which he held out to a cute Asian girl. "You met Will earlier. That's his girlfriend, Lila. See, I told you you wouldn't be the only new face." He scanned the crowd. "I'm not sure where Mom and Dad are, and I see some cousins mixed in, but at least you've got a little background. Shall we?" He held out a hand, inviting me to venture into the throng.

By the time we were called to dinner, my head was swimming with new names and faces, most of which I'd already forgotten. Will was one of the few I could remember, maybe because I'd met him first.

He took a liking to me and explained one way to keep them straight was that everyone was named after famous kings and queens in chronological order. "Biblical David is first, then your Alexander the Great, King Arthur, William the Conqueror"—he gestured to himself—"and Catherine the Great—but she insists we call her Casey."

I was about to ask how the odd naming system came to be when we were interrupted by the arrival of Alex's parents—a tall, tanned man with thick silver hair and the broad shoulders of a linebacker and a petite woman with precisely coiffed short red hair.

Alex introduced me to his father first. "Father, this is my girlfriend, Annabeth Coe. She's been the chief writer and strategist on the university's enrollment campaign. Annabeth, my father, the Honorable Oliver Grantham." He added in my ear, "He's a judge."

Oliver held out a beefy hand, and I blanched, anticipating the bone-crushing squeeze he delivered. "Pleased to meet you," he said stiffly.

Before I could respond, his wife stepped between us. She was a head shorter than me but carried herself with the grace of a ballerina. "I'm Evelyn, Alex's stepmother."

Introductions made, we sat, bowing our heads while the judge said grace, then he carved the turkey. As the trimmings were passed around the table, I began to relax, feeling less like the object of scrutiny. While we ate, Alex's father and David debated the upcoming election and how it may change the political landscape of the city and affect his judgeship.

Not being one for politics, I kept my eyes on my plate, wishing Alex was left-handed so I could hold his hand while we ate. Next to me, his sister, Casey, was prattling on about a concert she'd attended the night before, so I tuned in to that. I had seen one of the bands a few years ago, so at least that was something to which I could relate.

"Alex, you still coach crew for one those inner city schools, don't you?" Oliver's booming voice carried over Casey's story, drawing my attention back to him mid-conversation. At Alex's nod, he continued, "What do you think about this Common Core nonsense?"

"Well, I don't really deal with it much directly because I teach college students, but it is certainly affecting the way my incoming freshmen process information. And from what the boys on the crew tell me, it's making their homework harder because their parents can't help them with it. They—we—were raised on a completely different system, so it's hard to relearn the basics a new way at an older age. It's supposed to be a fair system that shows how well students are performing state-to-state, but all it seems to have done is cause problems for parents, teachers, and students. Where's the equity in that?"

Oliver chuckled darkly. "If equity is what you want, you should have become a lawyer. Maybe you could have advanced to a seat on the bench like me. Then you'd be the one to say what's fair and just." He sipped his scotch. "But no, you had to go off to your liberal arts studies and become a teacher."

"Not this again," Will muttered across the table.

Sensing an argument brewing, I took a few large swallows of wine.

Beside me, Alex tensed. "Father, I will not defend myself to you again. I know I'm the black sheep of the family because I chose a different path, but that ship has long since sailed."

"Perhaps, but you could have at least chosen to teach at Princeton or one of the other Ivies—a school worthy of the Grantham name."

"More stuffing, anyone?" Evelyn interrupted, offering the bowl with pleading eyes. I accepted, and she thanked me with a strained smile.

"So you're saying you'd rather have me eight hundred miles away than in the same city? I stayed here for you, for the family. I couldn't abandon the family after Mom died."

"Now we're a sacrifice you were forced to make? Please, son." He sighed. "Princeton is your alma mater. Think of the connections you could have forged. The biggest mistake you ever made was let-ting emotion—grief for your mother—cloud your judgment."

I stood, unable to listen to the argument any longer. "Mr. Grantham, I realize I don't know you or your family very well, but you are being terribly unfair to Alex. He is tenured at one of the top five universities in the country. Just because it's not classified officially as 'Ivy League' doesn't make it any less prestigious. During my work with the university, I've talked to plenty of prospective students, and they tell me they feel just as much pressure to get into this school as any Ivy League institution. You owe Alex an apol-ogy. He obviously thought of his family before himself when he chose his career path—one he loves and is very successful at, I might add—so father or no, you have no right to condemn him."

Silence greeted me as I closed my mouth and sat down. Heat instantly flooded my cheeks. Every pair of eyes was staring at me. Most wore expressions of shock. Evelyn looked at me, slack-jawed. Will was grinning as if he wanted to offer a slow clap of approval. Oliver's face was beet red.

"Regina never gave us these problems," was all he said before throwing his napkin onto his plate and storming out of the room.

∾

"Well, that's one way to make a first impression," Lila teased as we shoved through the glass doors to the veranda, where a fire pit burned brightly in the middle of a semicircle of overstuffed patio chairs.

"Oh, I doubt they'll ever forget me." I said, holding out my cup of hot cocoa for an infusion of Baileys. When Gemma barely dribbled it in, I motioned for the bottle. "You saw what just happened in there.

I'm going to need more than that to recover." I poured until the bottle glugged and my drink was more tan than chocolate brown.

"We like you though," Will put in on behalf of all the siblings.

"And they're the ones who really matter," Alex said, putting an arm around me.

I turned to him. "You're not mad at me? I feel like I should apologize for disrespecting your father."

"Nah, no harm done. He commands so much respect in his day job he feels like he's automatically owed it rather than needing to earn it like everyone else. You were the only one who could have put him in his place."

I shrank back in my chair, bringing a mittened hand to my mouth. "But will he hate me from now on? I don't plan on going away anytime soon." I smiled at Alex.

He returned my grin. "And I'm not letting you go."

"He may need to cool off a bit," Arthur said, "but I bet in the long run, you'll find he admires you for standing up for his son. That's what strong women do." He smiled at his wife. "Our mom was a strong woman. He'd want nothing less for any of his sons."

"Amen to that," Gemma said, holding up her mug for a toast.

Will appeared from seemingly out of nowhere, carrying a tray with two shot glasses and an old-fashioned brown bottle that reeked of alcohol.

"What in the world is that?" Lila asked, fanning her face.

"This, my dear"—Will leaned down to kiss Lila on the nose—"is the famous Grantham Goldmine. This is the stuff that made our granny and great-granny rich. Medicinal whiskey was legal to sell— provided the patient had a doctor's prescription. Just so happens that before the men in our family were lawyers, they were chemists who ran pharmacies. Every new member of the family has to taste it. It's tradition."

I wrinkled my nose at the dusty old bottle with its weathered, torn seal and peeling, faded label. Anything that came out of there surely had to taste like skunk water or worse. "Shouldn't we wait for the wedding?"

"Nope. Girlfriends count, especially on the holidays."

Gemma and Marcie nodded in unison.

"We've both been through it and lived to tell the tale. You'll survive," Marcie said.

Will handed me a shot glass of the amber liquid. I sniffed it gingerly. The ethanolic fumes took my breath away.

"Well, I haven't been responsible with anything else I've said tonight, so I'm certainly not going to worry after this." I held my glass up to Lila, who grimaced in solidarity.

"Ready?"

She nodded.

I threw back my head and opened my mouth, letting the liquid warm my tongue, my throat, and slowly my belly. I closed my eyes, savoring the surprisingly smoky, oaky flavor. It was rich, the kind of elegantly sumptuous flavor that hinted at expensive cigars smoked in mahogany-paneled rooms.

I opened my eyes to see Alex grinning at me. "Oh my God. That was amazing."

"Wow," was Lila's only response.

Arthur rubbed his hands together in glee. "All right, we've done the family thing. Now let's get to celebrating in earnest." He removed several highball glasses from behind an outdoor bar I hadn't previously noticed. "Who wants some?"

We raised our hands, and Will poured two fingers' worth into each glass, hesitating before Alex.

"Alex?"

He waved his brother away. "No, thank you. One is my limit, and I had that with dinner."

"Oh come on," David taunted. "You can slip just this once. It's not like you're in AA."

"Yeah, don't be a p—"

Marcie cut Will off with a look that could have frozen Lake Michigan. "There are ladies present."

"I was just going to say 'punk.'" Will sulked. "All right, all right," Alex said. "One. That's it."

Famous last words. One turned into two—or three if you were Will and Lila, who were dancing suggestively to music only they could hear—while the rest of us took turns trading dating horror stories. My cheeks hurt from laughing by the time it was my turn.

I counted off my travails on my fingers. "Let's see, I've been stood up, left for the guy's best friend twice—once was a girl, once was another guy—been the victim of many, many blind dates, one of whom ended up being my high school Spanish teacher—"

"Ew! No. No way that's true!" Gemma screeched through peals of laughter. "That is so wrong." She stuck out her tongue and fake hurled like a cat having a hairball.

I raised my right hand. "Swear to God. Granted this was like a decade after I graduated."

"Yeah, but still." She shuddered.

"Hey," Marcie drawled to Alex, "you've been awful quiet. Surely you have some dish to share. Maybe on this one?" She sloshed her drink in my direction.

"If you don't tell them, I will," I threatened.

He laughed. "I don't have any horror stories."

"Yet," I amended with a giggle. "It's only a matter of time."

Alex circled his head in a half nod, half shake as if unsure whether to agree with me. "You said it, not me." After a pause, he found the story thread he was looking for. "Well, she is a bit of a klutz." He proceeded to recount the night of Mia's birthday—when I fell down the stairs coming offstage—my less-than-graceful golf game on our first date, then added in the night I decided to try to be all naughty-maid sexy and seduce him in the laundry room. "She fell off the dryer and hit her head on the shelf holding the detergent. Needed six stitches."

"Truth." I pointed at my temple, where a fine white line would forever tell the tale. I pulled Alex close. "But at least you got to play doctor afterward."

"TMI! TMI," Casey squealed.

Alex was laughing so hard he was practically crying, face beet red. "Then there was the time we went ice skating in Millennium Park, and that jerk cut me off, forcing me down by the boards. When you tried to see if I was okay, you realized you didn't know how to stop and nearly sliced my finger off with your skate blade."

My smile evaporated. "We've never been skating, Alex. That wasn't me."

He turned glassy eyes on me, unperturbed. "Sure it was, babe."

My chest constricted. "No, I've never been ice skating. You and I talked about going when we got back to avoid the tourist rush, remember?"

He looked at me quizzically. "Are you sure? I could swear—"

Marcie looked from me to him and took the glass of whiskey from his hand. "Okay, you've had enough." She motioned between the two of us. "And neither of you are driving anywhere tonight. There's more than enough room for you to stay. Come on, soldier." She helped Alex to his unsteady feet before passing him off to Will.

"But if it wasn't Annabeth, who was it?" Alex asked as they ushered him in from the cold, one supporting each arm.

Marcie turned to make sure I was out of earshot.

I wasn't, but I couldn't get myself to move. I needed to know even though I dreaded it. *Please let it be from a movie, or maybe he's mistaking me for his sister or one of his in-laws.* I could have even handled a high school girlfriend. But even as I thought it, I feared I already knew the answer.

"It was Regina, dear."

∾

My head throbbed with the beating of my heart, and my tongue tasted like rusty nails. I didn't want to open my eyes because I knew any light, overcast or sunny, would send stabbing pain through my head.

"Oh, God, I think I died and someone forgot to tell me." Alex's thick voice came from over my shoulder.

"Uh-huh," I croaked, burrowing further into my pillow. My eyes popped open a few seconds later when I heard Alex bolt out of bed and half-walk, half-trip to the bathroom. Yep, I was right. Some invisible force was jamming an ice pick into my brain in time with my heartbeat. I squeezed my eyes shut and willed my stomach to be calm.

A perfunctory knock at the door was followed by Casey's head and a quiet whisper, "You guys awake?"

I motioned her in. But before I could answer, Alex loudly retched in the bathroom.

"I guess that answers that." She slowly backed into the room.

carrying a tray with two steaming mugs of coffee and a small plastic creamer container. "I thought you guys could use this."

I gladly accepted a cup. "You are an angel."

She smirked and shrugged. "The blessing and curse of being a light drinker is taking care of everyone else the next morning. But I don't mind." After a slight pause, she started to back away. "Oh, there're scrambled eggs downstairs if you get hungry."

I could have kissed her. "Thank you so much."

Reaching for the door handle, Casey nodded toward the bathroom. "Make him take aspirin and B-12. And both of you drink lots of water."

I grinned at her. "Thanks, Mom."

The caffeine was just starting to dull my headache when Alex reappeared, pale with a slightly greenish cast about his skin. He slumped into bed, smelling of minty toothpaste or mouthwash. "This is one of the reasons I don't drink more than one." He gladly accepted the mug I held out to him. "The other is that I get out of control and talk way too much."

I rearranged myself into a sitting position, knowing I wouldn't be able to stay upright for long. "Well, it could be worse. At least you don't get violent. How much of last night do you remember?"

He stared at the wall. "Bits and pieces. It comes in flashes."

"Do you remember telling the ice skating story?"

Alex sighed and hung his head. "Unfortunately, yes. I take it they told you it was actually about Regina?"

"Yeah."

"I'm so sorry, Annabeth. I really did think it was you. Maybe I conflated the memory with our future plans."

Or maybe you're still not over her. It doesn't seem like your family is. I kissed his cheek. "It doesn't matter."

He turned toward me. "Yes, it does. You are what matters now. I should never have had her on any part of my mind, conscious or unconscious."

"But how could you not? It didn't occur to me until I was lying here last night, trying to get the bed to stop spinning, that this was your first Thanksgiving without her under this roof. You were together for years, so she became part of the tradition. And here I am changing everything."

"That's still no excuse." Alex shook his head then groaned, hand to his temple. "Oh, not smart."

"Stop apologizing. You are forgiven." I set my cup on the nightstand and curled into him, laying my head on his chest.

"Did you really tell my dad off last night, or did I dream that?"

"Oh, that was painfully real. I'm not looking forward to facing him today." I buried my face in this chest, which muffled my voice.

"He'll probably act like nothing happened to save face."

"I hope so." I wondered if I should mention his reaction, and I decided to go for it. "He compared me to Regina, you know. That's probably why she was on your mind." I didn't believe that for a second, but I hoped it would soothe him.

No response from Alex.

I lifted my head. His eyes were closed, mouth slightly open, chest rising and falling in a gentle rhythm. He was asleep.

I slipped out of bed. Once in the bathroom, I downed aspirin and B-12, staring at myself in the mirror. Ugh, I really did look terrible— hair askew with brown frizzy curls pointing in every direction, ugly purple rings under my eyes. For a split second, my vision blurred, and I saw what I imagined to be Regina's perfect face staring at me.

I watched Alex sleep a moment before climbing back into bed. He and I were fine, but I wondered if I would ever be free of her ghost.

CHAPTER FOURTEEN

My hands and feet were numb by the time I flounced into the office—an hour late thanks to the face-gnawing, subzero Chicago cold and particularly icy streets. For the thousandth time, I wondered if I would be better off buying a car—not that I could afford one—and braving the insane drivers rather than relying on public transportation. Changing out of my snow boots and into flats, I said a silent prayer of thanks to whatever god had given me the sense to not try to walk to work today. I would have had frostbite on every part of my body.

"Hey, you made it in." Miles greeted me warmly, sliding into his desk chair across the eight feet of space that separated our desks. In his hand was a piping hot cup of coffee, which I took gratefully.

"Barely," I muttered. "Thanks."

"Rick wants to see us in thirty. Just thought I'd warn you."

I blew on the steaming black liquid. "Is this about the Warren account? If so, I should probably tell you some of my newest ideas for the magazine they want to create. I think we can help them make their employee communications interesting and fun."

"I have no idea what he wants, but he's called in Nick too, so it's got to be big. I think it may be the announcement."

My stomach plummeted. We'd been dreading this day for months, and it had finally arrived. I took a shaky breath. "Will Laini be there too?"

"I don't think so. Sounds like all the teams are meeting simultaneously with their respective bosses. She can't be everywhere at once." Miles put an arm around me. "Hey, we've been through worse. We'll be fine. With our talent, they don't dare fire us."

We went through the motions of reviewing a few projects, comparing mock-ups with designs awaiting approval, but neither of our hearts was really in it. We were counting down the seconds. Finally, Miles's computer dinged a five-minute warning.

Nick was already sitting at the small round table in Rick's office when we arrived. We both took seats.

Rick started in without preamble, leaning against the front of his desk as he spoke. "Glad you're all here. Since today is the last day before the agency closes for the remainder of the year, I wanted to tell you about some changes that will be happening in our department next year. The board recently decided we would be more efficient if we structured our teams a little differently, and the partners have agreed to give it a try. Right now, all of the creatives and account execs are on an even playing field, reporting to me as part of the creative team. They'd like to see what happens over the next quarter if we split into teams by clients. That means the writing and design teams, like you two—" he pointed to Miles and me "—will report up through their account executives—Nick—to the managers—in our case, Laini. So basically the account executives are now the supervisors of the designers and writers for their projects." He paused to let that information sink in, stroking his gray-and-white goatee as he prepared for whatever was next.

"What?" The word burst from my lips before I could stop it. "But Nick was just censured for his conduct with U of Chicago. Now he's getting a promotion? No way Laini signed off on this."

"She didn't have to. The board trumps her even though she's a partner."

"What does he know about production?" Miles asked, sending a pointed glare at Nick at the same time I asked, "Where will you be in this new structure?"

"Nick knows everything he needs to know—what the client wants, what they like, etcetera. Really, this is best. He's already the most intimately acquainted with the projects anyway, even more than I am sometimes." Rick turned his stern gaze on me. "I'm being transferred to New York to work with a startup team there to explore the possibility of a new office." He shook Nick's hand and patted his back. "Congratulations, Mr. Zarrino. I'll leave you three to discuss this transition as a team."

I stood frozen, feeling as if someone had just poured a bucket of cold water over me, as Rick left the room. This would be bad, very bad. Nick was insufferable at the best of times, and now he'd been given power over the next four months of my life . . . if not longer. Not to mention he was sure to repay me for the tongue-lashing I'd given him last month. *Shit. Shit. Shit.*

Nick turned to us. He was swallowing a smirk that likely could have powered the entire city. "Rick and I have discussed a few things, and Annabeth, given your current personal situation—"

God, he made it sound as if I was pregnant or had just contracted leprosy.

"I think it's best if we pull you both off the U of Chicago account."

"What? I've put the last six months of my life into that project. You know how much it means to me."

Miles raised his hand. "What did I do?"

Nick shrugged and held up his hands as though the whole situation were out of his control. "You're a creative team. What happens to one of you happens to both." He lowered his voice and leaned toward me. "Perhaps next time you'll take that into account before making certain decisions."

I wanted to hit him so badly I had to sit on my hands to stop myself. "You know better than anyone that Alex isn't my client anymore. That's why we hired you."

"But you're still writing for the university, so it counts. I'm sorry, but the firm has a reputation to maintain."

I wanted to retort about that being thrown out the window when they hired him, but I held my tongue.

Nick couldn't maintain his composure anymore, grinning like a used car salesman. "Don't think of this as a punishment, rather as an opportunity to work on new things. We'll meet at 9 a.m. on January third to discuss strategy for the upcoming months." He dismissed us with a wave. "Happy holidays."

CHAPTER FIFTEEN

I didn't have to sit on my suitcase to get it closed, but I was pretty sure the airline would make me pay a fee for overweight baggage.

Alex pulled the case from the bed and groaned dramatically. "You do know we're only going to be there two nights, right?"

I stuck my tongue out at him. "You try fitting clothes for an Iowa winter, toiletries, and presents for fifteen family members in one suitcase and tell me how you fare."

He held up his smaller suitcase with his other hand and swung it around with ease. "You've got me on the presents, but other than that. . ."

"Boys suck."

He kissed the top of my head. "But you love us anyway."

"Well, I love you anyway. There are a few I could do without."

"All right, time to set some ground rules on this trip," he said as I locked up my apartment and we headed down to his car. "Rule number one: no talking about Nick or referencing him in any way.

I know you hate him, but you'll have enough time to complain about him when you go back to work. The next two weeks are our time. I don't want any other men interfering. Got it?"

"My dad doesn't count, does he?"

Alex adopted a stern expression. "Of course not. Mr. Coe is the exception to all of our rules."

"Okay, but rule number two has to be that you'll put up with my mom no matter what she says. She's a huge fan of he-whom-we're-not-talking-about, and I can't control her."

"Thanks for the warning. But once she's been infected with my special brand of academic charm, she won't even be able to remember his name."

I laughed. "Believe whatever you like."

Two hours later, we were in our seats for the brief flight—we'd be in the air for less time than it had taken us to get to the airport and wait to board. I was having second—no, make that third—thoughts about inviting Alex to stay with my family for Christmas.

He noticed my preoccupation. "Rule number three: you are not allowed to overthink anything for two weeks."

I rolled my eyes. "You may as well be asking me not to breathe."

He squeezed my hand. "Everything will be all right."

It was mid-afternoon by the time we reached my house. Every time I came home, I had the same feeling of going back in time. As soon as we turned onto my tree-lined street, I felt like a high school student returning from a day of study, not a big-city girl coming home for the first time in a year.

Alex insisted on carrying all of our bags so my hands were free to hug my parents when they met us at the door. My mom was first out the door, her red-and-white polka-dotted apron dusted with flour, the scent of baking apple pie trailing after her.

"Annabeth, dear, you look lovely," she said as she hugged me. "City life agrees with you."

"Hi, Mom." I kissed her cheek, smudging away the flour. "Yeah, it does."

My dad was right behind her, ready to squeeze me tight before she even let me go. "How you doin', kitten?"

"Ugh, too tight, Dad." He loosened his grip. "I'm good, thanks." I arched an eyebrow at him. "Are you staying out of the chocolate chip cookies like the doctor told you? Healthy diet and all that?"

He gave me his best altar boy look and patted his protruding stomach. "Of course. But tonight is an exception. St. Nick wouldn't like it if I didn't taste-test his cookies. I mean, we have to have quality control, right?" He winked at me.

"Keep telling yourself that." I took a deep breath, knowing it was time to make the introductions. "Mom, Dad, this is Alex Grantham, my boyfriend."

Alex shook my dad's hand first. "It's nice to meet you, sir."

My dad gave Alex a once-over, appraising his worthiness for his baby girl. Alex must have passed muster because my dad's tone was jocular as he clapped Alex on the shoulder with his free hand. "You too, son. You too."

My mom was more reserved, as though withholding judgment. "Welcome to our home, Professor Grantham."

"Mom, this isn't *Downton Abbey*," I interjected.

Alex gave my mom a warm half hug. "Please, call me Alex, Mrs. Coe."

My mom made a polite murmur of acknowledgement but didn't ask him to call her Alice.

"Is Mirabelle here yet?" I asked, standing on tiptoe and trying to see over my mom's shoulder.

The mention of my older sister seemed to thaw my mom's demeanor somewhat. Her face softened as her eyes focused on me. "Yes. She and Chuck are in the den watching *White Christmas.*"

My dad gently guided my mom back into the house. "Let the kids in, Alice. They must be freezing."

We followed my dad into the foyer, which was decked out in its seasonal best. A twelve-foot Christmas tree held court in front of the bay window, festooned with sparkling gold and red ornaments, candle-like lights, and an old-world garland of wooden beads resembling cranberries, holly berries, and mistletoe that had been in our family for generations. Family lore boasted that one of my great-great-grandfathers had carved it for his first Christmas with his new bride and it had been handed down ever since. Behind the tree, the window seat held a ceramic nativity scene my mother had created with Mirabelle and me when we were little, when my mom was convinced she had an untapped talent for pottery.

Above our heads, the lighting fixture in front of the door was dripping with evergreen boughs, as was the banister leading upstairs. Alex and my dad dragged our luggage up the stairs, already chatting like old friends about their shared alma mater, Princeton. With nothing else to do, I asked my mom if she needed any help.

"No, of course not. Go be with your sister. But mind the time. We're having drinks at six before dinner is served."

"Okay, Mom."

I walked through the living room, pausing in the doorway of my father's den. It was still decorated with all of my dad's favorite things: photos of my sister and me at every age from infancy to last Christmas, memorabilia from his time on Princeton's rowing crew, a framed flag next to a case of military rank patches, photos of his family. I inhaled. The room still retained the ghost of rich tobacco that had seeped into the wood paneling decades ago, long before he gave up smoking a pipe for the sake of his girls.

Mirabelle and her husband had their backs toward me, facing the television. My sister was sitting very still, engrossed in the movie, but watching her husband's shoulders rise and fall just slightly, I had the strong suspicion that Chuck was asleep.

I took a silent step forward and proclaimed, "I'm here. Who wants to say hi to their favorite sister?"

Both of them jumped. Chuck snorted and looked around, obviously confused. Mirabelle practically tossed her bowl of popcorn on the floor in her haste to tackle me.

She squealed, picking me up and spinning me around. "Bethy! I'm so glad you're here!"

"I missed you too, Bella." If she was going to use my childhood nickname, I was going to use hers even though once her *Twilight* phase had passed, she'd sworn she'd kill anyone who called her that.

"Hey, Annabeth," Chuck said, his pudgy face lighting up.

I embraced him as well, whispering, "Last I saw, Dad and Alex were headed upstairs, but I have a feeling you'll find them in the living room if you're looking for a little male bonding."

"Yeah, I have to check out this boy toy of yours, see if he meets the family standards. I set the bar pretty high, you know." He pretended to preen like a peacock.

Mirabelle rolled her eyes and swatted her husband with a throw pillow. "Yeah, get out so we can have some girl talk." Once Chuck was gone, Mirabelle pulled me down next to her on the couch, putting the TV on mute. "So spill. I want to hear all about you and Alex." She handed me an untouched glass of red wine that I assumed was Chuck's. "Don't worry. He didn't drink it."

"What's there to tell that I didn't already say on the phone?"

"Yeah, I know, but it's different in person. So. . . big step bringing him home to meet the 'rents." She shoved my arm, her grin so wide it almost leapt off her face.

I set my glass on the coffee table, pulling my arms up inside my sweater and balling my fists around the cuffs. "You know, I never really thought about it that way. It was just natural for us to be together for Christmas. Dad seems to like him. Mom on the other hand. . ."

"She didn't like Chuck for two years, remember? I don't know who she thinks we should end up with, but it's never the ones we pick. Although we both know who she wants you to marry."

I rolled my eyes and reached for the wine glass then took a long swig. "Yeah. I warned Alex about that. I also promised him I wouldn't talk about *him* for two weeks."

Mirabelle snorted. "That should make for some interesting dinner conversation. But he doesn't have to know what's said between the two of us."

"Good point. So the good news is I still have a job. The bad news is Nick is my new boss, effective January third."

Mirabelle smacked my thigh. "No way."

Breaking my promise to Alex, I told her the whole sordid story while she listened, wide-eyed, occasionally interrupting with a disbelieving, "No!"

When I was done, she just shook her head. "I should have castrated him when I had the chance after graduation." She stared into the globe of her wine glass for a minute. "Don't you think it's a little odd that he knew where to find you?"

"Please, I know Mom told him. It wouldn't surprise me if she told him where I worked, even gave him my address."

"And your bitchy friend told him about the job?"

"Mia. Yeah. Or so she says."

"You don't honestly think nothing happened between them, do you? I mean, Mia is a hornball, and Nick's never been able to resist a pretty face no matter what she told you."

"You're probably right. But she hasn't mentioned him since, so I'm guessing it was a one-night thing. Poor Miles."

"Forget Miles." Mirabelle shook her head. "She has no respect for the girl code. Rule number one is you don't sleep with your friends' exes. You just don't. Tell me again why you're friends with her?"

I shrugged. "Behind her bitchiness and scheming, she is still a good friend. Besides I owe her. She really helped me a lot when I first moved to Chicago, when I didn't have any friends. Now she and Miles are so intertwined, and I don't want to hurt him just because his girlfriend can be unpleasant."

"Unpleasant? Help or no help, she really treats you horribly, Annabeth. I know that, and I've never even met her. This isn't the first time she's betrayed you, nor will it be the last. You just choose not to see it. Do you remember how she used you to get her hooks into that one client of yours from Estée Lauder because she thought he could help land her a gig as the face of their newest skin care line? You are lucky not to have lost your job over that. What Mia wants, Mia gets, consequences be damned."

"That's just her way. She's like that with everyone."

"Like that's an excuse."

"Hey, I don't like all of your friends. Hell, you had Lynda as your maid of honor, and she shaved off your eyebrows in high school."

Mirabelle covered her eyes with her hand as though the gesture could erase the memory. "Thanks for bringing that up—again. By the way, I'm still getting compliments on the engagement photo from your *HuffPo* article. I can't believe you were willing to put the tree picture out there for the world to see."

"Can you think of a better way to capture who I am?"

Mirabelle toyed with a curly lock of hair that had escaped from my ponytail. "Oh, honey, a single photo could never contain you. Speaking of, I've never seen you look as happy as in that photo you posted on Facebook the other day."

"The one of me and Alex from the photo booth? That was taken on our first date."

"Seriously, he's done you so much good. You consistently sound happy on the phone, you're glowing, and I haven't heard you cry in months."

I bit my lower lip. "Yeah, it's amazing how a little affection chases the loneliness away."

"Oh, I'd say from the glint in your eye and the flush in your cheeks that it's more than affection. You love him, don't you?"

I looked into her golden-brown eyes. "I think I do."

She hugged me again, holding me the way she did when we were little. "Do you think this could be the end of the letters? Do you think he's the one?"

I laid my head on her shoulder. "I really hope so."

We sat like that for a few moments, reminiscing about our girlhood wedding plans and how they compared to what we wanted as adults. By the time my mom's voice summoned us to the dining room, we were laughing so hard we were practically crying.

"What's with Mom having drinks before dinner?" I asked before we left the couch. "It's not like this is a fancy party. We all know each other. Well, except for Alex."

"She's obsessed with BBC America. She's determined to do the formal British thing tonight."

"Please don't tell me she's making us dress for dinner."

Mirabelle screwed up her lips. "You can thank me for that one. I talked her out of it."

"Seriously?"

"Seriously." She grabbed my hand. "Come on. Don't let her bother you. Remember, Chuck and I have your back."

We survived drinks, but dinner was turning out to be a minefield. Mom had decided that our traditional Christmas ham wasn't good enough, so she had made Beef Wellington, ignoring Mirabelle's protests that she had been a vegetarian for the last eight months. When Mirabelle slid her meat onto Chuck's plate, my mom took it as a personal affront. I was just grateful I wasn't the only one she was picking on.

"So, Annabeth dear, what's it like having Nick just down the hall from you every day? You two must have so much fun reliving the old days." Her smile was loaded with meaning.

I took a sip of water and glanced at Alex apologetically before answering. "Actually, we don't interact that much." I reached for Alex's hand under the table, and he gave it a squeeze. "And he's my boss now, so I don't expect we'll be chummy any time soon."

My mom frowned. "Really? But you're so close to your other coworkers."

"It's the nature of the role. Laini and I are strictly professional. And I wasn't that close to Jenna either."

"Has she had her baby yet?" Mirabelle asked, mercifully changing the subject.

"She's due around New Year's. She and Jake are hoping she'll have the first baby of the year. They could use the free stuff that comes with it."

"She's pretty young, isn't she?" my mom asked.

"Kind of. She's twenty-two."

My mom pointed at Mirabelle with her fork. "Speaking of babies, when are you two going to get started? You don't have all that much time left."

"Mom. . ." Mirabelle heaved an exasperated sigh. "We've been through this. Chuck and I have decided not to have children."

"I thought that was just a phase that would pass once you'd been married a while," my mom muttered.

"Alice, did you learn nothing from Annabeth's article? That's not how women want to be defined anymore."

I smiled at my dad, appreciative that he'd understood the point of my essay.

"Oh, that." My mom dismissed the reference with a wave. "How else am I supposed to feel when both of my girls are past their prime and yet my arms are devoid of grandchildren? I suppose all I can do is pray that God will deliver me from this test like the women of the Old Testament."

Next to me, Alex was shaking with suppressed laughter. I guess I'd forgotten to warn him about my mom's melodramatic side.

Ignoring my mother's histrionics, my father raised his glass. "I'd like to propose a toast to Alex and Annabeth. Besides being one of the most adorable couples I've ever seen, they've had great success working together. Alex was telling me earlier that the university's overall applications are up by thirty percent and the English department has seen the number of students listing it as their intended major double since the start of term."

I elbowed Alex. "You didn't tell me that."

He smiled. "We just found out."

"To Annabeth and Alex."

Everyone raised their glasses and repeated his toast. As I looked around the table, I was struck by how much love was in the house and how fortunate I was to have such a supportive family. When I caught Mirabelle's eye, I could have sworn there were tears in her eyes. Chuck winked at me. Only my mother refused to participate more than strictly necessary.

The evening carried on this way for another half an hour before the doorbell rang.

"Oh, whoever could that be?" my mother asked with feigned innocence as she rose and headed toward the door.

I glanced at Mirabelle. She shrugged.

"Well, hello, dear." My mother's exuberant greeting carried into the dining room. "Merry Christmas." She kissed whoever was at the door with a loud "mwah."

"Merry Christmas to you, Mrs. Coe."

I froze, the hairs on the back of my neck and arms standing on end. I knew that voice. It had echoed within these walls most of my life. No. She hadn't. She couldn't have. I grabbed Alex's leg under the table, my fingernails digging into his pants.

My mother returned, beaming. "Look who the cat dragged in."

Nick trailed behind her like a puppy, carrying two neatly wrapped boxes. He nodded to my dad. "Merry Christmas, Mr. Coe. Mirabelle, Chuck." He caught my eye. "Annabeth, nice to see you."

I gave him a mocking smile.

It was only then that he caught sight of Alex, whose expression had visibly darkened. Nick reached out a hand. "Alex, I wasn't expecting to see you here."

"I could say the same about you," he ground out while they shook hands.

I turned to my mother, whispering furiously, "You knew Alex was coming with me. Why did you invite Nick to dinner?"

My mother placed a hand on her chest as though to protest her innocence. "I was simply being kind to an old friend." She raised her voice so that everyone at the table could hear. "Nick is like a son to us. We couldn't in good conscience leave him alone on Christmas Eve."

Nick's parents had both died a few years back. The last I'd heard, his sister wasn't speaking to him, so he had no reason to be in this state other than my mother's incessant machinations.

"Why are you back home, Nick? There's nothing bringing you here—unless Alyssa finally forgave you," I said.

"Annabeth," my mother chided, aghast. "That is no way to treat a guest. Where are your manners?"

Nick ignored her. "She has, in fact, thank you. We've called a truce for the holidays. I hope you will extend me the same courtesy."

I looked at my empty plate, embarrassed to be called out by both of them, especially when they were right. I was being rude.

Mirabelle stood and cleared the plates. "Annabeth, be a dear and help me with these, won't you?"

I gave her a grateful smile and stacked dishes. When we were both in the kitchen, with running water and clattering dishes to cover our voices, I finally said, "What. The. Fuck? Is Mom insane?"

"Yes, but we knew that."

"Seriously, is she trying to kill me? Because she just might. Is there more wine? I'm going to need my own bottle to get through this."

Mirabelle nodded at the counter. "Three more bottles. But please, try to behave yourself. This is Christmas, and the two of you aren't children anymore."

I sighed. "I know. But do you have any idea how strange it is to have your ex-boyfriend who is now your boss and your current boyfriend sitting at the same table?"

She started to reply, but Chuck stuck his head in the door. "Um, Annabeth, you may want to come out here. Nick is up to his old tricks." He mimed incessant chatter by opening and closing his hand.

When I sat back down, Nick was regaling my parents with a tale of how he had "singlehandedly" convinced one of our celebrity authors at the October book signing to make a sizable donation to the university. "I just told him, 'Look at all these eager young faces. How could you not want to ensure several more generations have the benefit of learning from your writing?' Sometimes you have to appeal to their ego to get the job done."

"Too bad fundraising isn't your job," I said.

My mother glared at me but directed her words to Nick. "And what was your role in the event, my dear? Besides showing that writer some of your signature charm, I mean?"

Nick beamed like a schoolboy. "I helped Annabeth with every aspect of the preparations, did whatever she needed." When he saw my scathing look, he hastened to clarify, "She did most of the planning while I was still getting my feet wet, but I helped her with all the last-minute details."

"That's just like you, Nick—so dependable."

Alex nearly choked on his wine but quickly recovered. "Yes, we don't know what we would do without him." His voice held just enough sarcasm that Nick and I caught it but my mother was oblivious.

My father, visibly agitated, stood suddenly and asked, "Who wants dessert?"

Ten minutes later, we were munching on my mom's signature pistachio Bundt cake and sipping coffee. The apple pie I'd smelled when we arrived was for tomorrow, or so I was told.

"Do you remember the year the three of you decided to make this cake on your own?" my mom asked.

Mirabelle rolled her eyes. "Oh, God. Please, don't remind me."

Nick laughed. "We didn't have any baking powder, so we used baking soda instead."

"And the lid came off the cinnamon. I've never seen that much spice in one place in my life." I made a face.

"Hey, I did a pretty good job of scooping it out," Nick said.

"Not good enough. That was most awful cake I ever tasted," my dad said, shaking with laugher and wiping tears from his eyes.

"How old were we? Eleven?" I asked.

"Something like that," Nick said. "This cake has a ton of history to it. This is the same thing you served when Annabeth turned twenty-one, only you forgot to tell anyone you'd soaked it in rum."

"Yeah, thanks for that, Mom," I said. "It went really well with all the other alcohol people were plying me with that night."

"Yeah, Mom, you weren't the one who had to sit up with her and hold her hair back when it came back out," Mirabelle said, grimacing.

"You'll hear no complaints from me. I credit that cake with a lot of fun that night." Nick winked at me. "If you know what I mean."

I glanced at Alex, who had stopped eating and was slowly turning red. A cord of muscle stood out on his neck.

"Don't flatter yourself," I said. "I can't help that I was young and dumb."

"Hey, isn't that a line from a song?" Mirabelle asked. She thought for a moment then started singing the line from "Cherry Lips" about a girl who had just turned twenty-one.

Nick picked up the next lyrics, and soon all three of us were singing.

By the time we finished the chorus, I was breathless with laugher. "Didn't Garbage sing that when we went to see them?"

"Yeah, Shirley said they didn't usually perform it in America since it wasn't a single here." Nick shook his head. "Man, that was an awesome night."

"So many memories," my mom cooed, looking between Nick and me. "And more to come, I'm sure."

"I have no doubt of that," Nick said, grinning at me.

Alex politely excused himself. When he didn't return after a reasonable amount of time, I used the excuse of refilling the coffee pot to go look for him. I found him in the living room, looking at the photos on the mantel. Most of them were of Mirabelle and me as kids, but many of them also contained Nick.

"How can I compete with this?" Alex asked without turning around. "You have so much history."

I put my arms around him from behind, resting my cheek against his back. "And that's exactly what it is—history."

He humphed. "That's not what it sounded like in there."

"So we shared a laugh. We're old friends. It's going to happen. But nothing else is. End of story." I took his hand and turned him around. "My mom may be living in the past, but I'm not. I'm interested in the future—with you." I stood on tiptoe and waited from him to tilt his head down to mine. When he finally relented, I kissed him long and deep. "I can promise you Nick never got a kiss like that, with or without rum pistachio cake."

Alex laughed. "I hope not, or I really will have to throttle him."

"No need for that. But I do think our unwelcome guest has stayed long enough. What do you say we find a way to kick him out?"

"With pleasure."

We would open most of our presents tomorrow morning after coming back from dawn church services, but now that Nick had gone, we were gathered for my favorite part of the holidays. On Christmas Eve, after dessert and some time relaxing by the fire, we each selected one present to open. We believed that the gift contained a special meaning for the year to come.

We sat in a circle on the floor in front of the Christmas tree in the foyer. My mom went first, opening a box that contained a plush cashmere sweater from my dad. It was a deep forest green, and she declared it a sign of fortune and luxury to come. Mirabelle and Chuck chose a joint gift from my parents, which turned out to be a two-parter: a statue of St. Joseph and a check for several thousand dollars.

"We want to help you sell your house and make sure you have a down payment on the home of your dreams," my mom said.

My dad selected a gift bag from which he pulled a scrapbook Mirabelle and I had been collaborating on over the Internet. She'd done the actual design, but we both contributed photos, and I wrote the captions. It started with photos from when he and my mom were dating and continued through the present, with a placeholder near the end for a group photo we would take after church tomorrow plus a few blank pages for new photos.

"Thank you, girls," he said, voice quavering with emotion. "I say this means I'll have many more wonderful memories with those I love."

Alex picked the heaviest gift I'd packed. "I want to know what I almost broke my back carrying all the way here," he said, tearing into the green-and-red wrapping paper.

He uncovered a dark blue hardcover book sans dust jacket, the kind of tome you'd expect to see in a college professor's office. Embossed on the cover in gold letters was the title, *The Harry Potter Generation: A Study of the Influence of Young Adult Literature on High School and College Students*. It had just been published and was in high demand. Alex was obsessed with the author, John Fitzpatrick, whom he held in utmost respect as a peer and a kind of mentor.

"Open the cover," I instructed him.

It was autographed with a note about how impressed the author was with the coverage he'd seen on Alex's teaching methods and an invitation to collaborate on a future journal article.

"Oh, Annabeth, this beyond perfect. How did you get this?"

I grinned. "A girl has to have her secrets, but I'll say that my work with your dean has its advantages. I'm so happy you like it."

"How can I not?" He gave me a grateful peck on the lips.

I selected a small box wrapped in shiny silver paper that said it was from Alex. Slipping a fingernail under the tape, I arched an eyebrow at Alex, who was grinning like an idiot. I opened the first box only to encounter another. Tearing through another layer of paper, my heart began to race. The weight, size, and shape confirmed my suspicions. It was most certainly a ring box. My hands were sweating by the time I pried open the velvet lid. Inside was a beautiful white-gold ring made from two hands clasping one another. The cuff at the wrist of each hand had four tiny diamonds inlaid in it.

Alex took out the ring and placed it on the ring finger of my right hand. "This is called a Concordia ring. This particular one has been in my family since 1910, but they date back to Roman times. The ring is sacred to the goddess Concordia, who is the lady of harmony. She watches over all manner of relationships but has a special affinity for friendships that grow into deep love. I hope you will accept this ring as a symbol of my commitment to love only you."

Heat bloomed in my chest as love boiled up and bubbled over. I was so overwhelmed I could barely breathe. "Yes. Of course."

As I pulled him close and buried my face in his neck, the full weight of the meaning behind the ring started to sink in. It wasn't quite an engagement ring, but it was a close second. Alex was serious about us. After only six months, he was willing to make a deep commitment to me in front of my entire family. That was more than most men did after several years.

After we finally parted, Mirabelle pointed up. "Did either of you notice where you're sitting?"

We both looked up. Above us, a spray of white berries and green leaves hung from the ceiling.

I covered my face with my hands. "I've never been kissed under the mistletoe."

"Really?" Alex pulled my hands away. "Well, there's a first time for everything."

"You seem to be a lot of firsts for me."

"First and last, that's the goal."

I laced my fingers in Alex's wavy hair, one hand above each of his ears, and held his gaze so he couldn't look away from me. "I love you. More than anyone or anything in my life."

"You took the words right out of my mouth." He leaned in and kissed me.

After a minute of Mirabelle and Chuck catcalling, my mother interrupted. "All right, that's enough of that. We should all retire to bed. We have an early start in the morning."

Our group broke up then, heading to various sleeping arrangements. My sister and her husband disappeared in the direction of the den, likely to sleep on the pull-out bed, while my dad walked us up to the guest room my parents had made out of my old bedroom.

"Don't worry. We're not so old-fashioned that we expect you to sleep in separate rooms, although I have a feeling it would please your mother." He kissed my cheek. "I'm very happy for you, kitten."

"Thanks, Dad."

Alex held out his hand to my father, who pulled him into a hug. "You take good care of my little girl, you hear?"

"That's my mission in life, sir."

"Good man."

That night, as the house slumbered and I lay in Alex's arms, I sent a thousand prayers heavenward in thanksgiving for my good fortune and one that my mom's heart would embrace Alex—even if it took time. Her reserve was the one shadow on the gleaming starlight that was my life.

CHAPTER SIXTEEN

Three days later, after a quick flight back to Chicago to repack, Alex
and I were ensconced in a cozy little lodge in the mountains outside
Denver. My parents had given Mirabelle and Chuck a voucher for
an all-inclusive stay, but Mirabelle had quietly slipped it to me as we
were saying our farewells the day after Christmas.

"Bella, I can't accept this," I'd protested. "You and your hubby
need this time off more than we do."

"Well, be that as it may, Chuck's job has come calling, so we won't
be going anywhere."

Chuck stuck his head into our little circle. "Yeah. IT may pay
well, but being on call all the time sucks."

"Don't you love saving the world?" I asked.

"Oh, if only my work were so sexy."

Mirabelle held the envelope out to me again, shaking it slightly.
"Come on, take it. We don't want to see Mom and Dad's money go
to waste. They don't need to know what we did with it."

And so Alex and I were in a secluded lodge in the middle of the Rockies while Mirabelle and Chuck had returned home to North Carolina. The lodge was like a dream come true, with roaring fires and a hot tub in every guest room, gleaming timbers as tall as sequoias, fur rugs and blankets in abundance, and a nonstop supply of top-notch food and wine at our disposal with a single phone call.

Between this and the ring, I felt like a bride on her honeymoon. We spent the first two days of our stay in bed, cuddled together, while snow fell in giant flakes outside the floor-to-ceiling windows. When we weren't making love, we were watching movies on Alex's iPad or quietly reading side by side like some old married couple. It was heaven.

On New Year's Eve, we decided to venture out and mix with the other couples at the lodge's champagne bash. As usual, Alex was ready long before I was. While I hopped around, trying to get my heels on while pinning up my hair, he leaned against the edge of the sofa in the suite's sitting area, watching me with great amusement.

"How you women survive any event is beyond me. There's so much. . . preparation." He shook his head.

"Oh hush. You know you love the end result."

"That I do."

"Honey, will you get this for me? I can't seem to fasten the clasp." I held out my right wrist, from which dangled a silver-and-diamond bracelet, the two straps twined in an infinity knot—his latest gift to me. That was when I noticed he was absorbed in his phone. I placed a hand on his. "Is everything all right?"

He looked up, his dark blue eyes wide in the dimming light blazing through the windows behind him. "Yeah." He took my hand and led me over to the couch. "Annabeth, there's something I need to tell you."

I sat, fear knotting my stomach. I took an uneven breath.

"Back in May, long before we started dating, I applied for a guest lectureship at Oxford. It was a long shot. I'm American, and I don't teach the stuffy, overly academic classics, so I didn't think I had a chance. But it was an opportunity I couldn't pass up."

I was queasy, easily guessing what he was about to say. But I nodded, afraid if I spoke I might throw up on his fancy black suit.

"I just found out that I'm a finalist. They're doing interviews at the International Conference of Teaching and Learning next week since most of the candidates will be there."

I exhaled. He wasn't leaving—not yet anyway. I forced myself to sound as cheerful and supportive as possible. "Alex, that's great. Congratulations." I wrapped him in a tight embrace, savoring the spicy scent of his cologne and hoping this wouldn't be one of the last times I had the chance to do so. "You must be so excited."

He pulled away, running a hand through his thick flaxen waves. "In shock is more like it. I never thought I'd get this far."

"It's no surprise to me. You're a rising star using unusual teaching methods to make literature relevant in a digital world. Why should they not want you to speak at Oxford?"

"It's more than speaking. I'd be teaching there for a full term. I'm not sure what they'll end up assigning me to, but I applied for both teaching my methods to other teachers—probably graduate students, mostly—and applying them in a class for undergraduate students."

I furrowed my brow, trying not to show my dismay. "So how long would you be gone?"

"The terms vary a bit, but they're around eight weeks each." He readjusted so that he was facing me full-on. "I know this must be a shock for you. I never expected I'd be leaving someone behind."

I schooled my features into the picture of support. "Don't worry about me. It's only two months. If I waited this long to find you, I can live a few months apart from you. This is an opportunity of a lifetime, so don't you dare think about backing out now."

Alex took my hand and finally noticed the unclasped bracelet balancing on my wrist. He secured it then kissed my knuckles. "Are you sure?"

"Of course I'm sure." My voice brightened as I spoke. Genuine hope that he was successful in his interview bloomed in my heart. "I'll make you a deal—when you're off teaching in England, I'll finally contact that editor friend of yours. That way, while you're gone, we'll both be doing something toward our dreams. And who knows—if I can get the time off from work, maybe I can even come visit you."

He grinned at me. "It's a deal."

I stood. "All right then. We'd better get downstairs. We have more than the turning of the year to celebrate tonight."

CHAPTER SEVENTEEN

January

Ever since I was a teenager and Angela Chase, the main character on the teen drama *My So-Called Life*, said she equated the ticking of the *60 Minutes* clock to the end of the weekend, I've hated Sunday nights. But none quite so much as this one.

Not only was I facing the first morning of the new regime at work, but Alex was leaving for the conference too. I was so nervous that not even two glasses of wine could steady me. Alex, on the other hand, was the definition of calm and collected, watching TV as if this was any other night. It was driving me crazy. Finally, I kicked him gently in the ankle.

That got his attention. "Ow! What was that for?" "How can you possibly be so calm? Your interview is tomorrow morning. Why aren't you freaking out?"

"Because you're doing that enough for both of us." He grinned and pulled me down next to him, pinning my hands behind my back and covering my face in kisses.

By the time he came up for air, I couldn't help but smile back.

"I was going to wait to give this to you, but it looks like you need it now." He fished a long, thin rectangular block out of the pocket of his tan wool sweater and presented it to me.

When I looked closer, I realized it was one of those weekly pill boxes that older people keep their daily medications in so they know if they took them or not. "You're giving me drugs?"

"No. I'll leave it to you to medicate yourself. Open the one for today."

I popped open the lid on the far left marked with a capital S for Sunday. A small folded piece of paper jumped out at me, leaving a bed of dark chocolate Mini Kisses behind. I opened the page and read. "'This note entitles the bearer to a single wish fulfilled.'"

Alex leaned over and whispered a few racy suggestions in my ear.

My face flushed in response. "I'm up for that."

He pried my fingers from around the pill box. "And that's just the beginning. Each day has a little surprise in it to help you get through the week since I won't be here to help you in person."

I placed a hand on the side of his face and kissed him. "This has to be the most thoughtful thing anyone has done for me. How in the world did you think of it?"

"I could lie and say it was my own ingenuity, but I'm man enough to admit I found it on Pinterest."

"I think it's very sexy when a man is willing to admit to being crafty."

"Oh, you've seen nothing yet. Just wait until Valentine's Day. There'll be crafty things all over this apartment."

"Should I start calling you Mr. Stewart?" I giggled.

"Perhaps not, but that does conjure a lovely mental image of you in only an apron."

Biting my lip to hide a grin, I waited until Alex turned back to the TV. Then I bounded to the kitchen, grabbed the apron that hung on the oven door, and shed my clothes. A moment later, he had his wish.

I crooked my finger at him. "About that desire you were going to fulfill?"

"I think I said 'wish,' but I won't argue over semantics." He wrapped his arms around me, palms resting on my bare rear end.

"Oh, this sounds like the plot to a romance novel," I said, pulling his sweater up over his head. "The naughty cook who needs a lesson from the hot English professor."

He gave me a wolfish grin. "I like the way you think."

He carried me to the bedroom and made sure I didn't have any time that night to worry about what the next day would bring.

§

The last thing Alex said to me before leaving wasn't "I'll miss you." It was "Tu me manques," which his French aunt had taught him. It translated as "You are missing from me."

High on that bit of romance, as well as medicinally sedated, I was ready to take on anything Nick threw my way. That was until I actually saw him. One look at his smug expression across from Miles and me at our first weekly briefing made me want to rip off his face.

"Welcome back and happy new year," Nick began. "We've got a busy year ahead of us, so I'm going to need you both to bring your best work each and every day."

My phone vibrated in my lap. I peeked at it to find a text from Miles that said, *We do that every day, asshole.* I pressed my lips together to choke back a giggle.

"Annabeth, I know you were upset about being pulled off the U of Chicago account, but don't worry, we've got plenty of other meaningful work for both of you. I want you two to be the lead creatives on a project we just got celebrating more than a century of local Chicago music. In a former life, I used to be a musician. I also spent a few years as manager of a few local bands, so this project is near and dear to my heart, which is why I'm entrusting it to you."

My phone buzzed again. *More like you don't have a clue how to handle this.*

Nick cleared his throat. "Do I have to take your phones away?"

Chided, we both set them facedown the desk.

"As I was saying, I'll be meeting with the organizers of this summer's music festival tomorrow, so I'll know more then, but in the meantime, I'd like to see what kind of ideas you have to promote this kind of event. Let's meet back here tomorrow at nine to discuss, all right?"

I raised my hand. "I have a question. Are we contributing to the promotional strategy for this event or only functioning as a writer and designer?"

For a moment, Nick was thrown by my question. But like a consummate politician, he recovered his line of messaging. "Well, the three of us are a team, so you are part of the overall plan in that way. But as to your primary duties, they'll be limited to creating materials."

"But you still want our promotional ideas?"

"Yes. Three heads are better than one, right?" He chuckled.

By the time the meeting ended, I was quietly seething. Miles tugged on my sweater, directing me toward the parking garage instead of heading back to our cubes. With a chirp, he unlocked his car—a Christmas present from Mia—and shoved me inside.

It was eerily quiet and still.

"Let it out. No one will hear you in here," Miles said.

"Ugh! He's just so—just such—ugh! We're not really working on the account, but he wants our ideas? We don't get to talk to the clients, yet we're supposed to figure out strategy for him? Seriously?"

"He's in charge now. Right now, we don't have anything to go to Laini with, so we have to do what he wants. But give him time. He'll hang himself. They always do."

I punched Miles in the arm. "How can you possibly be so calm about this?"

Miles adopted his best Samuel L. Jackson look, cool and slick. "I told you; I'm quietly planning his demise. We could give him a list of bands that aren't even from Chicago, but that would be too obvious. No, we need to do our jobs like perfect little soldiers so that when he goes down, he has no one to blame but himself. So put on your best Pollyanna attitude and get back in there. It's only four months."

"Come on, April," I chanted under my breath.

∽

"Trouble in paradise?" Mia asked over lunch the next day.

My daily instruction from Alex's cure-all medicine box had been to take her out and have some girl time to help take my mind off of work.

I looked up from my phone. "What makes you ask that?"

"Well, for one, you haven't been this quiet since you two started dating, and two, I haven't seen hide nor hair of Alexander the Great since before Christmas. Did everything go all right with your parents?"

She'd been in Paris for Christmas with Miles, and I'd forgotten I hadn't brought her up to speed on everything that had happened since then. "Miles didn't tell you?"

She considered for a moment, a tiny furrow forming between her brows. "Well, he tried to, but you know how much guys listen, especially when it comes to matters of the heart. I feel like I got the story, but it was riddled with bullet holes."

I quickly filled her in on Christmas, including my mom's frosty reception of Alex, Nick's unexpected visit, our whirlwind trip to Denver, and Alex's interview. "I talked to him last night, and he was on cloud nine. He really thinks he's going to get it."

"That's great!" Mia's eyes were shining. "I mean, it sucks for you, but it's really great for him. Does he know when he'd need to leave?"

"No, not yet." I huddled closer to the indoor fire pit, suddenly chilled. "Trinity term starts in April, so I think he'll still be here for my birthday. Speaking of, will you be here for my big thirty-fifth bash, or are you off to London for Fashion Week?"

Mia's face hardened. "No, I'll be here. I didn't get a single callback for London. Can you believe it? Some of the designers had the nerve to call me old. One even suggested I start doing catalog modeling. Ugh. That's the kiss of death."

I really wasn't in the mood to appease her—she was thirty now, the equivalent of ninety in modeling years—but if I didn't, there would be hell to pay, and I didn't want to foster anger on her part. I cooed and said the appropriate flattering things, but I did notice that she skipped dessert when the waiter inquired about it.

"Anyway," she said, picking up our previous thread of conversation as we walked back to my office, "a few of the designers who favor me are doing runway shows in mid-to-late spring, so I'm hoping to show all those bastards at Fashion Week what they're missing."

"That's the spirit."

"Funny you should mention spirit. Miles says you're showing an awful lot of it lately with Nick. What's up with that?"

I shrugged. "He's an ass who only wants me for as much as I can further this farce of a career he's trying to build."

"That's not what I've been hearing," Mia sang, obviously wanting me to take her bait.

I bit. "And what would you know about Nick?"

"Well, he's really good friends with one of my friends' boyfriends, Terrance. Terrance says Nick won't shut up about you. He says Nick's still in love with you and claims Nick told him that leaving you in Rome was the worst mistake he's ever made."

I snorted. "I wouldn't disagree with him there. But the rest is bullshit. He's outwardly hostile to me. Miles too. Why in the world would he treat me that way if he actually liked me?"

I wanted to believe I was right, but yet, I wondered. It was the same thing Nick had told Alex. But then again, Nick was a really good liar, so he could have just been sticking to his story.

When we stopped at the corner, behind a throng of people waiting for the light to change, Mia grabbed my shoulders. "Annabeth, do you remember in grade school how the boys would pull on your ponytail or pinch you if they liked you? This is no different. He just doesn't know how to relate to you since you've been apart for so long, and now that he's your boss, it makes things all the more awkward."

I leaned in to sniff her breath.

She backed away, looking at me as if I had just grown three heads. "What are you doing?"

"Checking to see if you're drunk. That's the only explanation as to why you're trying to make me believe Nick has a crush on me."

Mia held up her hands defensively. "I'm just passing on what I've heard. I thought you might want to be prepared in case he does anything."

"He's my boss."

"He used to be your best friend. Crossing lines didn't bother him then. Why should he start caring now?"

I shook my head. "You are insane."

"Believe what you like, Pookie, but don't say I didn't warn you."

CHAPTER EIGHTEEN

To Whom It May Concern,

Another year has come and gone, and here we are, me writing this letter to you, you reading it at some unknown date in the future. It's been exactly a year since I vowed to do everything in my power to meet you. It's weird to write this and wonder if I've made good on that. I think so. I think I know exactly who you are. . . but yet, there's no way to know.

All there is is waiting, waiting to see your face at the altar, to slip a ring on your finger and promise you forever. Our wedding kiss will be the sweetest in history because that is the moment we'll both know for certain.

My eyes drifted down to the silver ring on my right hand. Exactly a year ago today, I'd met Alex. Could it possibly be him? Was he the one I had been writing letters to all these years? It certainly felt like it, but I was well aware that I was in love and that made my judgment less than impartial. Damn it. Why did this have to be so hard?

I picked up my pen, trying to recapture my train of thought.

Marriages can break; the wrong people can wed—it's no guarantee, but it's the best we've got. I have to believe that when we do get married, it will be for life. We've certainly had ample time to make our mistakes with other people.

So I keep writing, trusting in the universe, whatever gods or forces govern love. It can't just be a series of chemical reactions in our brains. Something that can bring forth life or drive people to the most atrocious of crimes can't be explained away by chance.

But why the wait? I ask myself that question every single day, wondering if today is the day. What if we've been through a series of near-meetings over the years, times when our paths just missed crossing? I can easily imagine us passing one another at the grocery store, neither noticing because I was looking at my shopping list and you were examining the label on a can of baked beans. Or us being one row apart at the bookstore, hands on opposite books, but one of us decided not to pull the book off the shelf, so we didn't see one another through the gap.

I shake my head as I write this, knowing you have all the same questions. I can't wait for the day we can talk and discover the answers. Until then, I want you to know that I'm still as sure as I was the day I wrote the first letter that you're out there. You are my other half, the twin of my soul I've been searching for through countless lifetimes.

"Hey, baby," Alex whispered in my ear, bending down behind me to kiss my earlobe.

I set the pen down to squeeze the hand he'd placed on my shoulder. "Hi. I'm glad you're home."

He squatted next to me so that his eyes were level with mine. "You sound upset." He reached for the letter. "What are you writing?"

I snatched it out of his reach. "No, don't. You can't read this." *Not yet.*

His forehead creased. "Why not?"

I sighed, not wanting to explain my tradition to him but not seeing any way around it. "Promise you won't laugh." I folded the letter and put it in the envelope I had decorated with a big thirty-five earlier.

He crossed his heart. "I will not laugh no matter what you say."

I turned in my chair to face him, bringing his hands onto my lap and covering them with my own. "I have this tradition, something I've done every year on my birthday since I was sixteen." I searched his eyes, not sure what I was looking for but not finding any indication that I couldn't trust him with this, my deepest secret. "Every year, I write a letter to my soul mate, the person I know is out there somewhere."

Alex didn't blanch or grimace. He didn't scoff or roll his eyes as Mia had. Instead, he smiled softly, eyes twinkling with something that looked like admiration.

"It helps with the loneliness," I babbled, unable to stop talking now that I had revealed myself to him. "I've been single a long time, and I just want whoever I end up with to know that he's been anticipated and loved since long before I saw his face, that I love him for more than what he looks like or does for a living or the money or power he may or may not have. I love him for him."

Alex kissed our intertwined hands. "I only hope you find someone who is worthy of all the love you've already given him."

But I already have, I wanted to say. My stomach twisted as some underlying current in his words activated the fear center in my brain. "Do you think it's not you?" I couldn't keep the worry out of my voice.

"I certainly hope it is me." He straightened, lifting me to my feet. "And I intend to do everything I can to live up to the faith you've put in this man." His lips pressed against mine for an all-too-brief moment. "Speaking of, you should be getting ready for your birthday celebration." He kissed my forehead and tried to disentangle himself from my arms. "You know the rules. Dress for the red carpet. I'll be here at seven."

Once he was gone, I wedged my twentieth letter into the box—yes, I'd counted them—only to find it was the last one that would fit. My stomach did a little flip-flop as my superstitious side read all kinds of meanings into that. Did this mean we would finally meet? That we already had? That I should stop writing them? Or did it just mean I needed a bigger box?

Shaking my head at my own silliness, I stepped into the shower and made sure to lather up with the peach soap Alex liked so much. Suddenly, I didn't want to be alone. As I toweled off, I texted Mia, hoping she was home.

Five minutes later, my door slammed, followed by, "You can't stand to be alone on your birthday, can you?" as Mia flitted into my bedroom.

I was standing in front of my closet in my bra and underwear, trying to decide which dress to wear. Most women, especially thirty-something non-celebrities, didn't have many fancy dress choices, but thanks to Mia's modeling gigs and Hollywood soirées, over the last three years, I had amassed quite a selection of couture frocks. It was a good deal; after all, it cost only a fraction of the retail price to have them tailored to my smaller frame.

"Hello to you too." I gestured toward the dresses hanging neatly in clear plastic bags. "Thank you for the hand-me-downs, by the way."

Mia waved away the compliment and made a dismissive sound. "I'm just glad someone could take them. I was running out of room."

I bit my lip so I didn't say something about most people not having that problem. I held up a burgundy dress. "What do you think of this one? Too Valentine's Day?"

Mia shook her head. "I think it's perfect. Alex is going to be busy on Valentine's Day, right? So you should roll that into tonight—make it an anniversary-Valentine's-birthday smash." She bumped my hip. "Just imagine how hot the sex will be."

I pulled the dress over my head, smoothing out the flared skirt. It fell just to mid-calf, making it nice enough for anything Alex could think up but not as restrictive as a formal ball gown. Mia came around behind me, making sure the scalloped ruffle at the neck lay right. When one part didn't behave, she dragged me into the bathroom and subdued it with a blast of steam from my facial machine.

"You'd be amazed the tricks you learn backstage at a fashion show," she said by way of explanation.

She insisted on doing my makeup and hair, which she braided into an elegant roll with a few strands curled into corkscrews around my face.

After looking me over a few times, she plucked a red silk rose out of an arrangement on my nightstand and pinned it behind my ear. "Now you're ready."

"Thanks for being my stylist, Mia."

She hugged me. "Happy to be of service."

"So, what are you up to tonight?" I asked while I put on my jewelry.

She shrugged. "Miles and I are going out. The usual."

"Nothing is usual with you."

"Touché."

When the doorbell rang, Mia beat me to the door, opening it with a growl that would have made Catwoman proud.

I peered around her, and there was Alex, looking every inch a movie star, more handsome than any James Bond Hollywood could dream up, in his finely tailored tux, gray vest, and matching tie.

"Damn! Are you sure you don't want to date a supermodel?" Mia asked.

Alex shouldered past her without a word, never taking his eyes off me. "Wow. You are officially the most beautiful woman on the planet."

I smiled. "Thank you. You're not so bad yourself."

Behind him, Mia huffed. "I'll take that as a no." She blew a loud kiss in my direction. "Happy birthday, dear." Then she slammed the front door with as much vigor as she had on the way in.

Alex shook his head before surprising me with a flourishing bow. "My lady, your carriage awaits."

Taking his arm, I let him lead me down to the street, where I found out he meant it literally.

I placed a hand over my heart. "I've never taken a carriage ride before."

His wicked grin melted my heart. "As I've said many times, I enjoy being your first." He reached into his breast pocket and retrieved two tickets. "That's why, tonight, I'm taking you to your first ballet."

I covered my mouth with my white gloved hands, careful not to get red lipstick on them. "Oh, Alex, I feel just like I'm in *Pretty Woman*, red dress and all."

"I hope I don't make you feel like a prostitute." He chuckled darkly.

"No, that's not what I mean at all. I feel like you've transported me into a fairy tale. *Pretty Woman* is a modern-day *Cinderella,* isn't it?"

Alex's brow wrinkled as he considered it. "I've never thought about it that way, but I guess it is. Lucky for you, look what ballet we're going to see."

I squinted, inspecting the ticket. "*Cinderella.*" I smiled at him. "I couldn't have done that if I'd tried."

"It's fate, I tell you."

Snuggled together under mounds of blankets, we pulled up in front of the glass-fronted Harris Theater just as a bus full of tourists in dresses and suits was letting out. A few of them stopped to take photos of us as though we were part of the event or a celebrity couple on display. As we made our way to our seats—impressively close to the stage—I wondered what tale they'd invented for us. We were obviously too old for prom. Did they think us part of a wedding party, or did any of them perhaps guess right that I was an incredibly lucky girl on the date of a lifetime?

"In case I forget to say it later, thank you for a lovely night," I said to Alex amid the low murmur of guests getting situated for the performance.

"You are most welcome. You deserve every moment. I'm so grateful to have you in my life, Annabeth." He entwined my gloved arm with his.

The orchestra played the opening notes of the overture, the curtain rose, and I was immediately transported into another world, one where everyone was tall, thin, and graceful and even Cinderella's "ugly" stepsisters were beautiful. My childhood love for dance reasserted itself as I watched the dancers float effortlessly across the stage, rise to impossible heights *en pointe,* and spin with dizzying precision. Envying their grace and fluidity, I made a mental note to work out more and maybe even investigate an adult ballet class. That would no doubt be an unmitigated disaster, but at least I could say I tried. By the second act, I was completely absorbed, as invested in the world, the story, and its characters as if I were reading a book. Thanks to the orchestra, every emotion was heightened—yes, I cried when the prince and Cinderella married amid a shower of golden confetti—and I felt as though I were floating with the dancers on the notes of music.

The dream-trance didn't end with curtain call.

"That was so beautiful," I said, gliding up to Alex outside the theatre doing my best ballerina walk.

He took my hand and spun me around. "You are beautiful."

Once my head stopped whirling, I saw that our carriage had been replaced by a sleek black town car. "I think our fairy godmother got it backward. Isn't it supposed to turn into a carriage?"

Alex laughed. "You may be right about that. But the car will have to do for now." He glanced at his watch. "It may be dark, but the night is still young, and so are we. Shall we head to our next stop?"

I slid into the car, wondering where that might be, but Alex gave no directions to the driver. He must have prearranged our entire evening.

I looked at him through my lashes and gave him my best pout. "Can't I have one tiny little hint?" I held up my fingers about an inch apart.

"I don't give hints to my students, and I'm not going to make an exception for you. You'll see shortly."

I huffed out my frustration.

Not long after, we pulled up to Navy Pier.

"Um, Alex," I said as he led me down the boardwalk, "aren't we a little overdressed?"

He stopped in front of one of the yachts. "Not for the *Odyssey*." He nodded toward the massive multileveled mini-cruise ship in front of us.

My jaw dropped. "We're going on there?"

After checking Alex's driver's license, the gangplank attendant unhooked the velvet rope barring our way.

Alex gestured for me to go ahead of him. "After you, my lady."

A smiling woman greeted us inside and took our coats while a waiter offered us each a sparkling flute of champagne.

"Watch out, Alex, I may get used to this," I teased as we followed the woman to what I assumed was the main seating area. She pushed open a large wooden door, and I stepped inside with Alex's hand at the small of my back.

"Surprise!" sang a chorus of voices.

My heart stopped, and for a moment, I couldn't take in what was happening. Familiar faces grinned at me. Then my mind reset itself, and I recognized my friends and coworkers.

Miles was the first to greet me, slipping an arm around my neck. "You didn't have a clue, did you?" He let out a satisfied chuckle. "He got you good."

I clutched at my heart, still fighting to recover. "Yes, yes, he did. I can't believe you were in on this the whole time." I whacked him with my purse. "You evil liar. Making me think you forgot my birthday."

"He wasn't the only one." Mia tottered over to me.

I pointed at her. "You. You knew the whole time we were getting ready, and you didn't tell me. 'The usual' my ass."

"Guilty as charged," she said with a flourish of her martini glass.

Alex touched my lower back, and I smiled at him. "We should probably take our seats. They will want to serve dinner soon."

Mia saluted him. "Aye, aye, Captain." She was still giggling as Miles led her into the larger banquet room.

Alex held out my chair at a specially decorated sweetheart table tucked into one corner. A single red rose adorned the center of the table along with two white tapers in glittering crystal holders. We could still see our guests but were secluded enough to feel like we were on a solo date at the same time.

"How is it that every time I'm with you, I feel like a princess?" I asked him while a waiter refilled our champagne flutes.

He took my hand, stroking my palm with his thumb. "That's the idea."

We had already eaten the best lobster bisque I'd ever tasted and were tucking into seared sea scallops when I noticed Nick sitting with Miles and Mia.

I leaned toward Alex. "Who invited him?"

Alex looked up. "I have no idea. He certainly wasn't on my list." Mia was scowling at him.

"Good to know I'm not the only one he annoys the hell out of."

"I think that's universal." Alex laughed.

I did my best to ignore him after that, but it wasn't easy. I felt his eyes on me, and I couldn't help but wonder what he was thinking. Ex-boyfriend/boss in the same room with current boyfriend was a dangerous combination at the best of times—Christmas had taught me that. Now here we were again.

When the dessert plates were cleared, Alex excused himself only to reappear in front of the band setting up in front of a small square dance floor. He tapped once on the microphone to make sure it was on. "Hey, everybody. Thanks for coming tonight and helping make Annabeth's birthday so special. Some of you may not know that she and I met a year ago today, so that makes this an even more important night for us."

Miles whistled, and a few people in the crowd cheered, making my face flush in embarrassment.

"Anyway, Annabeth, this song is for you, my 'Lady in Red.'"

The familiar opening bars of the song, played at every single wedding reception since it had debuted in 1986, wafted through the air and pulled me toward the stage as though I was under a spell. I smiled as Alex held his arms out to me, and I practically melted into them.

"Did I ever tell you this is my mom and dad's favorite song?" I asked, leaning my head against Alex's chest, eyes closed as we swayed to the music. "They even christened it their new wedding song when they renewed their vows. Dad says Mom was wearing red the night they met."

"It must be a lucky color."

We danced in quiet peace until the song ended, then Alex pulled me into a deep kiss.

When I opened my eyes again, Nick was standing next to us. "May I cut in?"

"I'd prefer if you didn't." Alex's tone was cool but polite.

"Come on, just one dance between old friends."

Alex's jaw throbbed in irritation, and he looked to me for guidance.

"Please?" Nick said.

Was it my imagination, or was he leering at me? Damn it. Mia was getting into my head already.

I faked a smile. "One song. That's it." The look I gave him said I wouldn't tolerate any funny business.

But I needn't have worried. Nick was courteous in his handling of me, keeping enough distance between us that even our eighth-grade teacher, Sister Agnes, would have been pleased.

"Happy birthday, Annabeth," Nick said, seeking my eyes.

I refused to look at him, preferring to watch the couples swirling around us. "Thanks."

"And I understand congratulations are in order for Alex as well."

My head snapped around so I was staring at him in wide-eyed surprise. "What are you talking about?"

Nick's lips formed a silent "oh," and he winced. "He didn't tell you yet, did he?"

"Tell me what?"

Nick looked around as though seeking escape. "You'd better ask him. It's not really my business."

I grabbed his chin, forcing him to look at me. "You brought it up. It's your business now. Out with it, Zarrino."

Nick rubbed his chin as I released my grip. "It's about Oxford—"

Alex appeared at my side then, wedging himself between us, his back toward Nick. "Is everything all right?"

I swallowed. "Nick just said you have news about Oxford."

Alex's shoulders slumped slightly. "I was hoping to keep that under wraps until tomorrow." He shot Nick a scornful look. "Let's talk about this somewhere private."

Alex led me out onto the deck, draping his suit coat around me for warmth and loosening his tie.

"Well?" I tapped my foot, unsure whether I should be furious with him for telling Nick something before me or scared of what I didn't know.

"I got final confirmation from Oxford this morning. They've asked me to lecture in Trinity term, which starts in April."

My stomach clenched. Here was my fear realized. "That's wonderful." I tried to force warmth into my voice, but I wasn't entirely successful. "Why did you think you had to wait to tell me?"

"There's more. They've invited me to stay the summer to do some research. John Fitzpatrick, the author of the book you gave me at Christmas, will be joining me to work on our journal article."

My heart sank like a stone to my feet. Staying the summer meant he would be gone five, maybe six, months. That was a lot longer than either of us had bargained for. I looked up at him, certain my disappointment showed in my face.

"When do you leave?" Even as I asked, an image of Regina accusing him of choosing his career over her formed in my mind. No, that wasn't what this was. This was totally different. It was an opportunity of a lifetime.

"I've got about a month."

I clutched his hand. "Well, then we'd better make it a good one," I said with mock sincerity that was painful to my own ears.

We stood in silence for a while, shivering and looking out at the black void of the lake, neither of us wanting to face the other. I couldn't stop thinking about what Regina had accused him of and wondering if that was what he was doing with me. But something else was bothering me even more.

"There's one thing I don't understand," I finally said.

"What's that?"

"How the hell did Nick know before I did?" I couldn't help the speck of spite that crept into my voice.

Alex ran a hand across his face. "We had a meeting with the dean today, and he mentioned that I wouldn't be here for the last few months of the project so Nick would need to plan around me. That's all. I swear."

I reached up to touch his cheek but only grazed his chin when he pulled away. "I'm sorry, Alex. This is just a bit of a shock. Then to have him of all people. . ."

"I know. That's why I didn't want to tell you yet."

"I really am happy for you."

He relaxed and pulled me to him. "I know you are."

I was also blisteringly mad at him for not texting or calling me the moment he found out, but taking it out on him now wouldn't do either of us any good.

We both stumbled as the ship slowly began to turn.

"They're heading back to port. We should probably go back inside for the end of the festivities," he said.

CHAPTER NINETEEN

The dreaded day was here. Alex was packing his suitcases, padding around his apartment—which he was subletting to a friend while he was gone—in bare feet, and grabbing this and that as final thoughts occurred to him. Neither of us had slept, too preoccupied by our coming separation to miss a single second of what time remained to us.

"Promise me one thing," I asked him, stopping his relentless march from the bedroom to his suitcase by thrusting a mug of steaming coffee at him.

"Anything." His whiskers scratched my chin as he pressed his cheek against mine.

"We're going to be honest with each other from now on. No hiding anything—not for surprises or to save the other's feelings. When you know something important, I know and vice versa."

"I promise."

While Alex was printing out his boarding pass, I slipped a small green-and-gold box into one of his bags. I'd wanted to wrap it but remembered TSA frowns upon that, so it had only a small bow on top with a note that instructed him not to open it until he was in his rooms at Oxford. It wasn't the only gift I'd left him—on his phone was a video of me doing a striptease that he would eventually find as well as little lighthearted odds and ends tucked in suit pockets or in the toes of shoes—but this was the big one. The one that I felt really showed my love for him.

All too soon, the phone rang, and I was putting him into the cab. Then the cab was pulling away down dark, rain-slicked streets. Then he was gone.

⁓

I should have taken the day off work or called in sick, but being the good soldier I was, I went back to my cold, lonely apartment and crawled under the covers. Two brief hours later, my phone chimed. I silenced my alarm without really waking up, which I regretted when I awoke again half an hour later, thoroughly late. I rushed around, throwing on the easiest outfit I could find: a pair of black slacks and a lavender cardigan over a plain white button-down. Not having time to do my hair, I brushed it up into a twist and slapped on some foundation, sheer eye shadow, and lip gloss.

Clopping into the kitchen in wedges only halfway on my feet, I slurped a cup of coffee and checked the time again on my phone. I had a text from Alex. It read, *Morning, beautiful. I miss you already. No matter what the day brings, remember to smile. You have a lot to be grateful for. I love you.*

The silly smile on my face stayed there all through my walk to work and was still lingering when Nick called me into his office.

He must have seen the stars in my eyes because he scrutinized me closely before declaring, "You were late this morning."

That was enough to flatline my good mood. "Yes, I was. But I intend to stay late tonight to make up for it."

He grunted dubiously. "Don't make a habit of it. I need to know I can depend on you to be here when I need you."

I fought the urge to roll my eyes and bit back a retort about him not being there for me thirteen years ago. "Well, you have me now," I said through facial muscles straining to maintain a professional expression.

"Yes." He placed his hands on the desk, fingertips touching like some real-life version of Mr. Burns on *The Simpsons*. "I need to know what you and Alex were planning for the National Poetry Month event in April."

"Isn't that in the notes I gave you?"

"It's mentioned, but there are no details."

"That's because we didn't get that far in planning before you took me off the account." I'd had a plan in mind, but I wasn't about to share that with the man who couldn't do me the respect of crediting my ideas.

"You can't be serious."

"I am. You'll have to plan something with the dean unless he appointed someone to serve as contact while Alex is out." My eyes flicked to the wall calendar over Nick's shoulder. "If they're still planning for an April eighth event date, you only have a few weeks to pull something together." I raised an eyebrow at him in silent challenge. "Tick-tock."

Nick shifted uncomfortably. "How am I supposed to know what would attract the poets of tomorrow to the school?"

"Use your imagination. That's what they pay you for, isn't it, oh esteemed account executive?"

"Annabeth, please." His eyes were pleading, an all-too familiar blue beckoning me to willingly walk into their depths with my pockets lined with stones.

I wasn't about to take the bait. I liked the safe, dry shore just fine. "Why should I help you? I'm only a lowly writer. You've made that more than clear. Besides, you reassigned me, remember?"

Nick reached across the table to grab my hands. "Please, Annabeth. I know I've been a jerk—"

I snorted. "That's an understatement."

He flinched. "I probably deserved that. Look, I just need a place to start—inspiration, if you will. Will you be my muse? You used to be so good at it."

The warmth in his voice hung in the air along with our shared memories of a time when he wrote lyrics and played bass with a local band. They'd been nothing big, but it had helped pay the bills and keep us college students in food better than ramen, so they'd thought they were really something. That was before our relationship, a time when he'd openly credited me with being his inspiration.

I sighed, giving in to the euphoria and dipping a toe into his waters. "Think about when you wrote music. That's a form of poetry. Use that as your starting place."

Nick thought for a moment, eyes distant. "Yeah, I like that. What else you got?"

I shook my head. "That's all you're getting from me. Unless, that is, you want to put me back on the account."

Nick leaned forward on his desk. "The partners are doing reviews in a few weeks to evaluate how the new structure is working, and I think it would be beneficial to both of us if they could see us working together as a cohesive team."

"Beneficial to us or beneficial to you?" I scoffed at my own naïveté. "You're afraid they'll blow on your house of cards and it'll come tumbling down. And you need me to secure this illusion of expertise you're so desperately clinging to."

"I do need you. I always have." He gave me his most helpless, stray-caught-in-the-rain look.

"Don't. This is about you as my boss, which you suck at, by the way. I'm happy to work with you as part of a team, as you say, and I've given you an idea. But I draw the line at pulling your ass out of the fire."

"Even if it means sacrificing your own career?"

I pulled my hands out from under his. "Are you threatening me? With what? There's no conflict of interest now that I'm not on the account. Even if I was, Alex is in England. It's a moot point."

"But I can easily build a case against you."

I stood and leaned over the desk, palms on its gleaming surface so that my face was nearly touching his. "Do your worst. You forget I've been here much longer than you and already have a track record of success. Other than snowing a gaggle of egomaniac doctors, you really can't say the same, can you?"

"Go to hell," he growled, his hot breath ruffling my bangs. "And get out of my office."

∽

Mia's idea of helping me get over my rough day was to pop by my apartment that night with a chilled bottle of vodka and her entire shot glass collection. Within an hour, we'd already rehashed the entire Nick debacle and were onto her latest woes—something about her bemoaning the end of her modeling career because she was over the big three-oh. But I couldn't concentrate on what she was saying. The vodka was making my sleep-deprived brain even hazier, and I kept thinking about how Alex was now somewhere over the Atlantic Ocean.

Mia snapped her fingers at me. "Hello. Earth to Annabeth. You aren't listening, are you?"

I looked up from my phone and blinked at her as though being ripped from a dream. "Not really, no. I remember the words 'London' and 'Betsy Sue,' so I'm assuming you're doing a fashion show for her?"

She tore the phone from my hands and tossed it into her purse. "He's not going to get cell reception at thirty thousand feet." She poured us each a shot and held hers up in a silent toast before downing its contents. "Seriously, he's on a plane, not a chair with balloons. He'll be fine."

I laughed and coughed at the same time, my lungs burning. I gasped. "Do me a favor? Don't say things like that while I'm drinking."

"Well, at least you're laughing. Jeez, you'd swear the man had never been out of the country before."

"It's not that. We've just never been apart this long."

"Not a fan of the whole 'absence makes the heart grow fonder' theory? Me neither."

"How do you and Miles do it? I mean, beside the fact that you have a guy or girl or both in every port."

She shot me a withering look. "My definition of fidelity aside, you just have to make time for each other. Just because you can't be in the same room doesn't mean you can't be together. Watch a movie or eat a meal together over Skype. Hell, sext each other. You still have to have sex while he's away. I'd suggest Nick, but I know you like that whole monogamy thing, so find a way to still have sex with Alex. When you have a camera, it's not that hard." She wiggled her eyebrows. "I'll even help you figure out where to position it in your room if you want."

I waved. "Seriously, even buzzed, I can't have that conversation with you."

"Oh, please, Sister Annabeth. If you can't talk to me, who are you going to ask? No one you know has as much experience with international relations, if you will, as me. Except for Miles, and I doubt you want to ask him for help."

I pretended to gag. "Oh, that's even worse than talking to you about it."

"Well then? Do we have a deal?"

I watched her, unconvinced. "Maybe." I ran a finger around the edge of my empty shot glass, trying to decide if I wanted to ask her a question that had been bothering me for quite some time.

She was watching me too. "I know that look. You want to say something but aren't sure how. What's up?"

I couldn't meet her eyes. "No, it's really nothing. Forget it."

"Nope. You're not getting out of this that easily. We're officially playing truth or dare. You"—she pointed at me—"get truth."

I crossed my arms. "Fine, but so do you."

"Here's your question. What were you going to say? And remember, you have to tell the truth."

"It's about your birthday. Do you remember kissing Alex?"

For a moment, Mia looked stunned, then her face lit up. "That's one of the few things I do remember." She fanned herself. "I would never forget a kiss like that."

I gaped at her. "If I wasn't drunk right now, I'd probably kill you for saying that."

She shrugged and grabbed at my pointing finger, missing the first time then finally twisting it. "It's good that you are then." A fit of giggles was building behind her rambling. "You know what else I remember? You falling down the stairs after we sang 'Jessie's Girl.' That was classic." She punctuated the statement with a snort.

"Mia"—I grabbed her shoulder, trying to get her attention—"I'm serious. Why did you kiss him? You knew I liked him."

"What are we, twelve? Seriously. He was hot. I was drunk. Put two and two together, and you get fireworks. I can't help that you're still jealous. Which, by the way, is just ridiculous. You've been together for how long now? He gave you a ring. And he's in another country. It's not like I can take him away from you from here."

I quirked an eyebrow at her. "And would you given the chance?"

"Is that a dare?" Mia loomed over me, halfway between sitting and rising. She stood, unsteady like a newborn doe. "What do you want me to say? If I say yes, you'll get mad. If I say no, you won't believe me. Your insecurity is maddening."

"I'm insecure? If you're Miss Confidence, why did you kiss him? Aren't you committed to Miles?"

Mia shook her head. "Because I can. He was there, and I wanted to. End of story. It's not like I had sex with him—although I tried. He said no."

"You what?" I couldn't believe my ears. Mia had done a lot of outrageous things over the years, but that topped them all.

"I had to at least ask. Even he'd said yes, you two weren't together yet, so you have no right to complain."

I pulled her back down to the couch. "No, you're right. I'm being stupid."

"So back to Nick. What are you going to do now?"

I shrugged. "Sit back and see if he hangs himself or if he's really trying to change. There's really nothing more I can do."

Mia stared off into the distance. "I just wish he was nicer to you. He wasn't at all like that when we met."

"Of course he wasn't. You got charming Nick because he wanted something from you—namely to get into your pants. I've known him long enough to see past that." I suppressed a fit of giggles. "In many ways, you two are a match made in hell."

Mia looked offended. "What are you talking about?"

"You both do whatever it takes to get what you want."

"Hey, that's called tenacity. It's a good thing." She thought for a moment. "Maybe that's what Nick is doing now."

"What do you mean?"

She shrugged. "Alex has basically removed himself from the picture. Maybe Nick is using this poetry thing as an excuse to get close to you. He really does like you."

"Uh-huh. Or maybe he's finally realized he's out of his league at work. Besides, he's got much more to make up for than being a shitty boss."

"I didn't say he'd be successful," she grumbled into her glass.

"Enough talk of men. It's Friday night, and we're in dire need of food." I wobbled over to the counter, opened a drawer, and flung a stack of menus at her. "Here, you pick the takeout place. I'll pay for the food."

The next afternoon, I nearly skipped to the computer when Skype rang. Alex's smiling face greeted me from his profile photo even before I answered. When I did, he was sitting in a high-backed chair in a dark-paneled room that looked—from what little I could see of a mullioned window and bookcase over his shoulder—exactly as I'd imagined an Oxford don's room would.

I couldn't help but tease him. "Cheerio, chap. All you need is a smoking jacket and you'd be right at home with C.S. Lewis."

Alex glanced over his shoulder at his new home. "Yeah, it's not exactly Chicago modernist, but it's comfortable."

I touched the computer screen, forgetting for a moment that I couldn't actually touch him. "I'm so glad you're there safe. How was your flight?"

He sighed, scratching at the shadow of a beard sprouting on his cheeks. "Long. Cramped. The usual."

"Have you slept?"

"No. I'm trying to wait until bedtime here. Not sure if I'm going to make it though." He held up the green-and-gold box. "So this little thing has been driving me crazy since TSA insisted on searching my carry-on at O'Hare. I've spent the last"—he counted on his fingers—"twenty-something hours wondering what is. Can I open it now?"

"Yes, you may."

He made a show of holding the box up to the camera so I could see that he was splitting the gold label I'd used as a seal. "I think I just popped its cherry."

"Wow, you must really be tired to be making jokes like that."

"Yeah, and I still have to sit at high table tonight. God only knows what's going to come out of my mouth. If you get a call tomorrow around noon, it means they kicked me out." He turned his attention back to the box and opened the lid. Nestled inside was a silver signet ring. On the flat face was the starburst of a compass rose surrounded by the Latin phrase *in me aquilone vero semper invenies.*

"In me, you will always find true north," Alex translated.

He was still staring at the ring when I said, "This way I know you won't get lost while you're there."

Alex slipped the ring on his left ring finger. When he looked up, his eyes were shining. "I wish I could kiss you right now. You have no idea what this means to me."

"I think I do if the care and love with which I chose it are any indication."

"We're going to be fine, you know. You and me. We'll talk every night. It won't be that much different."

"Thank God for technology, right?"

He raised an eyebrow. "Yeah, I've gotten an earful from Miles on how, um"—he cleared his throat—"useful that can be."

I giggled. "Me too, from Mia. Together, I think we know more about their sex lives than any two people should." It was his turn to touch the screen. He was trying to stroke my face. "I miss you already. When are you coming to visit?"

I rolled my eyes. "You just got there! But seriously, if I can, it will have to be after the partner review in April. Nick would rather take a vow of celibacy than make it possible for me to see you."

"Bastard."

"You said it."

"Well, I love you the same whether you're three thousand miles or three inches away."

"Same here. *Tu me manques.*"

∽

When the doorbell rang the following afternoon, I was still in my pajamas. It was Miles and Mia. Again.

"What do you two want?" I said with more than a little annoyance.

I loved them, but at some point, one would think they'd learn weekends were sacred alone time for an introvert like me. "I'm all out of chocolate chip pancakes."

Mia was huddled behind Miles as if she was using his body as a shield. It was very strange. "No, silly, we're not here for food."

"That's a first."

"We're here," Miles picked up the thread of conversation, "on strict orders from MI6."

I squinted at them. "Did you two do drugs last night?"

"I'm totally serious," Miles said. "If you will kindly let us in, we'll explain."

With a roll of my eyes, I stepped aside. They plunked down on the couch, a large box between them.

I pointed at it. "It's not ticking, is it?"

Mia smiled. "Nope."

"As I said"—Miles adopted a serious tone as if he were on one of those TV shows about the CIA—"we were given a clear mission, and it was to deliver this to you."

I perched on the arm of the couch. "And did this message self-destruct after you received it?"

"Nope. Mia destroyed the evidence by eating it. Girl will eat anything." Miles snickered, and Mia punched him in the arm.

"So what's in the box, and who sent it?"

"That's classified—need to know only, and we didn't need to know."

"You guys are really starting to weird me out," I said in partial honesty.

"Just open it." Mia pulled me onto her lap and forced my hands around the edges of the paper-wrapped box.

After inspecting it for any signs of who gave them this mysterious "mission," I tore open the paper. Inside was an expensive white-and-red striped decorative box, the kind in which an uptown woman might store correspondence or invitations to snooty parties. Lifting the lid carefully, I found a single sheet of cream stationery on top covered in Alex's elegant, Catholic schoolboy handwriting.

Annabeth, since there is much I cannot be with you for in body over the coming months, I wanted to make sure I was there in spirit when you needed me. I made this while I was waiting to hear the final outcome, knowing we'd have use for it eventually even if I didn't get in at Oxford. Please consider each one of these envelopes a work of love.

The letter ended with his signature and a quote from a Florence and the Machine song about finding a way around an ocean for the sake of love.

Speechless, I handed the letter to Miles. Mia craned her neck around me to see it.

Underneath, standing in neat rows, were at least two dozen multicolored envelopes. Selecting one at random, I pulled out a bright green envelope that reminded me of those glow sticks they used to sell at skating rinks in the eighties. I even had the urge to shake it to see if it would light up. In the upper left corner, where a return address would normally have been, were the words, "Open me when. . ." In lieu of an address, he had written, "you need a laugh." Below the words was a giant smiley face sticker. Thumbing through the others, I noticed they all bore the same return address but were meant for different occasions—everything from my moods to situations that might arise at work or in other areas of my life.

Typical Mia, she made a beeline for the only red envelope, which said, "Open me when. . . you're Fifty Shades of Horny." She waved it in my face. "I want to know what's in this one."

I made to grab it away, but she squirmed out from under me, scampering around the couch and holding it out of my reach like a schoolyard bully. She shook it. "Too small for even a silver bullet." Her face lit up with inspiration. "Someone's getting lucky online," she sang.

"Damn it, Mia. Give it back."

Miles calmly got up—unnoticed by Mia because she was too busy capering around—plucked it out of her hand, and tossed it to me. "My darling, we've completed our mission. We should probably leave Annabeth alone."

She gave Miles an incredulous look. "Why, so she can fondle her envelopes? Nope. This calls for a day on the town."

CHAPTER TWENTY

Friday couldn't come soon enough. In the last few weeks Nick had already called me out for socializing too much with Miles (which might have been true depending on one's definition of "too much"), being late twice (which I wasn't), and sticking my nose into projects that weren't my concern (Rick had always valued my opinions, so silly me assumed Nick would feel the same). At least I was finally learning the ground rules under Nick's regime. It seemed the only way was the hard way. But still I felt as if my every movement was under constant scrutiny, and I couldn't wait to get out of that office.

I was out the door like a shot at five, and within half an hour, I sat cross-legged on my bed with the computer at my feet. Several thousand miles away, Alex was telling me about his first few weeks navigating the labyrinth of rules—some spoken, some apparently floating in the ether—among the professors at Oxford.

"Did you know Oxford has its own time zone? Seriously. It's five minutes after Greenwich Mean Time. It's going to take me forever to learn that what I think is late is actually on time." He took a sip from the steaming cup of tea on the table in front of him. "Oh, and they have their own vocabulary too. I know every workplace has a certain amount of jargon, but this really is like being in a foreign country. Most of what I've heard has to do with rowing and proper dress, but there are other things. There's even a dictionary online."

"Really? I may have to study so that when you come back, I'll know what you're saying," I teased.

He laughed. "Yeah, just don't let me affect an accent like Madonna. Oh, and speaking of strange traditions, dinner at high table here in Merton College takes place in several different rooms. It's like a moving cocktail party with seating charts. I kept forgetting to take my napkin with me, and I spilled food on myself once, but all in all, it's great fun."

He carried on in this vein for quite some time. It was all funny and kind of amusing, but after a while, I found my mind wandering, even as my reflected image in the little window in the lower right corner of my screen maintained her interested expression. Only eight days remained before the university's poetry event, and as far as I knew, Nick still hadn't come up with anything. It wasn't my project anymore, but I still didn't want to see the school—and by extension, Alex—suffer.

"Babe, you don't look like you feel so good," Alex said, concluding one of his stories. "Do you want to keep the call short tonight?"

He had been talking for forty-five minutes already, so we really couldn't label this call short, but I wasn't going argue with him. "No, I was just thinking about something at work. Sorry. I should have been focusing on you."

"Are you kidding? I was just babbling. It's nice to have someone I can talk to about mundane things. Everyone here is so uptight, and I don't know who, if anyone, I can trust yet. Unfortunately for you, that means you get to hear it all. What's up in your world?"

"Oddly enough, it involves your world too. Kendra let it slip that the university hasn't liked any of Nick's ideas for National Poetry Month. At this point, they're either going to have to move it or cancel it."

Alex thought for a minute. "Didn't we send out save-the-dates around Christmas?"

"Yeah."

"I doubt they'll cancel then." He looked at me appraisingly. "I know you have an idea. Tell me what it is."

I cupped my jaw. "Does it matter? I'm not the AE."

"It matters to me."

"Well," I said, shifting to get more comfortable, "I was thinking about what you were saying a few months ago about popular music being a gateway into poetry. What if we showed them, in a very physical and auditory way, how poetry and music are connected?" I explained my idea of how the night could go. "We could even challenge them to adapt famous poetry to music and have a competition in the end."

Alex's face lit up. "I love it. Seriously. But can you pull it off in a week?"

"I think so. I already told Miles about it when I was complaining that I could do better. He's willing to help."

"I don't want to cut my time with you short, but it's still early enough that if I make a call, you'll be on it by morning. You're sure you can do this on top of all the other materials?"

"Yep. We'll keep it simple, invitation-only, but we give out a lot of invitations to key groups, like a rave. This is something people should want to go to, so we'll fire them up via social media and word of mouth, a very underground vibe. After all, at one time, poetry was dangerous. And it doesn't have to last long, just long enough to leave an impression."

"Okay then. Judging solely from the glow of your face, I know you'll make it happen. Record it for me so I can see it. I hate that I'm going to miss it."

"I will. And thanks for not thinking I'm weird for wanting to do this. I mean, we both know I'm weird, but I can be weird with you, and that means more than you can imagine."

As we disconnected, a half-remembered quote—I thought it came from Dr. Seuss—popped into my head. It went something like, "I am weird and you are weird. Eventually two people come together in mutual weirdness and fall in love." I admired the clasped hands ring from Alex. Dr. Seuss was right once again.

๛

The very next morning, Dean McAllister phoned Laini and insisted that if Smith and Grenwick wanted to keep their account, they would reinstate me as account executive. By lunchtime, Miles and I were sitting in the dean's office along with Kendra, hashing out plans for the fastest event we'd ever created.

I got back to the office in the late afternoon, disappointed that I wouldn't be seeing any of the sun-drenched, temperate weather the rest of the city was enjoying. But the extra hours would be worth it. I was determined to make the dean and Laini happy.

I still hadn't had a chance to thank Alex for his intervention, so while my computer was booting up, I dashed off a quick text, promising to text him since I wasn't going to make it home in time for our usual Skype call. When my phone dinged a few minutes later, I reached over, expecting a reply from Alex.

I had to read the text twice. It was from Alex all right, but it clearly wasn't meant for me. *Be ready in a few. Come up when you get here. It's open.*

I vaguely remembered Alex mentioning some event at his college that night, so I didn't think anything of it. But it was followed immediately by a second message. *Thanks again, Jolie.*

Jolie? Who the hell was Jolie? I imagined some gorgeous college girl with long legs and the kind of shiny hair normally only seen in shampoo commercials. Taking a deep breath, I told myself not to freak out. So he was texting another woman. . . so what? Did I really expect him not to communicate with other people while he was there? I should have just let it go, but I couldn't.

This isn't Jolie, I typed back.

A few seconds later, Alex's frazzled reply came. *Jesus, Annabeth, I'm so sorry. Running late and hit the wrong name on my list. Will explain all tomorrow.*

He'd better.

I was still staring blankly at my computer when Miles came back bearing a large pepperoni pizza from the place across the street. He kicked my chair. "What's up with you?"

"Nothing," I lied. "Just a little overwhelmed by what lies before us."

"Please, you thrive on this shit. What's really going on?"

Silently, I handed him my phone and let him read the text trail.

"Ouch. That's awkward. But it doesn't deserve all of this." His finger circled my disconsolate face.

"What if he's lying? What if he really does have someone else?" I cried, my trust issues spiraling out of control.

Miles hugged me. "You're being ridiculous. It's just the stress talking. You do know that, right? I've never met anyone who loves someone as much as he loves you. He wouldn't throw all that away for some girl."

"Are you sure?"

"As sure as I can be." His muscles flexed beneath my head, and a whiff of pepperoni and melted cheese assaulted me as he opened the box. "Now eat. It will help."

I took the piece of pizza he offered and nibbled at the crust. "How did you get used to Mia being gone so much?"

"It wasn't easy," he answered, pulling on a stretchy piece of cheese and popping it into his mouth. "I went through all the same things you are and then some. Then one day I got tired of second-guessing everything and just decided to go with it. I know who Mia is. As long as she comes back to me in the end, I don't care what else she does. It kind of comes with the territory—like dating a musician on tour. But Alex isn't like that. I bet you he swore off all other women the moment he met you. He's one of those chivalrous old souls." He took a bite of his pizza. "That reminds me, do you have any of those envelopes around here?"

I opened the middle drawer of my desk and handed him a stack.

"Nope, you pick."

I leafed through them and picked out a purple envelope with an image of a hooded figure on the front. It read, "Open me when. . . you feel like Dementors are sucking at your soul."

"Nice Harry Potter reference," Miles commented.

I took another bite of pizza before shaking the contents out on my desk. Three gold coins the size of half dollars rolled toward me along with something that looked like a stick and a folded sheet of paper. I opened the note and read it aloud. "'To banish the demons of sadness or rage, perform this ritual: eat at least one piece of chocolate (provided), look at this silly picture (see reverse)—'"

I flipped the page over to see a picture taped to the back. In it, an adorable cat was peeking through its upraised paws. The caption asked, "You still mad?" I laughed in spite of myself.

"He's good. You have to admit that," Miles said.

I turned back to the front and kept on reading. "'You back now? Okay, the last thing you need to do is point this wand and summon your Patronus.'" I picked up the wand—now that I looked at it closely, I saw it was actually a wand and not a stick—and waved it at Miles. "Do I really have to do this?"

"Yes. Alexander the Great says so." He crossed his arms. "Come on. Before the food gets cold."

I walked up and down the hall just to make sure there would be no witnesses, but almost everyone else had gone home for the night. Standing in the open area between the two cubes, I lifted my wand and took a deep breath, feeling extremely silly. I closed my eyes, then I chickened out.

Miles grabbed me before I got back to my chair. "Do you want to feel better or not?"

"Fine." I shook him off and closed my eyes again.

I raised my hand and said the words of the spell, imagining a stream of white light jetting from the tip and shaping into an eagle. When I opened my eyes again, I gasped. The tip of the wand was glowing.

"Whoa," Miles said. "I have to try this." He took the wand, and the glow faded. He repeated the procedure, and surely enough, the tip lit up. He shook the wand. "It must be battery powered."

He scrutinized it, turning it over and over. "Ha!" He stopped and pointed at a set of barely visible holes in the base. "It's voice activated. Watch." He repeated the words of the spell, and the wand glowed.

"Where in the world did Alex get it?"

"Internet probably. Hey, do you think this thing will help us create our materials faster?"

I took it from him. "It's worth a shot." I gently tapped his head with it. "Bibbidi-boppidi-boo. I am creative, and so are you."

He grinned and touched the wand to both of my hands. "Hocus pocus. May my words give your fingers focus."

"That was pretty clever for a designer," I said, winking at him.

Miles's soda fizzed as he cracked open the top. "Oh, honey, it's only six. Just wait until about midnight. That's when the creative's gonna come out up in here."

I smiled and said a quiet prayer of thanks to Alex. Jolie or no Jolie, Alex was definitely a keeper. He had just made my day from another continent.

∾

By six the next evening, I was so tired I could barely keep my eyes open. Miles and I had worked until around one the night before and reported back to work at seven in the morning to finish materials for a nine o'clock presentation to Laini. We'd spent all day revising and finalizing concepts, working through lunch to get "exclusive" invites into the hands of influential teens and leaders across the city, including a few DJs at radio stations popular with students. I'd wanted to stay to finish the event script, but Laini sent me home, and now I was so glad she had.

My brain was so fried I had completely forgotten about what Miles termed "Jolie-gate" until Alex answered my call not in his rooms, as usual, but on what appeared to be the front steps of one of Oxford's Gothic buildings. Behind him, students came and went through an oak door large enough for a mounted rider to pass through. At his side was a pretty young redhead with enormous blue eyes and pale skin.

Before I even had a chance to wonder who she was, Alex launched into his apology. "Annabeth, this is Jolie."

The cute girl waved at me enthusiastically, grinning like the "after" model in an acne commercial. "Hi, Annabeth. Professor Grantham told me you're a writer. I'd love to talk to you about your career sometime if you have the time."

I gaped at her, brain still trying to catch up to my mouth. "Of course," I managed politely.

"Jolie is John Fitzpatrick's daughter. He brought her along since she's going to be attending here beginning at Michaelmas term this autumn. She's only sixteen—quite a scholar this one."

Jolie's thousand-watt smile only increased, and her blue eyes shined under Alex's praise. "My dad is really enjoying the research he's doing with your boyfriend."

"What about you? How are you enjoying Oxford?"

"It's great. I can't wait to be a full student. I'm finishing my high school classes online. Plus, I'm doing an early research paper to try to test out of one of my courses here."

"I wish I was that ambitious when I was your age. Actually, I wish I was that ambitious now."

Her cheeks pinked at the compliment. "Oh, I'm sure you are. Dr. Grantham was telling me about your plans for National Poetry Month. I wish I could be there for it. It sounds really cool."

Her energy was infectious, and I sat up a little straighter. "Actually, we decided today that we're going to broadcast it live online. If you're willing to stay up for it, you're welcome to join us. Do you have a pen? I'll give you the URL."

"Sweet!" She wrote it down. "Can I share it with some of my friends?"

"Of course. Share away."

"This is so cool!" Behind her, faint bells tolled midnight, and Jolie's head whipped around. "Crap, I have to get inside. I don't want to break my dad's curfew before I'm even officially a student." She turned back to the camera. "It was nice to meet you, Annabeth. I hope we can talk again."

"Me too. Good night, Jolie."

After she flounced off into the darkened quad toward her own college, Alex adjusted the computer so he filled the frame. "She's the one I was texting last night. I forgot to pick up my dress robes from the dry cleaners, and we had an event last night. John offered to let me borrow his since he wasn't attending, so Jolie said she'd bring it up to me since she lives in the next college and John is staying at off-campus housing."

I shook my head. "I'm so sorry for doubting you, Alex."

He waved off my apology. "It's only natural. Although, honestly, if she's enamored of either of us, I think it's you."

I scoffed. "Me? How? She's only just met me."

Alex's expression turned sheepish. "I may have been bragging about you a bit. I think she's developed a little idol worship or maybe even a girl crush—whatever the kids are calling it nowadays. You made her day by inviting her to the poetry event."

As cute as Jolie was, I was getting tired of talking about her. I didn't want to waste any more of our precious time together, so I steered the conversation another way. "She said her dad is enjoying working with you. How's the research going for you?"

Alex sighed. "Slow. There's not a lot of time for it between two lectures, office hours, and grading papers." He ran a hand through his hair. "I'm already looking forward to the end of term so we can dedicate our time to it."

"And I'm looking forward to the end of summer so I can see you again."

"It'll be here before you know it. So two days to go before your big event. How are things?"

"Insane. I'm so tired I can barely see straight. We still have a lot to do. I have to do a run-through of the event with the crew and make sure all the details are in place. You'd think I'd have adrenaline singing through my veins, but it feels more like the sludge from an oil slick."

Alex grimaced. "Oh, I know those days. What you need is a good night's sleep. If I was there, I'd take you in my arms and hold you until you finally fell asleep." His face lit up. "Actually, I have an idea. Put on your pajamas."

I gave the computer a skeptical look. "What?"

"You heard me." Alex stood, and the screen shook as he carried the laptop—and me—inside.

I ducked out of range of the camera—I didn't know who could see the screen—and changed. When I was ready, I found Alex in his apartment, shirtless with the lights dimmed.

"Get into bed," he commanded.

I did so, positioning the computer so that it was next to my head.

Six thousand miles away, he did the same thing. We were lying cheek to cheek, only two computer screens between us.

He put a hand up to the camera. "I may not be able to hold you, but I can be with you as you drift off."

I touched his hand and closed my eyes.

He began to sing.

The last thing I heard before I surrendered to sleep was his promise that he'd never stop loving me.

CHAPTER TWENTY-ONE

Two days later, outside the theatre, I glanced one more time at the text Alex had sent me that morning. *Remember what Casanova said, 'Be the flame not the moth.' Everyone will love you.* I took a deep breath, doing my best to believe he was right. Granted anything would have been an improvement on Nick's lack of ideas, but I really wanted tonight to be a success.

I squared my shoulders and swung open the heavy door then took a deep breath as it hissed closed behind me. A sizable crowd had already gathered. Some of the older students and adults were sitting quietly or talking amongst themselves, while the prospective students preferred to lean across aisles, kneel backward on seats, and shout to one another. Normally such shenanigans would have annoyed me, but tonight these kids gave the event a celebratory air that was exactly what I'd been hoping for.

On stage, crew members clad head to toe in black were arranging stools and testing microphones with the gibberish intelligible only to roadies and soundboard technicians. Behind the standard red curtain, someone tuned a guitar. I climbed the spiraling staircase up to the sound and light booth.

"Hey, Annabeth," one of the students called before barking a lighting cue into her headset.

"You guys having fun?" I asked, setting down my messenger bag and fishing out my script.

"Not as much fun as we will be when this thing gets started," said an Asian girl with a flaming ombre dye job. "If they like this as much as I did, you're going to rock the house!"

"Seriously," the girl with the headset said, "you're making me think I should take a poetry class. I do need an extra elective in fall."

Ombre girl handed me what the theatre industry affectionately referred to as "the God mic." It was the microphone usually reserved for house-wide announcements such as casting changes and reminders to silence cell phones. But tonight, I was using it to play the role of narrator.

"Ready?" she asked.

I nodded.

The house lights dimmed three times in the traditional signal the show was about to begin. Minutes later, the whole theatre was plunged into darkness.

From out of the black, my voice rang out. "When you think of poetry, is this what you envision?"

A spotlight illuminated Dean McAllister center stage, dressed in his most professorial tan tweed suit with a red sweater vest and gold pocket watch. He recited the first verse of William Blake's poem "Auguries of Innocence" with as much vigor and enthusiasm as drying paint. I laughed along with the tittering crowd. He was hamming it up so much they knew he was doing it on purpose.

"Or maybe this is more of what you had in mind?" I intoned as the dean's spotlight faded and another fell on Kendra playing the role of hipster to a tee from the coffee house setting to her black turtleneck and beret.

She tilted her chunky glasses down on her nose and recited the same poem with a performance artist's rage and bizarre sensibilities.

> "To see a World in a Grain of Sand
> And a Heaven in a Wild Flower,
> Hold Infinity in the palm of your hand
> And Eternity in an hour.
>
> A Robin Red breast in a Cage
> Puts all Heaven in a Rage."

Here she roared for effect and hopped onto her chair, failing her arms wildly like a trapped bird.

> "A dove house fill'd with doves & Pigeons
> Shudders Hell thro' all its regions."

She jumped off her chair and flapped her arms as though she were flying. The spotlight went out, leaving the stage in darkness. Pulleys whined, and the central curtain rose.

"But did you know that poetry is often the basis for music? For what is a song but a poem set to music? Surely you've heard this version."

A lone guitar picked out a Spanish-style rhythm, and colored lights illuminated a tall blond singer doing his best Sting impression as he crooned "Send Your Love," a hit song whose first verse was based on the same poem.

I still didn't know how the dean had gotten permission for them to play this song, but I was grateful that he had no matter how much it had cost. Soon the audience was on its feet, clapping to the rhythm. A few girls were dancing in the aisles while others were even singing along.

The crowd cheered when the song ended, and I had to wait for them to quiet down before I could continue. "If you thought that was cool, tell me—how many of you ever thought of rap as poetry?"

A few tentative claps followed two hoots.

"Don't buy it?" I asked them. "Then check this."

Center stage was lit again, this time with two spotlights, one on Miles and the other on Kendra, both of whom were dressed in hoodies and jeans. Miles grabbed his mic and started rapping. It took a few seconds for the audience to realize he was reciting the same poem. Kendra answered with the second verse as though they were competitors, and by the middle of the poem, we had a full-on rap battle on our hands.

The kids were eating it up, getting out of their seats to stand in front of the stage as if they were at a concert, picking sides based on where they stood and jeering at the rappers and one another in turn.

When they were done, I asked, "Want to do it again?"

They yelled an enthusiastic "Yes!" and so we went through the same versions with Max Dunn's poem "I Danced Before I Had Two Feet," which was later turned into the song "I Danced" by the Violent Femmes.

While the band played, I crept down the aisle to backstage. When the final drum beats and cheers faded away, I stepped onto the stage and into the spotlight.

Fighting the urge to shield my eyes, I announced, "Now it's your turn. This is kinda going to be like the Broadway round of *So You Think You Can Dance*. You can either adapt Dunn's poem for a rap battle or write your own poem to be performed in any of the three main styles. No, Dean McAllister will not make your poem boring, but any of the others are fair game. As an added incentive, professors in the audience will judge each of the original poems for creativity. If they like yours enough, it'll be included in the year-end literary journal and will count as one of the writing samples required with your admission application."

Professor Aine Schopfman stood and yelled, without the aid of a microphone, "Plus, we have gift cards for iTunes and Starbucks for those who really wow us."

Below me, students where already dividing into groups and pointing at one another as they formed teams.

"Are you ready? You have sixty minutes. We'll be back here and online then. Those of you joining us online, you can compete as well. Just email your poem to the address on the screen. We'll cue you in when it's your turn. Oh, I almost forgot—both free verse and rhyming poems are fine."

The kids split up, some claiming seats in the theatre or on the stage while others followed the professors into the hall. I shut off my mic and wandered backstage, ready to wait ten minutes then mill among the groups to answer questions.

Dean McAllister greeted me with a huge bear hug before I even cleared the stage left curtains. "You were right, Annabeth. They love this. I doubt any of them have ever thought about poetry quite like this."

"I'm glad you're happy with it, sir. You seemed to be having quite a good time."

"Are you kidding me? I now have something I can threaten my

students with the next time they misbehave. 'Don't make me do the poetry teacher voice.'" He chuckled.

A group of university students nervously approached the dean in a cluster of long hair, perfume, and giggles.

"Dean McAllister, if we perform our poem, can we get extra credit in your Poetry and Poetics class?" the bravest girl asked.

"I don't see why not."

One of the girls squealed.

"Thank you," they chorused.

The dean turned to me. "What about you? You're a writer. Will you be performing anything?"

I gaped at him. I hadn't thought about it.

I glanced at my watch, but the dean placed a hand over it. "Don't worry about them. I'll make the rounds if you want to write."

An hour later, ten groups of would-be students competed, with four earning places in the literary journal and all getting gift cards. We had two online submissions. One was from Jolie, and it resulted in an argument among the professors over who would be her advisor if she decided to come to school here. The dean's freshman girls did a surprisingly moving a capella rendition of their poem that earned them a standing ovation.

Then it was my turn. I closed my eyes and let the words pour out in chant:

> "Hear me now, oh gods of night
> You who govern the moon's pale light.
> Listen, too, oh gods of noon,
> Who writ my path with words of ruin:

'Loneliness shall be her fate
Through endless ages shall she wait.
For one who never shall appear.
Lost, to pass away in greatest fear.'

Hear me now all powers above
For she you've cursed as found love.
The one thing that can break your vows
Here and now do I espouse.

For I have found my missing key,
He who shall for'ere be joined to me.
Harken now, your fears are true
I, in my weakness, have bested you.

For love has melted my heart as snow,
And given me more joy than you can know.
So may your own words now reverse.
That you may feel the bitterness of curse.

Be gone from me o' wretched bane,
And in your place may love remain."

When I opened my eyes again, the theatre was completely silent, as though the audience was afraid to breathe. In many ways, it was like a recurring nightmare. I actually looked down to make sure I wasn't naked. Nope. My clothes were all in their rightful places. Then someone clapped at the back of the crowd, a gesture soon picked up by others. Before I knew it, the whole audience was applauding. As ombre girl dimmed the spotlight, I took my bow.

I turned to where the webcam betrayed itself with a single speck of blue light and blew it a kiss. "I love you," I mouthed, knowing Alex would get the message when he awoke.

⌇

I stumbled into the office the next morning, eyes shielded by oversized sunglasses, a large gourmet coffee in one hand and fast food breakfast in the other. I hadn't gotten home until after midnight, and with the excitement of the event buzzing through my veins, it had been several more hours before I finally fell asleep.

Kendra accosted me in the hallway, practically spinning me around in a hug. "You are a genius. Do you know what our social media numbers look like? We were a local trending topic on Twitter last night for more than two hours, plus the university reported a significant uptick in traffic to our site. We had more than thirty thousand views on the live stream, and we expect that number to grow today as people continue to talk. We're doing several media interviews today, so you might be famous if they use the B-roll of your poem."

I pulled my sunglasses up into my hair. "Oh God, please don't. This should be about the students not me. No, you cannot use my footage. I forbid it."

Kendra's face fell. "But you were so strong, so fierce."

"I said no, and you are legally required to get my permission, which you don't have."

"No one wants to hear your shitty poem anyway," Nick called from the bowels of his office.

I stopped, confused as to what I was seeing. He was loading his few personal belongings in a cardboard box.

"What's yours called? 'Bitter, lazy, and fired'?" Kendra asked.

He gave a small sarcastic laugh. "Shut it, Kendra."

She kept on walking, calling over her shoulder, "I'm just saying if you had done your job in the first place. . ."

He silently flipped the bird at her retreating figure, then he glared at me. "I suppose you're here to gloat."

I crossed my arms and leaned against the doorframe. "Nope. Actually, I didn't know about it until just now. What happened?"

"I won the lottery." His voice was dripping with ire. "What do you think happened? Laini came in singing your praises with the board chorusing behind her. Hence, I no longer have a job."

"You're blaming me for your lack of planning? That's brilliant. Well, you can't say I didn't try to help."

"Just get out of here. I don't want to see you again."

I shoved off the wall. "Famous last words."

He looked up.

"Isn't that what you said to me after Rome?"

"Whatever." He slammed down the light switch and walked off in the opposite direction.

Miles was grinning when I finally made it to our shared space. "Ding dong, the evil bastard is dead," he sang. "So how does it feel to be belle of the ball?"

I grinned at him. "Pretty damn good actually."

Laini stopped in our doorway, arms folded but wearing a triumphant smile. "I see you made it through unscathed."

"It was just one night." I dropped my gaze to the floor, hoping to appear humble.

"I was talking about the last four months."

My head snapped up.

"Congratulations, Annabeth, you're officially an account executive." Laini held out her hand.

"I—what?"

"I knew he wouldn't last once the reorganization happened. And you've proven yourself. You can move into Jenna's old office on Monday."

"That's also Nick's old office. You may want to smudge it or do some kind of anti-voodoo cleansing ritual before you move in," Miles joked.

Laini snorted then left, presumably for her next meeting.

I sank into my chair, stunned.

Miles high-fived me. "See? I told you it was worth waiting him out."

"Yeah, yeah, yeah," I grumbled, already dialing my phone. "You're a know-it-all all right."

"Who are you calling?"

"Alex. I can't wait to share the news."

CHAPTER TWENTY-TWO

May

My phone dinged just before my alarm went off.

Peering groggily out of one half-open eye, I stretched toward the phone on my nightstand and promptly knocked it onto the floor. I cursed, leaned out of bed, and grabbed it, wondering what loving thought Alex had sent my way from across the pond this morning.

But when I finally focused on the screen, I sighed, shoulders hunching. It wasn't from Alex. It was from Mia.

As soon as I opened the text, a blurry image dominated the screen along with Mia's brief message: *I thought you should see this from a friend. Call me.*

I didn't need to enlarge the image to tell it was from one of England's tawdry gossip rags. At first, I thought the guy leaning into a tanned blond with long hair and a short camel skirt was Bradley Cooper, but then I realized this was no Hollywood star. I recognized him for a wholly different reason.

Fingers trembling, I touched the thumbnail, which obediently bloomed into a full-size mobile page, headline screaming, "Gotcha! Yank Professor Caught Snogging Mystery Woman at Oxford Bash." My veins froze, and my heart skipped a beat. It couldn't be. It just couldn't. But I already knew it was. Below was a photo of Alex, his head turned toward a leggy blonde with dark eyes and cheekbones that looked as if she could use them to slice bread. The pair most certainly appeared to be in the middle of a smooch. My stomach lurched, and I gagged, fighting the urge to throw up.

I had to take a few calming breaths before I could bring myself to touch the image again and read the corresponding story on the *Oxford Mail* website, which only made things worse.

It wasn't so much a story as a gossip-inducing caption. "We hear auction items weren't the only things up for grabs at last night's university donor bash. And newly arrived American professor Alexander Grantham certainly took home the prize. Who's the lucky lady? Here's a hint: one anonymous source says these two are no strangers."

I flopped back against the pillows and dropped the phone, trying to come to grips with what I'd just learned. It couldn't be true. Why would Alex suddenly kiss someone else? He wasn't the cheating kind. There was only one way to find out.

I picked up the phone and dialed his number. No answer.

"Okay, I don't blame him for not answering the phone. Who knows what crazies are trying to contact him," I mumbled.

Flipping open my laptop, I tried Skype. No answer there either. Maybe his computer was off.

I sent him a quick email. *Saw the photo. I don't blame you. Call me.* For good measure, I texted him the same message.

Then there was nothing to do but wait. I tapped my fingers

nervously against my pajama pants for a minute and practically jumped out of my skin when my phone rang. It was Alex. I just knew it.

I pressed the green button without even looking at the caller ID. "Alex, I knew you'd get back to me."

"It's not Alex," a solemn female voice informed me.

"Mia?"

"Yeah, how you doing, Pookie?"

"I—" I thought about it. "I'm in denial. This can't be true. I mean, I appreciate the warning, but the British press is always trumping these things up to sell papers, right? They found fresh meat and are just doing a hatchet job on him because he's not part of the 'old gents' club.' Right?" The line was so quiet I thought we might have gotten disconnected. "Hello? Mia, are you there?"

"I'm here. I'm just trying to decide how to tell you this."

"Tell me what?" I demanded, temper flaring.

After a lengthy pause, Mia spoke, her voice unusually quiet. "I was at the party. I'm sorry, Annabeth, but it's true. I saw it happen."

For a long moment, I couldn't speak. Once my brain whirred back into action, I tried to make sense of what she was saying. "You what? Why were you in Oxford? I thought you were in London."

"I was, but Nico Stasch—he's the designer I'm working for—got invited to this donor bash and needed a date. He went to the Ruskin School of Art at Oxford before he switched to fashion design, you know." She said that as though I should have been impressed.

"I—I still don't understand. You said you saw Alex kiss this woman?"

"Yeah." She lowered her voice. "Annabeth, she's not just any woman. Regina is—"

"Wait. What's her name?"

"Regina, Regina Forsythe. Listen, Annabeth, she's—"

"Alex's ex." Hot tears coursed down my face. I closed my eyes and swallowed hard. I took a few deep breaths to quell the urge to laugh and cry all at the same time.

All I could think about was those two being together. I remembered Miles and Alex telling me he had wanted her back. But that was over a year ago. Surely he couldn't still have feelings for her? He'd given me a ring; we were practically engaged. Then Alex's words when he'd accused me of having intentions with Nick rang in my head. 'You're in close proximity for long hours. Things can happen. Passions can take over.' If he'd thought that about me, he might be guilty of the same thing. What the hell had happened in Oxford?

I was quiet for so long it was Mia's turn to wonder if I was still on the line. "Look, Mia, I appreciate the warning, but I have to go. I have to call Alex."

"Don't bother. I can just hand the phone to him. He's right inside."

I hunched over as though someone had punched me. I shook my head, trying to clear it. Nothing was making any sense. "You're with Alex? Why?"

"I'm with Regina," she clarified. "I couldn't exactly leave her alone. I mean, we're not close, but she is a friend of my dad's, and she's really upset."

"They're together?" I practically yelled.

"Yeah, so?"

"So how do you think this looks to me? Put Alex on the phone."

"Ugh, hang on. I'm on the balcony. I have to go get him." Something rustled against the receiver as Mia moved. I heard indistinguishable voices then more rustling as she handed the phone over.

"Annabeth? Thank God. I want you to know none of it is true." For someone whose ex was in the same room, Alex sounded oddly relieved to be talking to me.

"Then why did Mia just say it was?"

"She what?"

"She just told me she saw you two kissing. Why would she say that, Alex?"

"I have no idea." He sounded nervous, or maybe it was just confusion. I was having a hard time judging. "She's been nothing but supportive since the picture came out this morning. What you say makes no sense."

I was kneeling on the bed now, fighting the urge to hop on a plane and throttle him. "No, you're the one who isn't making any sense. Your ex-girlfriend? How the hell did that just happen?"

"She was just there, at the event. She's an alumna, so she had every right to be."

"And you had no idea she was on the guest list. You just ran into her at the party, tripped, and fell on her lips, right?"

"What? No. That's what I'm trying to tell you. There was no kiss. All we did was talk, you know, catching up. I still remember where true north is."

I imagined him fingering the ring I'd given him. "I wouldn't put too much stock in compasses right now. It seems to me like up is down."

Alex sighed. "It does to me too, believe me. The photo has to be a fake."

"Sure it does. Because every paparazzo's dream is to sell a photo of a Midwestern professor snogging his ex. Yep, that'll go for millions. Come on, Alex. We have eyewitness proof, and yet you're trying to tell me Mia is lying?"

"Well, clearly something is going on. Are you certain you're not letting your jealousy get the better of you?"

I closed my eyes, pressing my free hand to the center of my forehead. "I'm going to pretend you did not just say that."

"What else am I to think? First, you practically rip my head off over a misplaced text to Jolie. Now you're telling me your best friend is lying to you about me when all she's done is be there for us in a very odd situation. Who am I supposed to believe?"

"Believe whomever you like," I said before I mashed the red "end call" button.

I looked at the clock and collapsed onto the bed, my decision made. There was no way I was going to work today. I needed time to sort all this out. I pulled a pillow over my head and wept. There was no way this could turn out well. I was either going to lose my boyfriend or my best friend.

❧

I finally poked my head out from beneath the covers when my stomach rumbled so loudly it couldn't be ignored.

"All right, all right, I'll feed you," I grumbled as I padded barefoot to the kitchen.

In my sour mood, everything was likely to taste like sawdust, so I didn't bother with a fancy meal. Out came the Cup-a-Soup, into the microwave it went, and back to bed I went, drinking it without really registering any taste other than salt. When I came back to bed with a glass of water, I grabbed my phone.

Somewhere in North Carolina, another phone rang three times.

"Hey, sis." My voice was already quavering, and my eyes were stinging. Damn it. I was hoping to at least get through the story without crying.

"Annabeth? What's wrong? Shouldn't you be at work right now?"

"Yeah," I said, twin tears racing down my cheeks. "But I have a case of girlfriend-itis."

Mirabelle's chair scraped as she pulled it over the ceramic titles in their kitchen. "I have to be at work by noon, but I can talk until then. What did Alex do?"

I forwarded the text from Mia. "Check your phone."

Mirabelle groaned. "I'm on my phone. What is this about?"

"Then get out your laptop and look at the gossip page of the *Oxford Mail*."

"Jesus Christ. What did he do, kill someone?"

"Yeah. Me." My teeth were chattering, salty tears still careening down my cheeks.

"Stupid son of a—" Mirabelle stopped herself. "How dumb could he be? Kissing someone else is one level of stupidity, but at a society event where he had to have known there'd be cameras? Wait. . ." I imagined her leaning forward to better inspect the image. "Annabeth, have you really looked at this picture? I mean blown it up?"

"No. Why?"

"Get out your laptop and do it."

I did as she asked. "What am I looking for, Miss Digital Queen?"

"Look at her mouth. She's talking, not getting ready to kiss him."

"Maybe he surprised her."

"Do you want him to be guilty? I'm starting to think you do. No, the angle of his head isn't right. He's not aiming for her mouth; he's aiming for her ear."

"Thanks for trying to cheer me up." I faked a smile even though she wouldn't be able to see it.

"I'm serious, you twit! What does Alex say?"

"That he didn't do anything. He thinks it may be Photoshopped or something."

She was quiet for a few moments. "No, it doesn't have the signature of a manipulated image, but I would still agree this photo was used out of context."

"But Mia said she saw the whole thing. She was the one who sent me the picture. She wanted to warn me."

Mirabelle snorted. "Fuck Mia. Of course she did. She wanted to be the hero. I'll bet you anything that she's somehow behind this. I've never trusted that skinny redheaded snake."

"But why would she—?"

"Because she can. Jesus, sis, have you not been paying attention? Mia does what Mia wants."

I didn't know what to say. I had called my sister hoping for some sympathy, and here she was telling me one of my closest friends was likely behind a relationship-ruining hoax? This was just too much. "I appreciate your concern, sis, but it is what it is. Even if it isn't true, I feel like my trust has been violated."

"It has, but not by Alex. Please don't take it out on him. Look, I know you're sensitive to this because of what Nick did to you. You've been wary for years, but it's time to get over that. Alex isn't Nick. If you're serious about wanting to marry Alex, you have to learn to trust him no matter what the risk because, I promise you, you will face much tougher challenges than some picture caught at just the right moment."

"You're right," I said quietly. "But I'm just not there yet."

"Well, you need to get there, or you could lose him. Just pick up the phone and give him a call. Did you ever think about how this must be weighing on him? Whether or not he's guilty, he's got to be worried about what this is doing to you. He loves you."

I sighed. "You're right."

"What are big sisters for?"

"Thanks, Bella."

After we hung up, I called up Alex in my contacts list, and my finger hovered over the green button for several minutes before I finally pushed it in. The phone rang and rang. There was a click as it was diverted to his school office phone with its formal greeting that sounded so little like the Professor Grantham I knew.

"Hey, Alex, it's me. Look, I'm really sorry for how I behaved earlier. I don't know what to make of the picture, but I do know you could use some support, and I want you to know I'm here for you. Please call me back. I love you."

∽

My phone rang again half an hour later. At first I figured it was Mirabelle calling with yet another piece of advice, but then I noticed it was a foreign number. My heart leapt with hope that it was Alex. Maybe now we could get this sorted out.

"Annabeth? It's Jolie," she said when I answered.

I grunted, not really wanting to talk to the one-woman Alex fan club.

"Look, I can't talk long. I kind of borrowed Alex's cell without telling him. But I had to tell you he didn't do anything. He's being set up. I don't know why or by whom, but it's true."

"And you know this how?"

"I was there."

"Of course you were," I muttered.

Jolie kept talking, ignoring my comment. "I was with my dad, but I saw Alex and Regina. They were just talking. It was really loud inside, and they were just trying to finish a conversation. That's all."

"I hope you're right, but I need more than your word to believe it."

"You've got Alex's too. What more do you need?"

I rubbed my eyes. "I know. But it's more complicated than that."

"How? So what if some of his students think he's cheating on you? The school has already opened a second section of his fall class since the first one filled so fast. If anything, this has made him more popular than ever."

"Wait—what did you say?"

"He's a popular teacher."

"No, before that. About a class in fall?"

"Yeah, Alex's Poetry and Storytelling in Modern Music class. I'm taking it. After the National Poetry Month event, everyone here is all about poetry, and it's one of the most popular lecture hall classes."

"And Alex is teaching it? You're sure?"

"Yeah, why?" She sounded confused.

"This is the first I'm hearing of it."

"Oh." Her voice was small.

I sighed. "It's not your fault. Is Alex around? He and I have some things to discuss."

There was a disturbance on the line. "Yeah. How am I going to explain taking his phone?"

"Tell him I called and you answered it."

She must have put her hand over the receiver because she sounded as though she was underwater when she called Alex's name and explained who was on the line.

Too quickly, he was there. "Hi, Annabeth. I got your message. I wasn't sure you'd call again after the way we ended things. I'm glad you did."

I leaned my head back on the headboard. "Part of me wishes I hadn't."

"Why?" Worry tinged his voice.

"I called to apologize and offer my support, but then I found out something very interesting. When were you planning on telling me you were staying for the fall semester?"

Silence. "Did Jolie tell you that?"

"Does it matter? Answer the question."

He sighed. "I didn't tell you because they just asked me before the whole picture thing happened. Everything else was wiped out of my mind. I haven't even said yes yet."

"Then why are they accepting registration?"

"It's just pre-registration to gauge interest. There's no way I would make this decision without you. You know that."

I squeezed my eyes shut, pressing them with the palm of my free hand. "Do I? First you forget to tell me you were accepted, let alone that they tacked on the summer for research, and now you don't tell me they offered to extend your time there by a term? That's a pattern, Alex. It's a pattern of lies I can't deal with. It sounds to me like Regina was right. You do put your career before your relationships. And you know what? It sucks."

"I never lied to you," he stressed, his voice rising. "And leave Gina out of this."

"Oh, she's Gina now, is she? My, aren't you two cozy. Like it or not, she's right in the middle of this. And by the way, lies of omission are just as bad as commission."

"Oh my God, Annabeth, how can you possibly not see that I was thinking of you in all of this? I knew each one of these things could upset you, and I was trying to avoid that. I never stopped thinking of you. Why don't you believe me?"

"Because you keep hiding things from me even after we promised to always tell the truth! And now with this whole picture thing. . . Regina is right there next to you while I'm an ocean away."

"How do you think I felt with Nick by your side every single day? I may have been jealous of his past with you, but I trusted you. You obviously can't say the same about me."

"No, it's not that—"

"Then what is it?" He sighed, and I imagined him running a hand down his face. "Look, we can't hope to keep up our relationship without trust."

I stared at the phone. "Are you saying you want to break up?"

"Of course not. But you're going to have to have some faith in me if we're going to get through this."

My heart was pounding. I couldn't just blindly take his word after all of this, not with her right there within arm's reach. "And if I can't?" I fought back tears.

"Then maybe we do need to reevaluate our relationship. You can't have lasting love without trust."

I couldn't speak.

"When you've figured out if you believe me and are ready to talk about this like rational adults, you know where to find me."

The line went dead. He was gone.

CHAPTER TWENTY-THREE

June

Alex and I hadn't spoken in almost two weeks, and I was beginning to think we were done for good. I was sure Regina had her hooks into him by now. Mia called every so often with updates, but according to what she said, things didn't look good. I tried to get some additional information, but the newspaper must not have gotten people as riled up as they would have liked, because they never did a follow-up. My only other source of information was Jolie, and even she wasn't taking my calls.

At work, things were busier than ever. I was pulling double duty as writer and AE until Laini found a replacement for my old position.

Miles and I were comparing mock-ups for an annual report for the Children's Hospital Foundation when my cell phone rang. The caller ID said it was Mirabelle.

I stepped away a few paces and answered. "Hey, sis. Before you ask, no, I don't need another pep talk about Alex."

"That's not why I'm calling." Mirabelle's voice was somber and strained.

I sat on the corner of Miles's desk, my left hand fluttering to my throat like a bird come home to roost. Something wasn't right. "What is it? What's happened?"

Mirabelle swallowed loudly. "It's—it's Daddy." A choked sob escaped her lips. "He died, Bethy."

"What?" Tears began to flow even as my mind grappled with her words.

"Last night." Mirabelle's voice was rough. "He must have had a heart attack during the night. Mom couldn't wake him."

"Oh, God," I moaned, bending forward to rest my arms on my knees, cradling my head in my hands. I rocked back and forth without really knowing what I was doing.

Miles must have heard my distress because he squatted so his face was even with mine and wrapped his arms around me. "Tell me."

"My dad." I choked and spluttered. "He's dead."

"Oh, baby, I'm so sorry. Do you want me to go with you?"

I nodded mutely, unable to form words.

Miles took the phone from me. "Mirabelle, it's Miles. I'm so sorry for your loss. How's Alice?"

Through the haze of my tears, I noticed people gathering in the doorway of our cube. Most wore compassionate looks, sensing something was seriously wrong, but a few simply looked annoyed. I wanted to beat each of them into a pulp, to take my pain out on them, make them hurt as much as I did, but I couldn't move.

In front of me, Miles made sympathetic sounds. "Of course. We're on our way." He tucked the phone into my purse then helped me to my feet. "Come on, dear. I'm taking you home to pack and then to the airport. I'll even fly to Des Moines with you."

"I don't want you to waste the money."

He placed his hands on my shoulders. "It's never a waste. My mom will be happy to see me. Come on. It's time for you to be with your family."

⌒

"Does it make me a bad daughter that I can't look at Mom today?" I asked Mirabelle as we waited at the soggy gravesite for the line of mourners to gather.

"No. We each grieve in our own way."

"It's not just that. Seeing her so upset makes my pain all the worse. It's like I'm taking on part of what she's feeling."

Mirabelle put an arm around my shoulders and hugged me. "She's your mom. It's natural that you don't want to see her hurting, just like I don't want to see you hurting." She kissed the top of my head.

I felt as though I should be crying, but I had used up all my tears over the last two days. No matter how hard my heart squeezed, nothing more would come out. All I was left with was a jagged hole where my heart used to be.

My cheek resting on my sister's shoulder, I watched the last of the stragglers pick their way across the soggy lawn to the three rows of white folding chairs that waited next to the open grave. Vaguely, I wondered if it was a rule that it had to rain at every funeral, nature grieving along with the family. But that couldn't be right; people died and were buried every single day, not just on the dreary ones.

"I believe we are ready to begin," the pastor said softly. "My friends, we gather here to say farewell to Randall Coe—a loving husband, devoted father, and proud American veteran."

Mom sobbed, and Mirabelle and I each took one of her arms,

helping to support her. Chuck stood next to Mirabelle, our knight ready to help whoever needed it most.

"Please bow your heads while we pray," the pastor continued.

I knew the prayer was supposed to provide some level of comfort and closure to us, the family left behind, but I really didn't hear it. My eyes were fixed on one person in the crowd. His head was bowed respectfully, his hands clasped in front of him, but his eyes weren't closed. They were fixed on mine. They were so blue and so sad.

Nick should have been the last person I wanted intruding on a day like this, but instead, my fickle heart warmed from seeing him standing in the crowd. He had practically grown up in our house and even occasionally addressed my father as "Dad," so it was only fitting that he was here. Remembering that this wasn't just my loss was tough; all of these people had a part of their lives missing now as well. In the face of that, a childish spat between two adults seemed insignificant.

After a few more prayers, the pastor called each of us up to say a final farewell to my father before the casket was lowered into the ground. Most people placed roses on their loved one's caskets, but we chose to use blue hydrangeas instead, cut from his very own bushes.

Suddenly, I was again the little girl who helped tend the flowers. "Do you think God will let him plant them as clippings in heaven?" I whispered to Mirabelle, twirling my flower between my thumb and forefinger like a child.

She squeezed my hand. "I don't see why not."

My mom held tightly to each of us as she stumbled to the casket. At first, she simply kissed her hand and placed it on the lid above where his face would be, but then she embraced the coffin as though she could hold him one last time. Chuck gently pried her away so my sister and I could say our farewells.

Mirabelle was silent as she placed the blue flower on top then backed away a few steps, but she never loosened her grip on my hand. I took a few tentative steps, then the world tilted once, twice, before righting itself again. He was really gone. My daddy, my hero, the man who had taught me how to ride a bike, row, and drive, would never again call me kitten. He would never see my wedding day or witness the birth of his grandchildren. It was too soon. He'd still had so much life in him. How could this have happened? Without warning, I sobbed, a keening sound pouring from my lips.

Mirabelle's arms came around me. She carefully guided me to a chair, where we both sat, her gentle rocking and soft coos settling my hysteria to a hiccupping sob. Wrapped in her arms, breathing in the floral scent of her damp hair, I watched the uniformed military men fold and present the American flag to my mom, tried to drown out the mournful notes of taps which made the loss so much more real, and stared vacantly as mourners filed past my father's gravesite. I was so numb and empty that everything felt as if it was happening to someone else, as if I was a spy intruding into someone else's life. Even when aunts, cousins, and relations I hadn't seen in years stopped to shake my hand or offer their condolences, I barely registered it. And the sad thing was I wasn't even on any drugs. My poor mom was medicated to the gills, but I had no excuse.

It wasn't until nearly everyone had gone and the casket was lowered into the ground that Nick approached us. The rain had ceased, so I could tell the wetness on his cheeks was born of grief. He paused in front of my mom, said a few words, and hugged her.

"Oh, Nick, my boy, Nick, it's so good to see you," she cried.

"You'd swear he'd just come home from the war," Mirabelle quipped.

I smiled for the first time all day.

Nick disengaged himself from my mom and greeted my sister warmly. But when he got to me, his eyes were wary, his touch tentative. "How are you, Annabeth?"

"I've been better," I said with a weary sigh. The little girl in me was gone; I suddenly felt every one of my thirty-five years.

"Why don't I take you ladies home? Mrs. Coe, I'm sure you'd like to lie down."

We'd opted not to have a post-funeral gathering, so that was the logical next step.

My mom patted Nick's arm. "You always know just what to do. Thank you, son."

∽

Mirabelle helped my mom inside while I sat in Nick's car, unsure of what to do next.

The hesitation must have shown on my face because Nick said, "You don't have to go in if you don't want to."

I bit my lip uncertainly. "But what if they need me?"

"Text them. Your sister can handle your mom. She's just going to medicate her anyway. She'll probably appreciate the quiet time alone."

"So what? We just sit here?"

Nick put the car in drive. "No. We go celebrate Randy's memory. He may as well have been my dad too, and I want to give him a proper sendoff."

Over the next two hours, we stopped at my dad's favorite hardware store, the service station where he'd gotten his car fixed since moving back to Des Moines in the late 1960s, his barber shop, and the independent bookstore where he'd done all of his Christmas shopping for "his three girls." We listened to story after story of good deeds he did, trouble he got into as a child, and quite a few off-color recollections of his wild, pre-army days. All over town, people were sad to hear of his passing. I'd expected to cry while hearing these personal reflections, but I found myself smiling instead.

There was one last place we needed to go, and neither of us needed to say it to know the destination. When Nick pulled into the parking lot, I felt as if I were five years old again. We'd spent so many weekends at this park with my dad—playing in the sandbox, chasing butterflies, chasing each other, just being happy and carefree kids. As we'd gotten older, I'd sold Girl Scout cookies here, Nick had had soccer practice at the adjacent field, and my dad had asked us to help in the community garden in the far lot. He taught us how to care for the plants and take responsibility for something outside ourselves. So many memories in such a small place.

Nick hopped up on the warm hood of his car and shook his head. "Man, that's how life should be. People mourn your passing, but they also remember you fondly." His face darkened. "I'm afraid not too many people would think kindly of me if I died today." He helped me up next to him.

"Maybe, but that's only final if you die tonight." I placed a hand on his. "There's always time to change tomorrow."

"Yeah," he said with a soft smile. "Actually, why wait? I can start with you. Can you ever forgive me for the way I've treated you, especially lately?"

I didn't know what to say. Not even my father's death could wipe away so many years of pain, not to mention what he'd put me through in the last year. "I don't know. Maybe eventually."

"Good enough." He seemed satisfied as he watched the sun slowly set, turning the sky into a giant Creamsicle. He leaned back on his arms. "What was your favorite memory of your dad?"

I flipped through many in my mind: the day he taught me to make scrambled eggs, reading in his den while he worked, arguing with him when I was thirteen that I was old enough to wear makeup, the day he dropped me off at the dorms at Drake, and on and on. Finally, I settled on one, a small giggle escaping even as my eyes misted over. "I'll never forget the father-daughter dance freshman year of high school."

"Oh, I was there when you and Mirabelle were getting ready for that. Your dress was hideous, all pink and poufy." He laughed. "You looked like a deranged ballerina."

"Maybe so, but his smooth moves on the dance floor got us crowned king and queen of the ball."

"I bet you still have that tiara, don't you?"

I blushed and examined my hands.

"I thought so." Nick flopped back on the hood, propping his head in his hands. "Mine has got to be when I went with your family to New England. When your dad showed us Princeton, then Boston, it was the first time history really came to life for me. Honestly, if it weren't for that, I doubt I would have passed American History." Nick gently tapped his fist on the metal. "I owe your dad a lot."

I gave him a half-hearted smile, fighting the tears threatening to return. "That's the thing I hate the most about all of this—the things we'll never say to him, never get to do."

Nick shed his suit jacket, laid it next to him, and loosened his navy tie. "What is it you regret?" He unbuttoned his cuffs and rolled them up.

I decided to get comfortable too. I turned onto my left hip so that I was facing him and kicked off my shoes before tucking my feet beneath me. "I really wanted him to walk me down the aisle." My mind conjured up a mental image of that, and the water works started all over again.

Nick pulled me into his arms and held me until I'd cried myself out. It was only then that I realized how comfortable I was. This was the way it used to be, the way it should have been and might have stayed if we hadn't gone to Rome. I breathed his cologne, savoring the musky scent of my teenage memories and longing to be back there again, when things were simple, when my dad was alive. Maybe, just maybe, things could be like that again.

I looked at him. "Nick—"

He placed a finger on my lips. His eyes scanned my face, reading the conflicting emotions there. Slowly, he leaned over and touched his lips to mine.

It was like stepping back in time. His kisses were morphine for my wounded heart, numbing the pain and grief with his familiarity. A wave of dizziness overcame me, and when I righted myself again, my tongue was searching for his, my hands unbuttoning his shirt, his hands tangled in my hair.

The next thing I knew, we were in the backseat of his car, undressing each other as fast as we could. I slid down beneath him on the sun-drenched leather, welcoming the heat of his body as his skin pressed against mine. Nick's touch wiped all the pain from my heart, all the memories and troubles from my mind, giving me oblivion sweeter than any alcohol could conjure. I reveled in the nothingness, losing myself in his touch.

I opened my eyes only when my leg cramped, and I shifted my position to alleviate the pain. Nick's kisses didn't miss a beat. If anything, he took my movement as a sign of desire, allowing his weight to press against me, silently telling me that soon there would be no going back.

A shaft of dying light caught my eyes, and suddenly, I was in a very different place on another hot summer day. All of my old concerns about Nick came rushing back as I relived Rome along with the memory of his recent cruelty.

What was I doing? This was no way of honoring my father's memory. He wouldn't want his daughter debasing herself just to escape the pain of his passing. He would want me to face it head on—with the man I truly loved not some poor substitute.

I pushed at Nick's shoulders, trying to get him to stop. "Nick, this isn't right. We can't do this."

He growled in frustration, slowly raising his head so that his hard blue eyes met mine. "Why not? You aren't with Alex. He's moved on. You should too. We're meant to be together."

"No, we aren't. We never should have tried."

"Annabeth—"

I shoved him again, moving him just enough that I could wiggle out from under his body. I grabbed at my clothing, dressing as quickly as I could.

Nick knelt on the seat, running his hand through his hair. "You aren't seriously doing this to me again, are you?"

"I'm sorry, but yes. You wouldn't understand."

He leaned toward me. "You're right. I don't. What's going on?" I grabbed my purse and yanked on the door handle, intent on walking back to my mom's house, but I didn't get far before he stopped me. "What did I do?"

"You were you. Every time, you manage to charm me, to make me forget. But it wasn't enough this time. I remember everything you tried to make me forget." I shoved past him and out into the twilight.

"What the hell does that mean?"

"It means we're done—for now and forever. Have a nice life, Nick."

CHAPTER TWENTY-FOUR

Miles sat with me on the flight back to Chicago, drinking with me until I could forget the last few days completely. Mia, freshly back from her stint in England, picked up our stumbling, giggling, pickled selves at the airport and tucked us each into bed—Miles at her place, me in mine.

Even when I was sober again, she cooed over me like a mother hen, making sure I had company when I wanted it during my bereavement. Miles took over the role of my chef, bringing in all my favorite fast foods and even cooking twice.

In honor of my first day back to work, exactly one week after I received the devastating phone call, he was making spaghetti from his nana's secret family recipe, one his mom had served for him when he'd spent time with her in Des Moines. He was at the counter facing into the living room chopping fresh tomatoes while I sipped at a glass of red wine on the couch.

"Have you heard from Alex? He sent flowers with his apologies, but he didn't call." I didn't bother trying to keep the disappointment from my voice. Just yesterday, a card had arrived from Alex along with huge arrangement of white roses and peace lilies. In the card, he apologized for not getting the news soon enough to send them to the funeral or be there in person and offered his condolences to my family and me. That had nearly undone me, reminding me of the two great tragedies in my life.

"Yeah, I've talked to him twice. He really is sorry about your dad and about what happened between you."

The rhythmic thwack of steel on the wooden cutting board rang out over the sizzling meat in the pot as I contemplated his words. "If that's true, why doesn't he call?"

"The phone works two ways, you know. He left the ball in your court."

"I guess," I groused into my wine glass. "Is he still maintaining his innocence in the whole picture debacle?"

"Yes. You know, I've been thinking about that." Miles scraped the mushy pile of tomatoes into a large sauce pot and stirred. "Mirabelle and I had a long talk while you were off making kissy face with Nick, and I think she's right about the photo being a setup."

I glared at him in response to the reminder about Nick. "Come again?"

He shook dried Italian seasoning into the pot. "Hear me out. Do you remember Mia's former bestie Demi D'Angelo?"

"Yeah, so?"

"I keep thinking of the nude photos of her and that photographer, Ernesto, that ended her career and her marriage. They never found who leaked them, but don't you think it was kind of suspicious that Mia suddenly started dating Demi's ex soon after?"

"I guess. But I'm still not following you."

Miles set the lid on the pot of sauce, turned down the heat, and set the timer on his phone. Then he grabbed his own glass of wine and plopped down next to me. "Don't you think it's awfully convenient that Mia just happens to be in Oxford? What if this is the same situation as Demi's but in miniature? Maybe she's trying to break you and Alex up."

I gave him the side-eye. "Wait, whoa. Now you're blaming your girlfriend? Did Mirabelle force-feed you her crazy juice?"

Miles smirked. "I'm serious. I love Mia, I really do, but even you have to admit this whole thing is suspicious. How did it make the papers? It's not like either one of them is married. You said yourself that he's not exactly a paparazzo's money shot. But Mia has resources and influence—and motive if her past behavior is any indication."

"But it could all be a coincidence."

"Maybe." He fingered the rim of his glass. "But with Mia, where's there's smoke, there's fire. Always has been. I've just chosen to ignore it before now."

I repositioned myself so I was facing Miles. "But why would she do it? It doesn't make any sense."

"Since when does Mia make sense? From what I've learned, she operates on one motivation—her ego. Her career and sex feed that. But she's getting older—you've heard her talk about her recent struggles to get work—and I think she's scared to death of losing what power she has. Gaining it has been behind all of her schemes to date. Now she has to fight to keep it—or in this case, take it from you. She wants what she can't have, namely Alex."

"Wow, you really do think she might be behind this, don't you?"

He held my eyes. "Sadly, yes."

"So, what does this mean for you and Mia?"

"If it's true, we're done. Even if it's not, I don't know." He shook his head. "Being back home with my mom put a lot of things in perspective for me. I thought a lot about how quickly life can change, whether someone dies or just walks out like my dad did. Seeing how happy my mom is with her new husband made me realize I'm ready for more. Mia has been fun, but she'll never be stable. I think that's what I need now."

I could only stare at him with an open mouth. This was quite a change from the guy who used to put up with Mia bragging about the other people she'd slept while he was sitting right next to her.

In the kitchen, Miles' phone chimed. I sprang up from the couch to go stir the sauce. Anything to move, to get away from the odd direction the night had taken. Could Mia really be so cruel? Was I that blind? And if so, what did that mean for me and Alex? The very thought that I could have ruined my chance with my soul mate because of her had me reaching for the wine bottle even though I knew I should have been reaching for the phone to call her. Tomorrow. I could feel her out tomorrow.

✍

By the time I was finally able to catch up with Mia on Saturday, Miles' theories seemed even more ridiculous than they had on Monday. Maybe he needed an excuse to leave Mia and that was why he had constructed that cockamamie story. That was what I was going with at least.

Over breakfast at a local café, I filled Mia in on everything that had taken place since we'd left for Des Moines. I knew she wasn't going to be happy when I told her what happened—or didn't—with Nick. But she didn't berate me for being a prude or roll her eyes at my issues. All she asked was, "If you aren't going to sleep with him, can I?"

I shook my head and closed my eyes, aghast that she would be so blatant. She'd met Nick nearly a year ago, and it was still eating at her that he'd rejected her—or so she claimed. I still had my doubts about what went down the night they met. As for now, they were two consenting adults, and if I had learned anything, it was that trying to reason with her was futile. "My permission has never stopped you before."

"Good point. Speaking of lovers, there's one more thing you should probably know." She popped a piece of melon into her mouth, watching me carefully.

Mia's expression betrayed guilt, an emotion I'd never seen on her before, and that turned my stomach to an acid pit. Was she finally going to admit to sleeping with Nick? Maybe she was asking permission for the act she'd already committed because she knew it was wrong. Or worse, what if she'd made another play for Alex?

"What?" I asked, but I so did not want to hear the answer.

"Regina is moving back to Chicago next month. She wasn't happy in DC, so I called my father, and he offered to take her on at his firm in July when one of the lawyers retires. I thought you should be prepared in case you see the two of them together."

"Well, aren't you a one-woman job corps?" I swallowed hard, trying not to jump to conclusions. "So they are back together?"

Mia shrugged. "I'm not sure, but things seemed to be heading in that direction when I left." She glanced at her phone. "Look, I hate to dump that on you and run, but I have to get to a fitting. Are you going to be okay?"

I nodded, and she tossed a wad of cash on the table to cover the bill before enveloping me in a hug. "You know where to find me if you need me."

I followed her out, my appetite gone, heading back to my apartment. Once inside, I sank into my favorite chair, mulling over our strange conversation. I bowed my head, scrubbing my face with my hands. This was the last thing I needed. Chances were good Regina and Alex would get back together whether they intended to or not. I knew firsthand how hard it was to resist the pull of history and familiarity, especially in times of upheaval. Chicago was a big city, but even if Alex ever forgave me, she'd still be around every corner, a specter haunting our relationship—as she had been from the night we met. I just hadn't realized it until now.

I was still staring off into space, trying to absorb this new information, when the doorbell rang. I thought maybe Mia had forgotten something, but when I opened the door, I was greeted by a FedEx employee holding an electronic pad.

"Annabeth Coe?" he asked.

"Yes."

The box he held wasn't big enough for flowers; it was only an airmail envelope. I wondered if he was going to hand me yet another condolence card from a friend or family member. I didn't think I could handle any more expressions of sympathy.

The FedEx employee indicated that I should sign the pad, and after I did so, he handed me the envelope.

I closed the door and looked at the return address with one eye open, half hoping and half not that it was further communication from Alex. I sighed. The return address was in Iowa.

I ripped off the indicated strip, breaking the seal on the thin cardboard. Inside were two sheets of paper: the first cream stationery and the other smaller and lined. The cover letter bore the return address of my father's lawyer, Barney Adamson. Leaning against the door, I read,

> *Dear Ms. Coe,*
>
> *As you were not present at the reading of your father's will, I enclose this letter per his strict instructions. You have my deepest sympathy for your loss.*

I shuffled the pages so that the lined sheet was on top. My dad's calligraphic handwriting was unmistakable. Even before I read a single word, my heart constricted, and I slid down the wall so that my knees were tucked against my chest. I heard his voice in my head as my eyes passed over the page, savoring his final words to me.

> *My little Kitten,*
>
> *If you're reading this, it means I'm no longer with you. I'm so sorry for leaving you behind, but this was God's will. I know you're sad, but try not to linger on it. I'm with God and my family now, and I'm happy. Life is full of beginnings and endings, and it was time for me to take the next step, one only God can ask us to make.*
>
> *I'm not sure when you'll receive this, but whenever it is, it will be too soon. There's never enough time to say the things we wish, so even if you're by my side when I go, I want to make sure you know a few things.*
>
> *First, I love you so very much, baby girl. You have always been my pride and joy. I love both of you girls, but you are my shining star. I've always known you were destined for something special,*

and you're well on your way. I'm so proud of the life you've built and the care you take with all your relationships. Keep on doing what you're doing, and if you ever have doubts, just ask yourself what your ol' dad would do, and I'll find a way to give you an answer.

All I want is for you to be happy, so I'll give you one last piece of fatherly advice: No matter what life throws at you, know that you are stronger. You can overcome anything. You'll never, ever be alone. I'll be right by your side for every moment just as I always have been.

Take care of your mom and sister for me. And remind your mom to water the hydrangeas when you talk to her each weekend. You know how she is. I love you.

Love, Dad

I looked up from the letter, blurry-eyed with tears. My chest was caving in again, and there was only one person I could share my grief with. I crawled over to the couch where I'd left my phone and called my sister.

"Mirabelle?" My voice was tiny, like that of a doll.

But she didn't need any more than that. "You got Dad's letter, didn't you?"

I nodded, not realizing for a moment that she couldn't see me. "Yeah."

Her voice cracked. "I got one at the lawyer's office. So did Mom and Chuck. I thought you'd have one too."

"Oh, Mirabelle, I miss him so much," I sobbed.

She let me cry my fill, staying on the line as a reassuring presence as I vented my grief. When I was spent, she sighed. "Even though reading the letter reopens the wound, I'm so glad to have a piece of Dad to hold on to."

I wiped my eyes and sniffled. "Me too."

"Chuck and I have been comparing notes. We can't quite figure out when they were written."

"Probably after his first heart attack."

"Maybe." There was a skeptical hint in her voice. "I don't know. These feel more recent to me. Does yours say anything about Alex?"

I shuddered involuntarily at the mention of his name. "Not specifically. Why?"

"Never mind. I thought if it did, maybe he wrote them after Christmas."

"Why Christmas?"

"Well, you two practically got engaged on Christmas Eve. I thought maybe. . . oh, I don't know. Forget it."

We were both silent for a while, absorbed in our own thoughts. I couldn't help but think how different things were now. But Mirabelle and I had been over that already. I didn't need to rehash it. Besides, she had better things to do than sit on the phone with her lonely sister.

"Look, I won't take up any more of your time. I just needed to talk to someone who understood. Thanks for listening."

"Anytime. What are big sisters for? Seriously, call me anytime, day or night."

"Thanks, Bella. I love you."

"I love you too."

I ended the call and tossed my phone onto the counter with a sigh. Was it a full moon? Mercury in retrograde? There had to be something going on because this was a suckfest by any standards. First Mia asks my permission to sleep with Nick, then she drops the bomb about Regina moving here, and now this letter. Could this day get any worse?

⌇

Around noon, my Skype rang with a number from Oxford, and my heart seized. I'd jinxed myself by asking that question hadn't I? I considered ignoring it—I really wasn't in the mood for a showdown with Alex—but if the universe was determined to continue to rain on my day, it would find a way no matter what I did.

I pressed the answer button. To my surprise, Jolie's smiling face greeted me. "Hey, Annabeth. I heard about your dad. I'm so sorry."

I smiled slightly. "Thanks, Jolie. How did you know?"

"Alex told me. Apparently Laini told the dean, and he told Alex."

"Ah. What's up?"

"I found something I thought you'd want to see. That's why I'm Skyping you instead of just calling. As part of one of my classes, I'm shadowing the public relations department. The other day, a bunch of us were going through photos from events over the last year to put together a donor report, and I found a few from the event where Alex and Regina were photographed. Now I can finally prove to you Alex is innocent, and you two can get back together like you belong. I can't stand seeing him so miserable."

I don't know which touched me more, that Alex was outwardly unhappy enough about our break up that Jolie noticed or that she cared enough to get involved. It was intrusive but cute.

Jolie held up a glossy eight-by-ten showing a group of smiling people. "Here's Exhibit A. According to the digital timestamp, it was taken at the same time as the supposed kissing photo. Ignore the people in the foreground. They aren't important. Look over their left shoulders. That's Mia and some designer." She pointed at the right side of the picture. "Now, look over here. That's Alex and Regina."

I leaned toward the screen, squinting. The basic shapes and hair colors were right, but I couldn't make out the faces. "Are you sure? I can't really see anyone."

Jolie lowered the photo and picked up her phone, thumbs flying over the keys. "Here, I'll text it to you. You'll be able to see it better that way."

A few seconds later, my phone dinged. We were both quiet while I opened the file and zoomed in. "I'll be damned. It is them."

"And look at Mia. What do you see about where she's standing?"

It look me a minute to realize what Jolie was talking about. "Her back is to them. Even if they did kiss, there's no way she could have seen it."

Jolie beamed. "Yep. And there's more." She clicked away at her phone again, and my phone dinged three times in quick succession.

I pulled up the photos one by one. "What am I looking at?"

"The first photo was taken right before the supposed kiss. You can see that they were talking. Now look at the second."

I did. It was of Alex and Regina, taken from over one of her shoulders. She was brushing her hair back behind her right ear, leaning toward Alex, face rapt in concentration on what he was saying. His lips were less than an inch from her ear.

"It's another angle on the supposed kiss. The time stamp matches to the minute. You can see that their lips are nowhere near one another."

I stared at the photo, my heart growing cold with guilt. This was proof Alex had been telling the truth all along. I reluctantly minimized the photo.

"And the third?" I pulled it up. Alex and Regina were posing next to each other, heads together.

"This one was taken one minute later by the same person. Look at their lips."

"What am I looking for?"

"Annabeth, you're a woman. Think. She's wearing dark lipstick. What would it look like if she'd just been kissed?"

I thought for a moment, remembering my own kisses with Alex before work in the mornings. I'd always had to reapply my lipstick. "Her lipstick isn't smudged or faded." My eyes traveled to Alex's full lips, my breasts tingling in response. "And there's no lipstick on his lips or face." I zoomed in on his right hand, which was around Regina's shoulder. His cuff was clean, as was the one at his left hand in his lap. "There's no smudge on either of his wrists as though he'd tried to wipe it away either." I set the phone down, turning back to Jolie. "You were right. I'm so sorry for not believing you. I've wronged you both."

Jolie held up her hands. "Hey, no worries here. I get where you were coming from. I'm the jealous type too."

"But you seem to like me."

She grinned. "Are you kidding? I love you. Alex is cute, but he's old. No offense."

I laughed. "None taken. So are you going to show these to Alex and Regina?"

"Already did. Them and the paper. Everything is cleared up. They're going to print a retraction and apology in the morning."

I breathed a sigh of relief. "Thank God. You are an angel, Jolie."

"Hey, I'm just glad I could help. You and Alex are so cool together."

"Do you think he'll ever forgive me?"

"Um, yeah. He's totally still in love with you."

"I should call him. Thank you so much, Jolie. I wish I could hug you."

"You'll be able to in fall."

My brow furrowed. "How? Has Alex decided to stay? And what does that have to do with me?"

"No, silly, I'm coming back to the States. I'm going to the University of Chicago. I've already told my dad that I intend to transfer unless Alex decides to stay here. Your National Poetry Month event cinched it. Dad said to tell you that your membership drive worked a little too well."

I laughed. "Tell him I never intended to poach you. Are you sure this is what you want?"

She nodded resolutely. "Yes. Everyone's always telling me how important mentors are as you find your way in life. For me, Alex is one, and I want to learn everything I can from him. I hope you'll be another."

"Of course. Ask me anything anytime."

"Sweet. Thanks."

"Is Alex around by any chance?"

Jolie shrugged. "I haven't seen him since Friday afternoon. But if I hear from him, I'll let him know to get in touch."

"You're a peach. And if you see Regina—"

Jolie held up a hand. "No need to say it. She's gone already anyway. Went back to the States according to her original schedule as though nothing happened, which really, it didn't."

I let out a deep breath. "At least that's over."

Jolie glanced at something off camera. "Look, I hate to cut this short, but I have to go."

"No problem. Thanks again, Jolie. I have to go confront my former best friend about her lies."

Jolie's eyes widened. "Kick some ass, Annabeth."

Thoughts zeroed in on confronting Mia, I didn't even see the woman with the moving boxes until it was too late. I barreled into her, sending her cardboard boxes flying and both of us tumbling to the white polished tiles of the lobby floor. My tailbone hit with a sickening shock that reverberated up my spine.

"Oh my God. I am so sorry," I said when I recovered, bracing myself on my arms and struggling to my feet. "Are you okay?"

"Yes. I think so. Not your fault," the blond woman said, dazed. "I should have been watching where I was going." She gestured to the boxes scattered around us. "Or at least carrying less."

I stuck out a hand to help her stand. "I'm Annabeth Coe. Please, let me help you."

She shook my hand hesitantly, giving me an odd look, her head cocked to the side as if she was trying to figure out something. "Nice to meet you. Yes, please. Thank you."

I scooped up one of the boxes and followed her into the elevator. She looked really familiar, but I couldn't quite place her. "Are you new to Chicago or just to the building?"

"A transplant, actually. I lived here for a while, moved away, and now I'm back. But this is my first time in this building. A friend helped me find a place to rent until I settle in."

The elevator climbed past my floor into the higher-rent suites. She must have been pretty well off to afford these digs.

"So what do you do?" I asked, curiosity getting the best of me.

The elevator dinged, and the doors slid open to reveal that only three units shared the floor, one straight ahead and one at either end of the hall.

The blonde gestured at the door facing us. "You can just set that down at the door. Thank you. To answer your question, I'm a lawyer, but I'm teaching adjunct classes at the University of Chicago until my new position begins."

"Really? I have a friend who lives in this building whose father owns a law firm, Jenner & Street. Perhaps you've heard of it?"

She nodded, smiling warmly. "I start work there in July. Your friend isn't Mia LaRue, is it?"

It was my turn to regard her quizzically. Perhaps we had met before. "Yes. What did you say your name was?"

She shook her head apologetically. "I'm sorry. I was so thrown by our collision I forgot to introduce myself. I'm Regina Forsythe."

∽

Regina proved more delightful and enlightening than I ever could have dreamed. After I helped her unload her rented van, we ended up having lunch together, talking at length about the photo scandal and Mia's involvement. She'd had no idea the lies and half-truths Mia had been feeding me—her rekindled relationship with Alex was news to her—so I was relatively certain Alex was in the dark as well.

Well, it was all about to come out. While we were at breakfast, Mia had told me where her photo shoot was and invited me to come visit if I got bored. That was an offer she was soon going to regret.

I swung open the heavy glass door leading into the photographer's studio. There weren't nearly as many people hanging around as I'd imagined. I'd been expecting a crowd of people oohing and ahhing and telling Mia to "work it." Instead, the only people around—besides her and the photographer—were an assistant dressed in jeans and a concert T-shirt, who watched everything with an appraising eye, occasionally saying something to his boss in low tones, and a makeup artist with exactly the multi-tone hair and wild makeup I'd envisioned.

I stood around for several minutes before anyone noticed I was there. Good thing I didn't own a gun, or Mia would have already been dead.

The assistant strode over to me, an air of self-importance wafting off of him like bad cologne. "May I help you?" He crossed his arms and looked down his thin nose at me.

Mia noticed us and called him off. "Chester, she's with me. Chill."

After a few more frames, the photographer called a break, and Mia strode over to me.

"Come to see what the fashion world is really like?" she asked before sipping from a bottle of sparkling water procured from a craft services table laden with more food than any model would ever eat.

It was my turn to cross my arms. "Actually, no. I came to ask you why you lied to me."

She gave me a quizzical look. "Which time?"

"When you told me about the picture of Alex and Regina."

Another woman joined us, a stylist judging by the way she held shirts and jewelry against Mia with a critical expression. After trying a few combinations, she shoved a pair of hot pink leather pants at Mia along with a white blouse and leopard-print jacket.

"I still don't know what you're talking about," Mia replied as she kicked off her shoes and quickly stripped to her bra and underwear.

"Yes, you do. I'm giving you a chance to admit it."

"And I take it I'm supposed to be grateful?"

I gave her a pointed look.

She shimmied into the leather pants with an ease that would have made any other woman jealous. "I give. What did I do?"

"You told me you saw Alex kiss Regina when there's no way you could have." I waited for a reaction, but she gave none as she continued dressing. "And I have proof."

That got her attention. She stopped fiddling with her collar and cocked an eyebrow. "Really?" Her tone was skeptical. "This I have to see." She waved away the ministrations of the stylist.

I pulled out my phone and thumbed through each picture, all of which had time stamps. I didn't want her to have any wiggle room. "This is the one you sent me, only it's the original. The newspaper supplied it to Regina on threat of a lawsuit. See the time code?" I flipped through the next two, giving her the same explanations Jolie had given me. I ended with the one showing her back to Alex and Regina. "What do you have to say for yourself?"

Mia bought herself some time by allowing the makeup artist to powder her face and reapply her cherry-red lip gloss. When the girl finally moved away, she said, "So I made a mistake. So what?"

My eyebrow shot up of its own accord. "A mistake? Is that what you call swearing to me you had my back when you were really lying to me while at the same time telling my boyfriend you believed in him?"

"Where did you hear that?"

"Well, Alex said it first. But someone else confirmed it. You'll never guess who I literally ran into today in our building—Regina. Not a smart move putting her up in our building where she and I could easily cross paths. Or was that the whole point, to try to create drama between us?"

Mia didn't answer, just sank down on a stool and fiddled with her bottle cap.

"You wanna know what I think?" I said, knowing I had her in a corner.

She rolled her eyes. "Enlighten me."

I sat on the edge of the craft table. "You've wanted Alex from the get-go when you thought he purchased you at that auction. Don't think I didn't notice you hit on him every chance you got. Once he was in England and pretty much out of the picture, you hinted that Nick still had feelings for me, hoping I'd go back to him while Alex was away. Then when you found out you'd be attending that party in Oxford, you saw an opportunity to accomplish your goal by using your old family friend Regina as part of the trap. How am I doing so far?"

"Wow, you're a regular Veronica Mars, aren't you?" she scoffed.

"I'm willing to bet a year's salary that you were the 'anonymous source' quoted in the paper. I'm also willing to bet you or someone you know was behind that perfectly timed photo. God knows you have enough connections to people with cameras and even to some paparazzi who are used to making things look different than they are. Once you'd broken the news to me, all you had to do was sit back and let events take their course. Unfortunately for you, Alex didn't take the Regina bait, then someone else got involved and exposed your lies."

"Did you cook up that little theory all by yourself?"

"Nope. I had help. Miles got me thinking, and then Regina and I put the rest of pieces together over lunch. It wasn't that hard once we had both sides of the story."

"Miles knows?"

"Every dirty word."

For the first time since I'd met her, Mia looked as if she might cry. But instead she turned on me. "You think you're so perfect, don't you? You and your little conspiracy that makes everything my fault. Did it ever occur to you that Regina might have been lying to you today? I mean, no, she didn't kiss him, but she sure as hell wanted to. She was a willing victim in this, more than happy to see the two of you split. In fact, she's probably planning how to get back with him now, especially since she's neutralized you as a threat by befriending you."

"Is that supposed to make me jealous? Suspicious? Because I'm done with that. I trust Alex. If he wants her, he can have her. And don't change the subject. This is about you being guilty."

"You don't get it, do you?" Mia shook her head. "You had everything. Alex and Nick were both begging for your attention, and you didn't appreciate either of them. You deserved everything you got."

"Look, Mia, all I want you to do is admit what you did. At least then I'll know where I stand. An open enemy is better than a false friend."

"Mia, time to come back, love," the photographer called from a set that had been completely transformed into a trendy club.

"Be right there," she called before turning back to me. "You should leave."

"If that's how you want things to be, fine. But you'd better hope Alex doesn't decide to sue you for slander. He's got a solid case, and I bet Regina would be willing to represent him."

Mia turned her back on me. "Go fuck yourself."

It had been a long day, but there was still one thing I had left to do.

Pushing through the door onto the sidewalk, I dialed Alex's number. He and I needed to talk. One ring. Two. Three. . . five. Voicemail. I growled and hung up. We were not going to do this by message. I would try Skype when I got home.

Back at my apartment, I was pleasantly surprised to find Miles in the elevator when I stepped in. "Going up?"

"Yep." He held up a brass key. "Taking my stuff back from Mia's and leaving her the key. I'm done." He patted the empty blue duffle bag hanging from his left shoulder.

"I'm sorry to hear it, but good for you. You deserve a woman who values you for the wonder that you are." I kissed his cheek. "Come by my place when you're done. We can commiserate together."

He gave me a questioning look.

"I'm calling Alex. Or at least trying to. I already tried once. I don't know if he's just busy or screening my calls."

"Seems like a day of reckoning for both of us." Miles reached into his pocket and held out his phone. "Here. He'll answer if he thinks the call is from me."

"Sneaky. I like the way you think." I took the phone just as the elevator lurched to a stop on my floor. "I'm serious. Stop by when you're done."

Miles eyed me dubiously. "If I hear yelling, I'm out."

"Har har. Hopefully it won't get to that point."

I dumped my purse on the couch and flopped down next to it, staring at Miles's phone. I didn't want to do this. I didn't want to hear Alex's voice because my heart would break all over again. I didn't want to admit to how wrong I had been, how much I had wronged him. I didn't want to tell him about Nick—God knew I'd lose him for sure then. But yet, I wanted to do this. I had to hear his voice one more time, to fix it in my memory so that I'd always remember the good times. I wanted Alex to know how sorry I was and that I finally trusted him. At least that way, he'd know before he walked away forever.

I took a deep, ragged breath and navigated to Alex's name in Miles's contacts. I closed my eyes as I pressed the connect button and listened to the phone ring.

As soon as he answered, my heart double-timed it as though it could run away and avoid whatever was about to happen. "Hey."

Alex was quiet for a moment, long enough for me to fear he had or was going to hang up on me. "Hi." His voice was barely above a whisper.

"You said to call when I could talk to you like an adult."

"I shouldn't have said that—"

"It was exactly the right thing to say. You were right. I was behaving like a child. But things have changed. I've changed. I'm so sorry, Alex."

He let out a noisy breath through his nose. "I'm listening."

I filled him in on everything that had taken place since we'd last talked, including meeting Regina, confronting Mia, and once I could no longer avoid it, what had nearly happened with Nick. "I'm such a hypocrite. As if taking Mia's word over yours wasn't bad enough, I committed the very same sin I wrongly accused you of."

"Even though we never said the words, we were broken up when you did what you did with Nick. There's nothing to apologize for. We're both adults. We know that life sometimes throws us curves, and sometimes we react in strange ways."

"Strange is an understatement."

"Grief makes people do crazy things. I'm so sorry to hear about your father, by the way. I would have been on the next flight if I could have gotten away."

"I understand, really. Look, I've talked enough about myself. How have you been through all of this?"

His laughter was dark, sarcastic. "I won't lie. It's been rough. The worst part was not understanding what was happening or why. Everything was going along so well, then all of sudden there was this photo and you hated me."

The pain in his voice was so raw that tears pricked my eyes and fell before I could stop them. "I never should have listened to Mia. None of this would have happened if I hadn't. The last thing I ever wanted to do was hurt you, and now I have—multiple times. Can you ever forgive me?"

"Yes. And do you know why? Because you've changed. You proved it by not freaking out that Gina lives in your building and will be working at the university—at least temporarily. I can hear it in your voice. The uncertainty is gone. You know what I have all along—that all we have to do is trust one another."

"Would it break your trust if I asked what really happened that night? With the picture, I mean."

Alex chuckled. "No, not at all. You've been honest with me, so I should do the same. Clean slate and all that." He paused, and I imagined him running a hand through his hair while he framed his thoughts. "It was a chance meeting. When that picture was taken, Gina was apologizing for the way she ended things between us. She didn't want to have our breakup on her conscience anymore. I think it set us both free, if you want to know the truth. No more unfinished business."

"It sounds like we've both gotten closure in the last few months."

"It's about time."

"So where does this leave us?"

"Hurt, but I think we'll be okay," he said. "We both need time to process everything that's happened. I'll be back in the States next month. Why don't we see how things are then?"

It wasn't an affirmation that we were back together, but it wasn't the hellish fight I had been dreading or a shattering breakup, so I would take what I could get. "Okay. Thanks for hearing me out and giving me a second chance, Alex."

"Always. *Tu me manques.*"

CHAPTER TWENTY-FIVE

July

I hadn't realized just how dependent I'd been on Mia until she was out of my life. Suddenly, I was alone. I saw Regina every so often, but she was too busy working to do much. Miles and I wallowed together occasionally, but he was more of the suffer-in-silence-then-move-on type and was already testing the waters of the dating scene again.

I, on the other hand, was stuck in limbo, waiting for Alex to return. I needed to make an effort to get out and meet people, but I was content to lock myself at home and work on the edits Alex's friend had given me of the first Millie mystery. That was enough until I knew what was what with Alex.

But all that changed when Angela knocked on the edge of my cube and handed me a small envelope. "It was just delivered for you."

"By who?"

"A bike courier. You know, that cute guy who sometimes flirts with Kendra."

I slipped my nail under the glue and pulled out a single sheet of paper with a solitary line of typed text.

There's one letter left in the box. Read it.

"It can't be," I said to myself.

I'd just put the box in the hall closet yesterday. It was empty. I'd opened the last envelope before we left for the airport the day my dad died. It had said, "Open me when. . . your world is falling apart." Along with a few pieces of chocolate, it contained a beautiful handkerchief with my initials monogrammed into it and a photo of Alex and me from our first date. I had clutched the small square of linen all the way through my dad's funeral.

What if that wasn't the box referenced in the note? What if my imagination was truly running away with me? But if it wasn't from Alex, who was it from? And what did it mean? I closed my eyes and held my head, trying to decide if I was losing my mind.

Miles came up behind me and rubbed my shoulders. "What's up, Pookie?"

I glared at him. "Don't ever call me that again."

"So the right to that name doesn't pass on to your next best friend? Damn."

"No. It's time to let it die. It goes the way of your relationship—right down the tubes."

"Okay then. And thanks for the reminder that my ex is a lying psychopath. Seriously, what's gotten your panties in a twist?" I handed him the note, which he read with a snicker. "You know what this means, right?"

"If did, I wouldn't be sitting here."

"It means you need to get home and look in that box."

"But—"

"No excuses. Trust fate for once, would you?"

⌇

Was it my imagination, or did the doorman wink when he greeted me? I shook my head in the elevator, seriously contemplating getting on medication if these kinds of things kept up.

I stopped in my tracks when the elevator doors opened. On the floor at my feet was an old, beat-up paperback, its spine cracked as though it had been abused. I picked it up. It was *The Princess Bride*, open to the scene toward the end where Westley and Buttercup finally have their epic kiss. I smiled. It was one of my favorites. I guessed one of the Millers' teenagers from down the hall had dropped it on their way to school.

Two steps later, I stopped again. A playbill for *Rent* was open to the song list, and "No Day But Today" was highlighted in garish yellow. This was getting weird.

I unlocked my door, still wondering what I was doing here. Chasing after an anonymous note was insane, but there I was. I dumped the book and playbill on the couch and tossed my keys down next to them. I went over to the closet and withdrew the striped box Alex had sent me months ago. It was just as light as before. Nevertheless, I took a deep breath before opening it, looking at the Concordia ring I still couldn't bear to remove.

"Okay, Concordia, if you exist, here's your chance to prove it," I whispered, slowly pulling off the lid.

There it was. A single white envelope bearing the words, "Open me when. . . you finally know. . ."

I turned it over, surprised to find that unlike all the others, the message continued on the back flap. ". . .we're meant for each other."

My stomach did a small somersault. Alex had been here. In this country. In Chicago. In my apartment. I felt like hitting myself upside the head. *Stupid, Annabeth. The book and the playbill are from him. Hello, they were clues.* He must still care for me even after everything. Why else would he fly across an ocean to deliver a note? And why go through all the trouble of leaving clues if he didn't want me back? Suddenly, the room felt as though the heat was on full blast, and my hands and feet started sweating profusely.

I tore open the envelope. Inside was a handwritten note with a quote from *Rent* in block letters at the top. It was from the song he'd highlighted in the playbill, the closing number of the show, a beautiful anthem about letting go of past mistakes and regret and embracing the only thing we're guaranteed in life—this very moment. Beneath that was written, *Go into the bedroom. You'll find further instructions there.*

Intrigued, and so nervous I thought I would puke, I did as instructed. On the bed was a gorgeous floor-length silk gown the color of a blooming pink rose along with a pair of teardrop pink-diamond earrings and a pair of silver slingback Christian Louboutins.

Normally, I'd have assumed those were Mia's latest castoffs, but given we weren't speaking, that was highly unlikely. When I picked up the dress and held it up in front of the mirror, I noticed a small note pinned to the sash.

Dinner at 8 p.m. Wear this. Be ready by 7:30.

It was signed simply *A*.

The limo pulled up to the Hancock Building at the stroke of eight. The driver got out to open my door.

"Ninety-fifth floor," he instructed with a slight tip of his cap.

The Signature Room. Butterflies took flight in my stomach again as my imagination ran through a range of increasingly unlikely scenarios while an elevator shot me up to the ninety-fifth floor.

The doors opened to reveal Alex in a tux with a tie, vest, and pocket square that matched my dress. I practically ran to him and flung my arms around him, kissing him as if he were a sailor just home on leave.

When I finally ran out of breath and pulled away, still on tiptoe with my arms around his neck, he grinned. "Hello to you too."

"I take it this is your way of saying things are okay with us?"

"They're more than okay. Consider this a starting-over date." He kissed me again then glanced around at the gaping crowd. "We have all night to catch up. Why don't we take our seats?"

He offered his arm like a gentleman out of a movie and led me to a table by one of the many floor-to-ceiling windows wrapping around all sides of the restaurant. The table was covered in candles and a long arrangement of hydrangeas varying from midnight blue to deep purple interwoven with lily of the valley. Off to one side, a bottle of champagne was chilling in an ice bucket.

Alex pulled out my chair then took his seat across from me. "Well, what do you think?"

I shook my head. "I think I'm dreaming," I said, thoroughly convinced I was.

Alex smiled, and my heart lit up. "No, you're very much awake."

"I don't deserve this."

"Love isn't about what we do or don't deserve. If it were, we'd all be alone. It's about forgiveness and second—and third and one hundredth—chances and being there for one another in good times and bad. As my note said, I've come to realize there's no time in life for regrets. All we have is today."

A waiter approached us, introduced himself, and informed us that our pre-selected meal would be served shortly.

After he poured us each a glass of champagne and departed, I held out my hand to Alex. "Please forgive me for not trusting you."

He placed his hand in my palm. "But you did. Regina lives in your building, and you're actually friends with her, of all things. If that's not trust, I don't know what is. Plus, you trusted me enough to come here tonight."

"But this was something so simple."

He smiled. "Baby steps."

"Then maybe we should talk about something bigger. Tell me about this new class at Oxford."

"I'm not going to take it. Don't worry."

"Maybe you should—if you want to. I'll be okay here without you one more term. It's only two months, right?"

Alex nodded. "Yes, but are you sure?"

I smoothed the napkin in my lap with my free hand. "I am. And this time, I promise to hear you out if they want to give you another extension—no matter how long you wait to tell me."

"And I'll try not to be the center of any more compromising photographs." He chuckled.

I squeezed his hand. "It's a deal."

Over a main course of lobster and fresh vegetables, Alex told me about the end of his first lecture term and his research with Jolie's dad. They'd ended up uncovering another topic, so they'd submitted two articles to two different journals.

"We should hear about our original idea in about a month. The other journal has a more stringent review process, so it could be up to six months on that one. But the best news is that John has asked me to co-author a book with him, and Oxford University Press has already agreed to publish it."

"Seriously? Oh, Alex, that's wonderful." I raised my glass. "We should toast to that."

We clinked our glasses together. As Alex raised his to his lips, I noticed a thin line of sweat had formed above them and was also making his temples shine.

"Are you okay?" I asked, concerned that he perhaps didn't feel well.

"I'm perfect." He flashed me his famous grin, the one that had made my heart melt that night at the Drake more than a year and a half ago. "Actually, I have something for you. It's from London." He reached into his suit jacket and produced a small velvet box.

My heart leapt into my throat then promptly stopped. Oh my God. This was it; he was going to propose. After all we'd been through, he still wanted to marry me. Was I ready? What would I say? I couldn't breathe, and the tall glass walls seemed to be pressing in around me.

The lid opened with a creak under Alex's gentle pressure. I'd been expecting a diamond ring but instead found myself staring at a white gold chain with a small fortune cookie pendant. My heart zoomed back to my stomach and hit my feet with a thud that made me nauseated.

I did my best to blink back my disappointment and keep my voice level as I fingered the tiny charm. "It's beautiful."

I started to take the necklace out of the box and put it on, but Alex stopped me. "Don't you want to see what your fortune is?"

"It has one?" I turned the cookie around in my fingers. It was no bigger than the fingernail on my pinkie. "How is that possible?"

"Just open it."

I looked again and saw tiny hinges I hadn't noticed before. I pulled gently, revealing a thin scrap of rolled paper. I held it up to the flickering light of the candles to read it. "Your life will change when you next meet his eyes."

Confused, I sought Alex's gaze only to find he was no longer sitting in his chair.

He had gotten down on one knee and was holding out a ring. "Annabeth Coe, will you do me the honor of becoming my wife?"

Every nerve in my body sang, urging me up out of my chair. I knelt beside him and kissed him. "Yes," I answered between tears of joy.

He slipped the ring on my finger, and we kissed again. I was vaguely aware of the entire restaurant applauding.

When we were back in our seats, he said, "Do you remember when we met that you said you thought this was the kind of place Al Capone would have hung out? Well, I wanted you to have a ring that would have made him jealous."

I gazed in wonder at the round diamond countersunk into the white gold band. It was edged on both sides by filigree lilies that looked as if they would have been at home in a Tiffany lamp. "It's—I have no words."

Alex took both of my hands. "I wish with all my heart that your dad could have been here tonight, but I want you to know he gave his permission. I was already planning this at Christmas, and I talked to him then. When we broke up, I felt like I was somehow letting him down, but I didn't know how to make things work. And then I received his letter."

My whole body tensed. "What letter?"

Alex looked at our hands, rubbing my knuckles with his thumb. "It was a few weeks after he died. I—I guess he wrote it sometime between then and Christmas because he addressed me as your future husband. He obviously wasn't aware of our breakup."

I shook my head slightly. "No, I didn't tell them. I didn't want my mom to know."

"In the letter, your dad told me that my number one duty to you was to watch over you, to love you and be there for you. He told me how much he loved you and that now it was my duty to take his place in loving you. I spent a lot of time thinking about how quickly our lives change—in the blink of an eye. His did, yours did, and so did mine. I just didn't know it yet."

"That's an understatement."

"Your dad's words made me realize just how short life is and how ridiculous we were being by letting Mia's antics drive us apart. What you and I have comes along once in a lifetime. I couldn't let another moment go by without setting things right and making sure you never left my side again." He gestured to the blue hydrangeas. "Since your dad couldn't be here in body tonight, I thought it only fitting that he was here in spirit. In many ways, this is all his doing." He fingered one of the small bells of the lily of the valley. "My mom is here with us, too."

A tear trickled down my cheek. "Thank you. I can't tell you how much your thoughtfulness means to me."

"You have the rest of our lives to try—starting in Oxford."

"What do you mean?"

"If I'm going for Michaelmas term, so are you. You've been saying you want to study creative writing. Why not audit a few courses while we're there?" He leaned across the table to kiss me. "You don't think I'm going to leave you here now, do you? What if I meet another ex? Who will keep my lips chaste?"

I almost spit out the champagne I'd just sipped, and I covered my mouth with giggle. "I—I'm grateful, but what about my job? I can't just leave."

Alex's grin was cunning. "Actually, you can. Laini has already approved your sabbatical. She said it was the least she could do after all the work you did for our campaign. After that, she said you can work remotely. That is, if you even want to work at all. You've always said you want to be a writer. Now's your chance."

"I—I don't know what to say."

"Say yes."

"Yes." I stared at him in wonder. "Are we really going to start our lives together in England?"

"It's just a new chapter. Which reminds me—I should have plenty of reading material on the plane ride over."

"I don't follow."

"Twenty years of letters should take some time to comb through, I'd imagine." Alex gave me a playful look. "Then we'll start a new tradition. We'll write one together on our wedding day then do the same thing on each anniversary. After all, we have a new story to tell for future generations."

I smiled, my heart warming that he wanted to expand the tradition I hadn't even known I was starting for him when, as a sixteen-year-old girl, I'd first set pen to paper. "It will be a chronicle of our love."

He kissed my hands. "One that began with a letter addressed 'To Whom It May Concern' and won't end until the preacher says, 'Dust to dust.'"

Before You Go . . .

Thank you for reading this book. If you enjoyed it, please leave a review on Amazon and/or Goodreads. Word of mouth is crucial for authors to succeed, so even if your review is only a line or two, it would be a huge help.

To be the first to find out about future books and insider information, please sign up for my newsletter. You will only be contacted when there is news, and your address will never be shared.

Previous novels include:

Daughter of Destiny (Guinevere's Tale Book 1)

Camelot's Queen (Guinevere's Tale Book 2)

Future releases include:

Madame Presidentess (historical fiction about Victoria Woodhull, the first American woman to run for President) – July 25, 2016

Mistress of Legend (Guinevere's Tale Book 3) – Late 2016/Early 2017

Please visit me at **nicoleevelina.com** to learn more.

I love interacting with my readers! Feel free to contact me on Twitter, Facebook, Goodreads, Pinterest, or by email. You can also send snail mail to: PO Box 2021, Maryland Heights, MO 63043.

Acknowledgments

Even though this is very much a work of fiction, this book is very, very personal to me, so I first want to express my gratitude to everyone who reads it. The fact that you connected with this story—its characters, situations, or whatever drew you in—helps me know I'm not alone in the world.

As you may have noticed, many of the places in this novel are real landmarks in Chicago. The Drake Hotel, University of Chicago, Navy Pier, the Harris Theater, the *Odyssey*, the Hancock Building, and its Signature Room are all places you can visit. I discovered them on several trips to that amazing city. Thank you to the staff and student volunteers at the University of Chicago for the tour, answering my questions about the English department and showing me what Alex's office may have looked like.

Courtney, this all began with you and a Civil Wars song. Thank you for being my best friend, sounding board, advisor on the male mind, and title consultant!

Thanks to my beloved editor, Cassie Cox, for helping me shape this story into something beautiful. Thanks also to Jenny Q. for the beautiful cover and to The Editorial Department for the elegant layout. I would be remiss if I didn't thank the judges of the 20+ contests this book went through under its original title of *He Loves Me, He Loves Me Not*. I may not know your names, but this book couldn't have been what it is without your feedback and guidance; even if you hated it, your comments helped.

This book wouldn't be what it is without my fabulous beta readers, especially Kerry, Kay, Courtney, and Suzanne, who all pushed me to go beyond my comfort zone to make it better. Thanks also to betas Tessa, Jessica, Terry, Lee, Liz, and Colleen for your overwhelming enthusiasm for this book and its characters.

Thank you to Mat Devine/Kill Hannah for the constant musical inspiration. Even though the band is no longer together, you're immortalized in these pages. Mat, I hope you someday find the one you've been searching for. In addition to inspiring the title of this book, your music has helped me be more patient during my own search.

And as always, thanks to my parents for their constant love and support. Dad, thank you for helping me see a father's perspective on a son-in-law's responsibilities to his wife. Mom, thanks for listening every step of the way and always offering suggestions. Last but not least, thanks again to Connor and Caitlyn for letting my attention be diverted into Annabeth's world for a while.

Nicole Evelina is a St. Louis-born historical fiction and romantic comedy writer. Her previous releases include *Daughter of Destiny* and *Camelot's Queen*, the first two books in a historical fantasy trilogy that tell Guinevere's side of Arthurian legend.

Been Searching for You is her first foray into romance/women's fiction. Her goal in writing romantic comedy is to create strong female characters who are role models for women of all ages in stories that are fun and romantic. These women represent the modern independent female spirit and are meant to appeal to women who feel they're outside of the norm of society whether by age (her heroines are almost always over thirty), race, sexuality, or natural inclinations—those things that make us feel like freaks. She hopes her readers can find something in her books that makes them think, "Oh, thank goodness, I'm not alone."

Nicole is one of only six authors who completed the first week-long writing intensive taught by #1 New York Times bestselling author Deborah Harkness in 2014. She is a member of and book reviewer for the Historical Novel Society and Sirens, a group supporting female fantasy authors, as well as a member of the Romance Writers of America; Women Fiction Writers Association; the St. Louis Writer's Guild; Women Writing the West; Broad Universe, a group promoting women in fantasy, science fiction and horror; Alliance of Independent Authors; and the Independent Book Publishers Association.

When she's not writing, she can be found reading, playing with her spoiled twin Burmese cats, cooking, researching, and dreaming of living in Chicago or the English countryside.